Cyra
Chaos Star Trilogy
Book 2

Ebony Olson

EBANDMUSE & PUBLICATIONS

EBANDMUSE
PUBLICATIONS

Published 2024

Published by EbandMuse Publications Sydney, Australia

http://ebonyolson.com/

Chapter One

It was hours past sunset when I dragged my body onto the jetty out front of the darkened cabin. Lying there exhausted for a moment, I fought the need to just close my eyes and sleep. I'd been attacked again, this time by an Elite Guard.

Flashes of Utz as he tried to kidnap me played in my head. How long had it been? Was Luther, my companion and guardian, home yet? Had he discovered the betrayal of one of his closest guards? It didn't matter. I couldn't go back to the palats. I couldn't trust those who were meant to protect me.

Trying to get up, I groaned with weakness and lethargy. I'd gone nearly the entire day without food or sustenance, something my body would have struggled with even without two other lives to sustain. The thought of my unborn children drove me to my feet, and I stumbled down the well-maintained jetty to the familiar cabin door.

Searching my fingers above the door frame, I found the key and managed to still my shaking hands long enough to get the door open and lock it behind me. I scrounged around in the dark to find the lantern, blowing across the top to activate the light within. Sitting at the table, I continued to breathe on the lamp until the carbon from my lungs was sufficient to make the lamp burn bright enough to see the entire inside of the cabin.

It had been years since I'd been to the cabin. My need to keep my lovers secret from the general public, to keep my reputation untarnished in the eyes of the Praldian people and their archaic ideas about females and sex before taking a companion, had once made it a regular stop for me. This cabin belonged to the Cyran trader who taught me much more than how a Cyran liked to tumble between the sheets.

Using the table to support me, I made my way to the food locker and opened it, hoping the cabin was still in use. Luckily for me, it was, and only recently by the looks of the food inside. I didn't bother with preparing a proper meal. I merely grabbed and ate until I couldn't eat anymore. Then I pulled out a bottle of clear water and drank it dry.

Once I did all I could to see to the health of my offspring, I crawled over to the bed, removed my wet robe, and slipped into the sheets. I was asleep before my next exhalation.

"The Queen be thrown into a black hole!"

Blinking up into the Cyran face above me, I tried to raise myself to sit but couldn't. Whimpering, I fell back onto the bed.

"You're safe, Princess, do not try to move yet. Let me silence the alarm, and I will be back."

I should have known Ethelred would have his cabin alarmed. Moving to a power box, he flicked a switch and shut the door before pulling out a comms unit. "It's Ethelred, passkey lax faller. It is just a false alarm. Yes, a kattdjur got in through a hole in the wall. Thank you."

Putting the comms unit away, Ethelred returned beside the bed, bringing me a water bottle. He was the same large build as all Cyrans and kept his hair short like the Royal Guard he'd once been. Big and strong and so very intimidating, if you didn't know his compassionate heart.

"So, Princess, what brings you to the wetlands?"

"I need somewhere safe to be. I couldn't think of a better place." Taking the water that Ethelred offered, his smile warmed me.

"Well, I would say make yourself at home, but by the looks of it..." He raised his eyebrows at my nakedness beneath the sheet before he picked up my robe. "I will hang this to dry for you." Ethelred looked at his comms. "It is late, but I know a market that's still open. I will get some food to see you through the night."

"Ethel—" I hesitated. "I need Hälsodryck, or I will be unconscious by morning."

Pausing, Ethelred stared a moment longer than was polite. He shook his head. "Of all the times to get a woman pregnant, he chooses to do it on the eve of war. I know some people. I will see what I can do. Go back to sleep, Princess."

"Ethel, if this will put you in a bad spot?"

Ethelred smirked as much as a Cyran's mouth let them. "Prince Saboa got back to the palats hours ago. Everything has been in chaos since, but no one knows why. I have not been contacted by Commander Stark or the Prince yet. So, your being here is not an issue. But as soon as either of them calls me, I will be honor bound to reveal your location, Zira. You understand?"

With a nod, I closed my eyes again. "How long does that give me?"

"Depends how bad it is."

"One of my Elite tried to sell me to a power-hungry Avalonian and planned to kill my unborn children."

Ethelred cursed so severely that I blushed for him. "As long as it takes them to work it out, Zira. I'll give it between sunrise to lunch tomorrow at the latest. I will be back within the hour." The door shut and locked, and I drifted back to sleep.

I was only vaguely aware of Ethelred returning and lifting my head as he put a bottle to my lips. I sipped the Hälsodryck until the bottle was taken away. Then I was conscious enough to recognize a body slipping into the bed with me and folding me in large arms.

It wasn't until a comms unit beeped just before sunrise that I was able to fully wake. Movement behind me alerted my brain and forced me to open my blurry eyes to see the strong arm around me collect their comms from the bed, raise it up, and read the message.

With a sigh, Ethelred kissed the top of my shoulder. "They found the Elite's body at the mouth of the våtmarker channel just a short time ago. I have been called to appear before the Prince after breakfast. Your robe should be dry by now."

Climbing out of bed, Ethelred placed my dry robe next to me before turning his back to dress.

"I didn't interrupt your evening, did I?"

Ethelred laughed, his voice filling the cabin. "You are my Princess, you can interrupt the best sex of my life, and I would not begrudge you. But even before that" – he turned to smile at me – "even as my friend. If you need me, I am there, Zira. Just like you were for me."

I blinked away tears, and Ethelred growled. "Now, do not start doing that, or I will have to take pity on you and pleasure you until you scream, and we both know how much trouble that will get me in with the Prince."

My belly flipped over at the memory of sex with Ethelred, and I sighed. "Don't start making those sorts of offers, Ethel. You know I can't, and right now, my desires are uncontrollable."

Ethelred's face became sympathetic before a devilish glint entered his eye. "For the first time ever, I envy my Prince. Imagine the burden of an insatiable, beautiful wife?"

"Most Cyrans would not find me so."

"But the Prince does, and I always have, Zira, since the day you soothed my loss."

The tease was gone from his voice now. Anything that prompted the memory of Ethelred's wife stirred his grief. It was how we'd met all those years past. I had just come of age, and he was a trader mourning the loss of his wife. I gave Ethelred a shoulder to cry on. He gave me some fantastic and invaluable experience on how to be with a Cyran male. Not to mention our mutual knowledge, which led to successful business arrangements.

"Do you regret your choice, Ethel?" I wouldn't have been game to ask it five years ago.

"Choosing Berdine over my career in the Royal Guard?" Ethelred started making breakfast. "I would have made Elite if I did not meet her and break my celibacy before the five-year stint. Still, six months with Berdine was worth an eternity of being seen as a failure."

"The Prince doesn't see you that way."

Ethelred smiled. "No, thanks to a certain lady, my business became very successful. At times, the Prince and his Commander see my training as a Royal Guard and my chosen profession as very valuable. Like when the Princess vanishes into vapor."

I cringed at the reminder of my predicament as he handed me the flask of Hälsodryck.

"I only managed to get the two flasks last night. The black market on this stuff is not exactly flourishing since you funded the free disbursement to pregnant women at every clinic. I lucked upon a dealer who just happened to pick up a couple of bottles while he was freeing a clinic of some more valuable product last night."

"I really don't need to know, Ethel." Taking the bottle, I skulled the remaining mouthfuls before replacing the lid.

"You said children."

"What?"

"Last night, you said the Elite tried to kill your unborn children. It is very unusual for an Avalonian to have multiples?"

I nodded as he took the empty flask from my hand and replaced it with a plate of food.

"The last flask is not going to last you long. Any idea where you will go, since your Prince will be arriving here soon after breakfast?"

"No idea. The only place I've ever felt safe is the estate."

"Bad idea! Not only will the Prince be watching it, but also your enemies."

"I've nearly been taken three times from the palats. Each time gets closer to succeeding. I honestly don't know what to do."

"Can I make a suggestion?"

Meeting Ethelred's eyes, I nodded. If anyone knew where I would be safest, it was him.

"No matter who your enemy is, not even the Elite would raise a hand against you while the King offers his protection."

I swallowed the ball of fear that suddenly collected in my throat. "I wouldn't even know how to get off-planet, let alone into the King's palats to beg for his protection."

Ethelred smiled as he sat down with his own plate of food. Of all the people who thought to smuggle someone off-planet and into the King's palats, Ethelred was probably the only person who could.

"Well, is it not lucky you crawled into my bed last night, Princess?"

Shaking my head, I smiled. "Let's reframe that when you inform our Prince how you found me."

Giving me the Cyran equivalent of a grin, Ethelred pointed to my plate. "Eat your food. You're going to need your strength."

Chapter Two

"Expect many guns pointing at you before you get your bearings," Ethelred warned. He locked a precious-looking bracelet around my wrist. He'd already pre-set the destination for me. "They will not be able to stop you transporting into the King's chambers, but they will see you coming a couple of minutes out. They will be ready to kill a possible attacker."

"I'm having second thoughts about this plan."

Ethelred smiled at my furrowed brows. "Just get low and announce who you are as soon as your feet hit the ground. It is your first long-range teleport, so expect to feel slightly disoriented."

"Anything close to the Cyran elevators?"

"Worse."

"Well, getting low won't be a problem. I'll probably fall on my royal behind when I land."

"Just make sure you do it gracefully. It is, after all, the first time you are meeting your King." The humor from Ethelred's face drained away. "I am not kidding, Zira. They will shoot you if you even blink on arrival. You land. You acknowledge your King. Then announce your status and why you are breaking the law and transporting directly into his chambers." Ethelred stopped to consider for a moment. "He may have a lover in there with him."

"Blackness! What if he has the Queen?"

"Not likely," Ethelred dismissed quickly. "She is still angry with him about her hair. He will have to go to her chambers to get time with his wife for a while."

The Queen had made a promise to the Prince about the treatment of his traitorous half-sister Padget. When the Queen broke it, the King took Brutnalöfte on the Prince's behalf. Brutnalöfte was the law of broken promises. In Cyra, a broken promise can have payment extracted to equal physical consequences. It made Cyrans very wary about making any promises at all. It was why joinings were a contractual agreement instead of an oath.

Ethelred's comms unit buzzed. He read the screen and gripped my hand tightly. "The Prince has finished breakfast; I have to go. You remember everything I told you?"

Slightly anxious about this entire plan, I nodded my head with no other option.

"Give me five minutes, Zira, not a moment earlier or later. They will monitor the transportation channels, but the King will be on the comms to the Prince by the time they trace yours." Ethelred kissed my cheek. "I have to go." Touching his wrist, Ethelred activated his personal transportation channel and vanished from in front of me.

I moved to the table and picked up the last of the Hälsodryck. Tucking the second bottle into my robe pocket, I swallowed the rest of the other. Then, with a deep breath and shaking hand, I touched the device at my wrist.

The loudest crack echoed through my head, my stomach lurched as the world around me blurred, and I thought I just might grace my King's presence by puking at his feet. I clenched my teeth as my nails dug into the palms of my hands in an effort not to be sick. I'd just started to think I was never coming out of the channel when my feet hit a hard surface, forcing me to stumble forwards and land on my knees.

Cyra

The click of weapons ready to fire was the only sound as I threw my arms over my head. "I am Princess Zira of Avalonia, joined to Prince Saboa of Cyra. I seek our King's protection from my domestic and foreign enemies," I announced, keeping my eyes downcast.

For a scary moment, I wondered if I'd put my trust in the wrong man and I'd been delivered to my enemy. I could almost hear the laughter of the Barbarian echoing around me, but it never happened. Swallowing my fear, I looked up to find myself surrounded by Cyran Elite and their weapons.

"Blackness! It is the Princess," one muttered, lowering his gun and stepping aside to give me my first glance of the King, whom I'd only seen as a hologram before.

Luther was the spitting image of his father. Overly tall, muscled, broad-shouldered, black hair, darkest blue eyes, and the sun-kissed complexion all Cyran's had. King Saboa was only older and slightly less muscular than his son.

The King was shirtless and just sealing his pants. Still on the bed sat a Cyran woman, around my age, with nothing but a sheet wrapped around her. Her blue eyes were so big and wide that I wondered if they might pop out of their sockets.

I dropped my arms to my womb, and the following words from my mouth were strangled by tears. "My King, I don't know who to trust."

King Saboa's face relaxed as he stepped forward and offered me his hand. "Trust me, child."

Taking his hand, he helped me stand and placed a gentle hand on my upper back. "Elite Penrod, order the staff to ready the Prince's chambers. Elite Rcky, the Princess is shivering. She is dressed for the weather in Praldia. Fetch one of my cloaks for her, then call up Hildebrand and Wolfe. They will guard her until her Elite arrive."

Stepping back, panicked, I tried to pull away, but the King held my hand and gave it a gentle squeeze. When I cringed. He turned to examine the burns his son's amulet had caused, and a growl erupted from his throat.

"I swear to you, Princess, not a hair on your head will be at risk while you are in my palats. Didrika?" The girl on the bed dropped her sheet and was beside her king immediately. "Get dressed. You will tend the Princess during her stay."

I didn't realize I was looking so particularly at Didrika until I noticed the evidence of her time with the King running down the inside of her thigh. Heat crept into my face, and I quickly turned my head away.

King Saboa laughed and gave Didrika's thigh a squeeze. "You have excellent timing, Zira. A moment earlier, and I might not have been in such a forgiving mood at your gumption to transport directly into my chamber."

"I do not believe the Princess set the destination of her arrival, my King." A Cyran older than Luther stepped up beside me and inclined his head to the bracelet on my wrist. "Since the Princess is still in her bedclothes, I assume she did not take the time to stop for an ornate piece of jewelry during the latest attack."

King Saboa took my wrist in his kind hands and examined the bracelet. "I believe you may be right, Wolfe. Interesting friends you must have, Zira, that they can provide you with the technology to transport off-planet and directly into my chambers."

The King laughed when I dropped my gaze to my feet and pressed my lips firmly together. "I see the reclusive Princess still managed to get up to some mischief before my son tied you down. Zira, meet Elite Wolfe and Elite Hildebrand. They will guard you until your companion arrives." He indicated the two newcomers.

Elite Rcky wrapped an oversized pelt coat around my shoulders as the King stepped away to a door in the wall. "Get her fed and rested. Luther is going to be beside himself when he gets here."

"This way, Princess." Elite Wolfe held out his arm for me. I frowned at it, but when he merely lifted his eyebrows, I placed my good hand on his muscular forearm and let him lead me from the King's chambers. Elite Hildebrand, who was around the same height and build as Hartwin, took up my other side while Didrika stepped in front of us and led the way.

Outside the King's apartments, the floor was the black stone they called Is, crackling beneath our feet as if we were walking across fragile ice on a frozen lake. The corridor was reasonably empty. The external glass windows showed the palats lit up against the early onset of darkness. The snow floated to earth to join the carpeted layer over the palats grounds. I shivered. I hadn't seen snow since I was a child in Avalonia. Praldia never got cold enough, even in the depths of winter.

My eyes kept drifting up to Wolfe. "Is it my height or size that worries you, Princess?"

"If I can't trust my own Elite, why should I trust anyone else's?"

Hildebrand ruffled, but Wolfe merely lifted a brow as if in agreement. "We have served the crown of Cyra for over half our lives. We would die to protect you, Princess."

"And how long did Elite Utz serve before he decided my blood could not sully the Cyran throne?"

Didrika turned on her heel, anger radiating through her. "Elite Utz was the one who attacked you?"

I wanted to cower at the venom in her words, but I held her glare, realizing there was something personal in it for her.

"Yes."

Didrika looked to Hildebrand than Wolfe. Wolfe nodded agreement to her silent question. Didrika turned back to Hildebrand. "Go inform the King. The Prince might know already, but if not, he should know before he leaves."

Hildebrand bowed his head and ran back to the King's chambers. Didrika took his place at my side. When she took my other hand gently in her firm grip, I noticed the Chaos Star marked on the back of her hand.

"You're Elite?"

Didrika smiled. "Few would see the woman behind the King a threat, Princess. So many devalue a woman's strength." Her smile grew. "There are several women in our Royal guard, but I am the first and only woman to become Elite." Her eyes flicked to Wolfe before returning to our surroundings.

Glancing up at the man, I witnessed a father's pride evident in his eyes. "You have no issue with your daughter sating her King?"

Wolfe chuckled. "What better place to protect her King from?"

"Admittedly, your arrival did catch us by surprise. I do not think the Prince himself would have the gonads required to transport directly into his father's chambers, especially at bedtime." Didrika smiled. "No wonder he fell for you, Princess. Beautiful and fearless."

"I'm anything but fearless."

"Fully trained Elite would have wet themselves coming out of a long-range teleport to find them surrounded by readied weapons. You bowed to your king and proclaimed yourself Princess. The King is probably considering marking you Elite purely out of respect for that feat alone," Didrika acknowledged.

"We are here," Wolfe announced. He pushed open a door into a well-furnished apartment. Inside, staff rushed to spruce the suite ready for the Prince. At my arrival, they stopped and stared openly. A glance from Wolfe set them back to task.

The outer quarters of the apartment were tastefully decorated, even if it was a lot more ornate than Luther's apartment at his palats. When I glanced up at the chandelier, the world spun. Wolfe caught my body against his and looked worriedly at his daughter.

"I'm sorry, I'm fine. I just need to stop for a drink." Removing the flask of Hälsodryck from my pocket, I flipped the lid taking several mouthfuls to find the bottle empty. "Crap!"

Wolfe looked at his surprised daughter. "Go tell the Kingthe King and organize food now. I will see the Princess to bed."

"Please, let that mean that you will tuck me in and kiss me on the forehead goodnight and not something else?"

Wolfe chuckled as he lifted me into his arms. "Would you like it to mean something else, Princess? It must be decades since I have rolled an Avalonian and never one so beautiful as you."

14

"Avalonians are monogamous," I murmured to his shoulder, where my head rested perfectly.

"I am aware of that, Princess, but I was not sure if you were."

"Because the Prince isn't?"

Wolfe didn't answer.

"I know the Cyran way, Elite Wolfe. I may have adopted some practices that are not of my people, but that is not one of them." When Wolfe tensed, I sighed. "That doesn't mean I hold the Prince to my ways either."

Pushing open the door for the bedroom, Wolfe lowered me onto a bed that stood three times as high off the floor as any bed in Praldia. "Elite Wolfe, I might need a ladder to get down from the bed later."

Wolfe smiled. "I will commission a slippery slide for you, Princess."

The doors to the room flew open, and Wolfe turned, ready to attack.

"Is it true?" The Queen demanded. "Did Utz attack you?"

"Yes, my queen."

"Did he know you carried my grandchild?"

"I told him before he attacked, my Queen."

"What were their plans for my son's unborn child?"

Saboa's mother stood radiating anger at the foot of the bed. Tears poured from my eyes as I curled my body protectively around my womb. "They meant to kill him, my queen."

The Queen assessed me a moment. "Would you have let them?"

Mouth falling open, I stared at her, stunned by the accusation.

Lifting an overly manicured brow, the Queen shrugged one shoulder as if it was to be expected. "You were forced to marry my son, Zira. I doubt you planned to give him this child."

Gritting my teeth to stop myself from spitting at the Queen, I inhaled deeply before responding. "I may not love the Prince, my queen, but I respect and admire him. I would never allow anyone to harm my children no matter who the father or what throne, if any, they were in line to inherit."

The Queen smirked. "Is paternity suspect?"

I was about to snarl an insult in answer, but I didn't get the chance.

"No, it is not, Mother. Paternity has been tested, and the child is legitimate." Luther stormed into the room, sparing only a glare for his mother before he swept me into his arms and held me tightly. "Would you please stop getting abducted every time I leave the palats, Zira?"

I knew he meant it playfully, but the stress of the last twenty-four hours came crashing down the moment I was in his arms. "I'm so sorry, Luther. I was scared and didn't know who to trust. Hartwin and Chas were unconscious, and Utz opened the transportation channels ready to take me to the mercs who bought me, and I-"

Luther rubbed my back. "Zira, breathe. Ethelred filled me in as soon as we were told you made it here safely. I am worried about some of the friends you keep." When I didn't laugh, Luther held me tighter before drawing back. "Hartwin and Chas, keep my companion safe while I speak with the King."

"One of your Elite just tried to abduct her," the Queen started.

"Hartwin has known Zira since she was a child, and Chas sees the beloved cousin mercilessly killed by the Barbarian. They would die for Zira and were handpicked by me to be my Elite. Utz was your pick, Mother. But, by all means, remind me of that."

The Queen chewed her lip before drawing herself to full height again. "I am glad the Princess is safe. I will see you all at breakfast." The Queen turned gracefully and walked lightly from the room. When the doors shut behind her, Luther took a breath and turned to me again.

"Wolfe, Didrika, and Hildebrand will also stay with you tonight. The rest of your Elite will join us in the morning."

"Luther-"

"I have to go speak to my father, Zira. We can talk when I get back." Luther went to move away, but I clung to him.

"Luther, I need you here."

He touched my face tenderly. "Hartwin will keep you safe."

"No, Luther. I need you!"

"My Prince," Wolfe spoke softly. "I believe your companion is Avalonian, with child, and absent from you for over some time. The Princess is asking for her companion, not her guard."

Standing straight, Wolfe looked at Didrika and Hildebrand before inclining his head to the outer chambers. "The King is not so tired. He will understand your needing an hour with the Princess to ensure her health. We will wait outside. Food will be ready for the Princess before she sleeps."

Without waiting to be dismissed, Wolfe and the other Elite left the room; our Elite followed them out, leaving Luther and me alone. "Oh, I like him!"

Luther touched my cheek tenderly. "He is old enough to be your father. He is old enough to be mine!"

Mouth falling open, I stared wide-eyed at Luther. "I didn't mean like that!"

Luther smirked. "Are you well? Were you hurt? Ethelred assured me that other than exhaustion, you were unharmed."

Taking his face in my hands, I kissed Luther to quieten him. "I'm fine. Our sons are fine. Now, fuck me."

Chapter Three

With a shiver, I cuddled into the warm body behind me. They took a deep breath and pulled the blankets up higher around me. Releasing a contented sigh, I rolled over to snuggle my face into Luther's neck. I placed a kiss on his hot skin, and my hands on his chest before the clothing and the sudden tensing of his body alerted me.

Pulling back in confusion, I found Chas watching me, eyes slightly wider than usual. "Sorry, Princess. You were cold and restless after the Prince left but seemed to settle with someone holding you."

Dropping my head back down, I sighed. "Has Luther been gone all night?"

"Yes, Princess. Hartwin is out organizing your breakfast and your Elite. Didrika is searching for clothing you will feel comfortable in."

"Chas, please don't take this the wrong way, but I need it to be Luther in this bed with me at this exact time. Can you call him while I have a bath?"

Slipping out of bed, I moved over to the sunken bathing area in the room. I was shivering before I made the bottom step. The bath started filling with hot water when my bare feet hit the stone floor. I jolted when a thick cloth fell over my shoulders and wrapped around me.

Chas's face was set in a frown as he stepped past me and tipped a carafe of colorful oil into the tub. "You just climbed out of your bed naked before me, Princess. Are you sure you are well?"

Glancing down inside the King's cloak he'd wrapped around me, I realized I had walked from the bed naked. When I looked up, Chas stood before me, his eyes piercing as he met my gaze for the first time. "Chas?"

The warmth of his touch on my abdomen made me flinch. Chas cupped his hand over my womb. "You do not trust your Elite. That is hard for us, Princess. Of course, now Utz has given you more reason than before not to trust us. But to know you are with child for weeks and kept it from us. We are your protectors. We cannot protect what we do not know."

"Hartwin and Anberon knew."

"Are you and Hartwin lovers?"

"No." I held back the sob that wanted to escape. "No, there'd been no one in my life for years before I joined with Luther. It's only been him since."

Chas moved even closer to me and lowered his mouth to mine. The kiss was gentle, chaste. Chas licked his lips as his eyes settled on mine. "You are going to need to take a lover, Princess. I know it is not your people's way," he cut me off before I could voice the protest that burst to life in my head, "but you are a Cyran Princess now. Our ways are not as restrictive. No one is saying you need to publicize what you do or who you do it with, but the Prince will not be able to serve you as needed during this stage in your life. Especially here in Cyra, where he has an älskarinna whose needs he must also address."

Tensing all over at the mention of a mistress, I turned away from Chas angrily. "I know there are other women, Elite Chas, but I do not appreciate you rubbing them in my face."

Chas turned me to face him, his hand gently cupping my face. "I do not say this to hurt you. Hartwin will keep quiet to protect your emotional state, but you need to know the facts. I know what an Avalonian woman with child needs."

"Elite Chas-"

"Hartwin cares for you, but unless the Prince asks it of him, he will not give you what you need. You need to broach this with the Prince. For him to at least appoint a surrogate for when he cannot be your companion. And for your sake, Princess, you need to have a say in who that is. I do not care if it is not me, but I do care for you, and I need to know you are being looked after properly."

"Chas, I assure you-"

"Do you even know what it does to an Avalonian woman with child denied passion? Coupling is a form of sustenance during this stage. It is like starving yourself, Princess. It won't kill the baby, it will take everything it can from you, but it will be a slow and torturous death for you."

Frustration licked up my spine, tickling my triggers, but I had enough control not to activate any. "You're telling this to the wrong person, Chas. I'm not refusing my companion. He's off keeping his Cyran lover happy and denying the mother of his children. Why don't you go find your Prince and give him the speech, because giving it to me is not going to make any difference."

Throwing the pelt from my shoulders, I stepped into the bath. Chas had seen me naked now, damage done. I'd only settled in the tub when the doors opened and Hartwin marched in. "Chas, the King, has called a meeting with the Elite. Zira will have to come with us."

"I only just got into the bath."

Hartwin's facial expression was sarcastic enough, but then he added, "Oh, well, of course, take your time, Princess. It is only the King. He is known for his patience. I am sure he will be happy to wait on you to feel ready."

"Did everyone swallow a bowl of rövhål for breakfast?" I grumbled. Before either could respond, I ducked under the water and rinsed my hair before standing up and stepping out.

"Zira!" Hartwin grabbed a towel and wrapped it around me.

"Why is it so cold inside? You'd think the palats would be heated."

Hartwin's brows flattened. "Is she in shock?"

"She's shivering and absent-minded, both signs of malnutrition," Chas corrected. "She needs her husband to comfort her and a good meal. Did we get clothes for her?"

Hartwin scowled as he picked up the pelt cloak. "Go see if Rika is back while I get her dry,"

Chas wrapped the pelt around me and walked out into the outer apartment. Hartwin turned me to face him, caressing his hand along my jaw. "I know what Ethelred told us, but what didn't he tell us."

I leaned my face into the warmth of Hartwin's hand and sighed at the comfort of his touch. Remembering myself, I pulled away. "I can't be near you right now, Hart. I can't control my desires, and I yearn for your touch just as much as Luther's. It's a terrible idea for us to be alone together."

Pressing his lips tightly together, Hartwin considered me, then stepped closer and tugged the cloak tighter around me. "The Prince has ordered that I stay with you in his absence, Zira. We have no choice but to be near each other."

Hartwin pulled me into a tight hug as I shook my head, his body warming me throughout. Choking on a sob, longing, a heavy weight on my chest slowly suffocating me. "Luther knows what happened last time. Why is he doing this to us?"

"Because right now he wants someone he trusts with you. One of his Elite just tried to kill you, Zira. He is not putting you at risk again."

"Instead, he'll risk our honor? Why isn't he here with me?" Even to my ears, I sounded emotional and needy.

The door opened, and Chas led Didrika in, a dress over her arms. "Come on, Princess. Let us get you dressed, so you do not keep the King waiting."

Hartwin kept his arm around me to help me up the steps and back to the bed where Didrika placed the dress. "Thank you, Rika.

Could you bring some food in, please? The Princess can eat before going. Otherwise, she may end up too weak to stand on ceremony."

"Of course, Hart." Didrika stepped out of the room.

Chas removed the cloak and towel from me while Hartwin readied the dress for me. "The Queen has an Avalonian for a maid. It is not fitting attire for a Princess, but luckily, the Queen likes even her staff to dress well in court." Hartwin explained as he touched the close tab. "Thankfully, the dress is still loose on you even with your belly starting to grow."

Didrika returned with a food tray; Wolfe and Hildebrand followed her, shutting the door. "We will take the back passage, Hart. Broadcasters have been lurking since the news of the Prince's arrival. The King wants to keep the Princess out of sight until we find clothes more befitting his daughter."

Giving Wolfe a nod, Hartwin draped the pelt cloak over my shoulders while I ate quickly. Hartwin led me towards the outer rooms as I grabbed the last bite. Instead of walking out of the apartments the way we arrived last night, we turned and went through another set of inner doors.

We entered a large bedroom containing many beds and a sunken bathroom with multiple showers. "This is the Prince's Elite Guard's room. Normally, there would be a few sleeping if they were night shift, but the King has summoned us all."

At the other end of the room was another inside door. We entered to find a luxurious bed and very ornate furnishings. It was so obviously a woman's place by the colors, but also the smell of perfume. The bathroom looked the same as the Guard's room but contained a large bath big enough for several Cyrans to share without touching off to one side. Hartwin didn't offer an explanation, and I instantly had a sense of who occupied this room.

"This is the Prince's current älskare room," Chas adopted Hartwin's tour guide voice. Hartwin, Wolfe, and Didrika all stopped to glare at Chas. "What? Do you think the Princess is stupid? I saw her work it out before I said it."

23

"Then why vocalize it?" Hildebrand huffed roughly.

"Because the Princess needs to know she can trust us. That means being honest with her. We are her Elite now, not the Prince's. Who are we protecting by lying to her, the Princess or the Prince?"

Wolfe smirked. "You have a point, Chas, but the Princess is already overly emotional. Let us not push her buttons. I hear the Prince has already had to repair significant damage to his palats after his companion let loose her emotions."

Indicating that we should continue, Hartwin then led us to a hidden passage in the back of Luther's Mistress's room. Holding the door for us, Wolfe gave me a large Cyran grin. "Even the Älskarinna does not know about this passageway. She is distracted and lured from the chamber if there is a reason to use it."

Taking my elbow as we stepped down the stairs, Hartwin stayed beside me through a myriad of passageways, lending me his warmth and reassurance that I was safe in his hands.

Finally, we exited into a tiny alcove that held multiple doors opening off it. Wolfe waited until Hartwin securely shut the door, then opened one of the other doors and led us into the King's private audience room. It wasn't the throne room where broadcasters were permitted. It was more like his staff meeting room or strategy room.

The room was full of Elite guards, all in uniform. At the front was a small dais for the King to address his Elite. At the bottom of the platform, Luther stood talking to a beautiful Cyran woman several years older than me. I watched as he fingered her short-cropped blonde hair and felt my stomach flip.

"Knowing is one thing; seeing is too much." Turning quickly, I stepped back into the chamber and spilled my breakfast into a basin on the wall.

A large hand started rubbing up and down my spine while another held my hair out of the way. Peering up, Chas watched me with sympathy in his eyes. "Is he angry with me? Is that why he stayed away and now flaunts a lover in front of me?"

A door closed behind me. Glancing over my shoulder, I spotted the King stepping in from a different entrance, Elite Rcky and Elite Penrod behind him.

Observing my position over the sink and the tears in my eyes, the King cleared his throat. Chas stepped away as the King came closer. "I remember when my wife Galiena carried Luther. She usually was not fazed, or at least would not show it, by most things considered natural. But while my son grew within her, the wrong look could see her grieve like a widow, a false step could see her angrier than an injured Saber, and a misthought word could bring her undone."

The King indicated where I still bent over the basin. "Has the early sickness started already?"

Closing my eyes, I turned to the sink and tried to cover the sob I couldn't prevent with a deep breath.

Sweeping my wet hair behind my ear, the King lowered his voice, so it was just between us. "Wash your face, child, and escort your father into the room."

Splashing some fresh water in my face as instructed, I straightened and accepted the handtowel the King offered me to pat it dry before taking his arm that he held ready for me.

Chapter Four

T he King smiled at me as he strode into the room, the Elite
making a path for us. At the bottom platform, I stopped
walking. I may not be Cyran, but even I knew that the dais
was only for the King and the future Kings of Cyra.

When King Saboa raised a brow at Luther, he smiled weakly and
stepped away from his älskarinna to meet us. Luther's eyes were all
for his father, acknowledging me only with the barest of glances. It
wasn't warm or inviting.

The bloom of companionship germinating in Praidia withered
around the edges, and I looked away to steel my emotions. Ensuring
my spine was straight, I held my body poised and pretended Luther's
behavior wasn't as hurtful as it was.

"I apologize for stealing your companion, Luther, but as King, it is
my duty to be seen with the most beautiful woman in the room."

I didn't dare look at the älskare's reaction or Luther's. Instead, I
curtsied and moved to the other side of the room where Wolfe,
Didrika, and Hildebrand gathered. Hartwin and Chas followed me
and took up posts before me when I set myself between Didrika and
her father.

When I turned, I noticed the high arch of Wolfe and Didrika's eyebrows. The same surprise echoed from the King and Luther's faces. In fact, everyone in the room stared at me before raising eyebrows at Luther.

Swallowing my discomfort, I looked up at Wolfe. "Did I do something wrong?" I whispered.

He leaned to my ear as the King smirked and climbed the dais. "Usually, the King's Elite take his side of the room, and those that belong to the Prince take the other, Princess. If the Queen were here, she would usually stand here. As his wife, you would stand below your companion."

Huh, I'd declared my displeasure with my companion just by wanting to be away from him. I smiled; I couldn't help it. "Well, the Prince should not have brought his älskarinna to stand in my place. The King escorted me; I will stand for him."

Wolfe choked on his laugh, drawing the King's attention again, his eyes narrowing as his guard whispered in my ear. "And here I had been led to believe the Royal Womb was made submissive and delicate, so she could not hold herself upright when the winds of politics would make her bend to their will. No, this is not you. You are not as delicate as you appear. Are you, Princess?"

My mouth twitched with satisfaction as I met King's piercing gaze but kept my words just for Wolfe. "The Elite talk. What does the Prince's Elite say I am?"

Wolfe leaned closer long enough to breathe, "scary," in my ear, straightened, and faced his king. Why that made me grin, I couldn't say, but it strengthened my resolve. I was not going to let Luther tame me like everyone expected.

Luther observed me and gave an uncertain look over his shoulder at his älskarinna before taking the three steps up the dais to stand beside the King.

"Daughter, come stand with me." The King held out a hand with a gentle smile towards me.

Gasps sounded all around the room. Luther nearly pitched off the dais. Didrika gave me a gentle push forward to Hartwin, who held my elbow while I ascended the steps to take the King's hand.

"But, only the King or future ruler may stand on the dais." Luther's älskarinna stepped forward, unable to swallow her jealousy.

"Thank you for reminding me of the laws, Adima," King Saboa raised a warning brow. "As you can see, the King stands. My son, the future King, stands. But let us not forget that before now, no companion of the King or future king has been royalty herself. Even the Queen of Cyra was born only a politician's daughter. Like yourself, Adima." The King accentuated the 'only' reminding Adima who she was in the process.

"My son has married a Princess of royal blood. Their children will be royal twice over. No, I believe it is right to have the Princess beside me. As the future Queen of her planet and race, she will soon outrank her companion and rank equally with me."

Surprised by the acknowledgment, I curtsied low while I responded. "You honor me greatly, King Saboa. Even if I become the Queen of my people, you will still be my father. Therefore, the respect of a daughter will always come before the equality of crowns."

King Saboa smiled, taking my hand and encouraging me to stand tall once more before his features turned stern. "As most of you are aware by now, the Princess came to me last night fresh from another abduction attempt, this time by one of her own Elite."

Scowls broke out on nearly every face around the room.

"The Princess has no reason to trust a single person in this room. She was forced into her contract with my son and her current circumstances, which she finds chafing at her patience as binds would her tiny wrists."

A look of sympathy filled Adima's eyes as she turned to Luther, confusing me for a moment. Luther shifted with discomfort and developed a keen interest in the chamber's back wall.

That's when I understood his absence and his flaunting Adima in a place he knew I would be. He'd told her or let her believe he was forced to marry me equally as I was him. I almost scoffed audibly but buried it deep as anger flooded my veins.

"I have promised the Princess my protection," the King continued. "I have sworn that no harm shall come to her while she is under my roof or guarded by those who I raised to the rank of Elite. You are all my Elite whether you guard my son the Prince, my wife the Queen, or the Princess. If you betray any you are set to defend, you betray me, and I will not stand for it."

The King locked his gaze with Luther, who gave a slow blink to answer his father's unspoken question. Inhaling deeply, the King stared down at his Elite. "As such, the Princess will stay here in the safety of my palats. At least until the threat to her security has passed."

Luther's Elite exchanged side glances, but you wouldn't have known they reacted other than that flicker. Still, the King didn't miss it.

"The Prince will travel back and forth to Praldia, but for the time being, we will have double the traditional Elite stationed in the Prince's quarters when he comes home. Adima, I will have to ask you to give up your current lodgings. That room is intended for Elite." Adima's eyes nearly popped out of her head in fury. "You can take up lodgings in the staff wing or return to your family's residence. The choice is yours."

"How can I serve my Prince if I am not here when he needs me?"

"The Princess is here now. The Prince only has use of you when he visits alone."

Glaring at me, Adima smirked wickedly and gave the King a brilliant smile. "Of course. Maybe I should visit Praldia while the Princess is here to ensure the Prince does not get lonely there." Adima gave Luther a coy smile and batted her eyelids.

Tilting his head, King Saboa caught my eye and inclined his head infinitesimally towards the woman in silent command. Luther's mouth opened slightly in surprise. Stepping forward, I gave the delusional woman the most sympathetic look I could muster.

"Älskarinna Adima, you are apparently misinformed if you think the Prince would be lonely in his palats. He has a lover there also. She has been given leave to enjoy the company of others until he requires her again. I believe it would be unfair and hurtful for the Prince to bring a foreign ánægjuhóra-"

Beside me, the King covered his sudden laugh as a cough, putting his fist in front of his mouth. At the same time, Chas almost blew a raspberry, trying to contain himself. A few others, like Luther and Wolfe, had much milder responses. The reactions revealed to me the few in the room who spoke enough Avalonian to know that term. That is to say, they might be fluent in my homeworld's language.

Pausing at the disruption, I hesitated while King Saboa gestured I continue, but Adima wasn't about to let it pass. "What does that mean?"

"Apologies, that's the Avalonian title for a woman in your elevated position once Luther married." Glancing between the King and Chas, Adima wasn't sure, so she looked to Luther, but he kept his focus on the back of the room.

"The point being that Luther's Praldian lover is already well placed within the palats to fulfill those needs." I met Adima's eyes, ensuring she understood that being his mistress was a replaceable position. I wouldn't have done so except for her spitefulness when I walked onto the dais.

"I doubt my stay will be ongoing. And I'm sure the Prince will give you leave to take another lover like his ánægjuhóra in Praldia until I leave."

Giving Adima a curt nod, I turned my back on her to look at Luther. He gave a slow blink of approval as I walked past him. I wanted to swipe my nails down the side of his face so he could feel the hurt I was feeling, but I clenched my hands together in front of me to restrain my instinct.

It only worsened when Luther stepped down from the dais and took Adima's hand. He whispered something in her ear, kissed her cheek, and returned to stand by his father. Adima chewed her lip, then curtsied and left the room through the far doors.

The King waited for Adima to leave before continuing. "Other news that may have reached your ears is that of the Princess's health. I will confirm the Princess is with child and has been for several weeks now." I watched the surprise register with Commander Stark and most of our Elite.

"This confirmation—in fact, any rumor of the Princess's condition —is not to leave this room. It will not be spoken about or hinted at after you leave here. If the suggestion even graces the pages of a Skvaller, I will trace it back to the leak. That person and his or her family will suffer the penalty of high treason. We are at war. Any gossip or innuendo will not be abided until we have found peace and the threats against my family have ceased. Is there anything I have been unclear about?"

When no one dared even to breathe, the King relaxed his shoulders. "Elites Wolfe and Hildebrand," the King took one step to address the two soldiers. "Elite Utz's sad departure has left the Princess short an Elite guard. I ask you both to fill the slot until the Prince chooses a new member."

"As you wish, my King," both men replied, bowing to knee before rising again.

"My King." Didrika curtsied, though I'd half expected her to go to her knee. "I beg permission to escort the Princess during waking hours. I believe she has been devoid of another woman's company since the joining and could use a bit of variety in her house."

When King Saboa raised a brow, Didrika smirked. "Shall I rephrase it to daylight hours, my King?"

King Saboa chuckled. "By all means, Didrika. You have my leave to make girly talk and braid the Princess's hair during the daylight hours. Let it be educational for you to spend time with a female of another species. Just remember, Avalonians are excessively emotional."

"So are Cyran women, my King," Didrika debated. "Here, we see emotion as weakness. In Avalonia, emotion is strength. Perhaps, I will get a better understanding of why our species view emotions so differently?" Didrika curtsied and stepped back beside Wolfe, who was trying hard to hide a smile.

King Saboa looked to Luther. "A night in my palats, and three of my favorite Elite are already ready to sign with your companion. The offer Utz accepted must have been a small fortune to tempt him when so many of your Elite obviously adore her?" The King's eyes passed by Chas and Hartwin.

"I believe they paid him a king's ransom, Father," Luther growled, striding off the dais and towards the exit doors. His Elite followed automatically. My Elite waited until Hartwin gave a silent command. They all filed out of the room, leaving those I came with standing alongside the King's Elite.

"Go about your business," King Saboa ordered his men.

Taking my hand, King Saboa kissed it as most of his Elite filed out. "You are an intriguing woman, Zira. After handling Adima, I believe you will make an excellent Queen. More importantly, you will be an exceptional mother to my grandchildren. I will be absent from lunch, but I expect you to join us for dinner at nightfall. Good day, Princess."

"Thank you, and good day, my King."

Elite Rcky and Penrod followed the King back into the chamber, which gave him access to the hidden passages. Hartwin came up the first two steps of the dais and gave me his hand to assist me down the giant steps. The remaining Elite filed around me to take me back to my room.

"We will take a different passage back," Didrika smiled. "We should not disturb Adima while she packs."

"I still do not understand why he put aside Clotilda for that high and mighty slyna?" Hildebrand conversed as they walked.

"Language," Hartwin growled. That made Chas and Wolfe chuckle. "What?"

"Considering what the Princess called her in front of the King, it was mild," Wolfe answered before turning to Hildebrand. "Your partiality is because Clotilda played with the Elite in the Prince's absence, but Adima thought she was too good for you."

"What did the Princess call Adima?" Hartwin asked Chas.

"Ánægjuhóra roughly translates to pleasure whore," Chas explained, causing Hartwin to gape and give me an admonishing look. Ignoring him, I continued to watch where we were going, noting landmarks to try and memorize these passageways.

"It's how Avalonians refer to a mistress who is used purely for sexual gratification," Chas explained further. "You must remember that they are a species that mate for life and their marriage contracts require monogamy. For them taking a mistress for physical pleasure is greatly frowned upon."

"Is there any other reason to take a mistress?" Hildebrand asked.

Nodding his head, Chas opened a door and turned us onto a new passage. "Sure. The most common being áhugakona. It translates for us as mistress of interest. In Avalonia, it's a friend of the opposite sex who you have common hobbies or interests with that your companion may not enjoy. So, you take part in those activities with your áhugakona instead. An intimate relationship may develop after some time. At this time, they would declare the mistress their sálufélagi to protect their honor, but most are purely platonic."

"What's sálufélagi?" Hildebrand asked.

"Soulmate," I answered, my eyes drifting to Hartwin for a moment. "It's rarely used, even for your companion, because it declares that person as your everything. Your heart and soul. It is the only time a marriage contract can be declared void in Avalonia."

We walked a few steps in quiet. "Though, perhaps I was wrong to call Adima ánægjuhóra. For her, at least, I feel that there was more than sexual pleasure."

"Yes. There was status and the hope of becoming Queen," Wolfe agreed. "But don't mistake ambition with love. I believe you called it correctly, Princess."

"As I said, slyna," Hildebrand grumbled.

Cyra

"Any fool could see Adima sought a contract. She had no right as Royal älskarinna, ever. A true älskarinna knows their place." Didrika glowered as we climbed a set of turret stairs. "Luther knew better. He let his dick think for him with that one."

The rest of the journey back to the Prince's apartment was a thoughtful silence. When we returned, Luther was still absent. A flame of anger lit up inside me. As the morning turned to afternoon, that fire grew into an inferno of hurt emotions.

Chapter Five

"**A**re you ready to go to dinner, Princess?" Didrika stood smiling as the page that announced dinner exited the apartment.

Didrika's smile slipped a little as I stood slowly, feeling as weary as I'm sure I looked. "Truthfully, I'd like to sleep for a week, but that probably means I need the food."

"If a Cyran ate half as much as you have today, she'd be buying new clothes to fit her tomorrow. Is it normal for Avalonians to eat so much?" Didrika asked, supporting my arm as we started towards the door just as Chas entered the room from Elite's dorm.

"The more powerful an Avalonian, the more they eat," Chas explained. He held out a glass to me, which I took and drank with a relieved smile. "The royal family are the most powerful Avalonians. An Avalonian woman with child needs Hälsodryck to support the child's sustenance needs. The Princess needs regular meals and a unique brew of the Hälsodryck. But none of that will matter if denied intimacy by her companion."

"Chas, that's enough." Hartwin took the empty glass from my hand and thrust it back to Chas.

"Wait. You're saying the Princess is exhausted because the Prince hasn't fucked her today?"

"Crass, Rika!" Hartwin started leading me towards the door. "But correct. Avalonians are emotional and crave intimacy as much as food during this time."

"That's why King Saboa dismissed the älskarinna." Wolfe touched his daughter's shoulder as he explained. "He knew the Prince would be starving his companion by bedding the älskarinna instead."

"Plus, the King wanted to get rid of her and remind her family that having a daughter as an älskarinna does not entitle you to special favor," Hildebrand smirked.

"There is that, also," Wolfe agreed.

I turned to Wolfe. "Was the Prince forced to marry me?"

"Zira, Luther's feelings were explained to you," Hartwin interrupted.

"Then why would Adima sincerely believe the King's cunning forced us on each other?" I saw the denial in Hartwin's eyes before he even opened his mouth. "Don't lie to me, Hart. I saw it. As much as Adima despises my existence, she feels sympathy for Luther and me with our joining."

"Princess." Wolfe stepped forward. "The Prince and the King often put on a public show of opposition to make their plans more palatable for their people. Like this morning, when the King dismissed the älskarinna. Be sure the Prince and King had planned and agreed to their method before the meeting."

"So, Luther wanted to get rid of his älskarinna?"

Everyone nodded.

Wolfe gentled his voice as he stepped near. "The Prince petitioned the King to take you as a companion years ago. The King was initially skeptical, but when he found out who you were, he relented and gave his blessing. They just didn't plan on your parents preventing his courting you. When the Prince finally had no more barriers between your union, he came home, and he and his father put on a show for the palats staff. The King told the Prince that he would not kill an innocent child; instead, with the revelation of who you were, the Prince would marry you and protect you and be happy to do so."

"It's true, Princess," Hildebrand confirmed. "I was there when the Prince first told his father he had met a woman, still not old enough to join, who had made him feel like no other woman had. And when your parent's death as traitors gave the prince a way to make you his, the King asked if he were still sure. The Prince declared he'd never desired a woman for anything more than the warmth of her body until he met you, and only you have ever touched him this way."

"Honestly, Zira, how often do you need the reassurance of the Prince's feelings for you?" Hartwin scolded.

"Hart!" Didrika got in his face. "She is a born Princess whose male heir will instantly rule her planet. A planet embroiled in civil war. She has every right to doubt every man who shows her interest. Especially when the person in question knows she needs him and has only seen her once since she returned safely from being attacked."

"He is the Prince and has duties to attend to, Rika. You know where he's been all day," Hartwin argued.

"I do. I also know where the Prince was last night when he should have been in his companion's bed, Hart. I don't blame the Princess for doubting his affection for a minute. He left his Elite to comfort his companion when there was no reason for him to be anywhere but her side."

"Enough!" I steeled myself against the storm of emotions flooding my system. "Thank you, all of you, for your reassurance and honesty, but can we just go to dinner now, please?"

Throwing open the door before anyone could react, I took two steps into the corridor. A broadcaster stepped out from behind a pillar further down the hall and started taking stills. The Elite surrounded me a second later, Chas and Hildebrand stalking in front towards the broadcaster, who hastily rushed for the exit.

"Wonder who he paid to get in?" Didrika grumbled.

"Want me to catch him and ask?" Chas chuckled.

"Tempting, but we have a duty to attend to." Didrika looked me over. "Thank god Luther had some of your clothes transported for you."

Giving Didrika a nod, I didn't point out that the dresses delivered today were new. They had a looser waistline to hide the small bump growing in my abdomen.

As we walked down the stairs, I noticed more broadcasters pressed against the glass that insulated the open corridor from the cold outside. In centuries past, the palats walkways were open to the elements, and in the cold season, they would have to rug up just to get to breakfast.

The exposure to cold ended when Luther's grandfather conquered Glacier, a planet renowned for turning the crystal sands into thick transparent glass walls.

More stills were taken, and probably some vids. Unlike Praldia, where the broadcasters would yell queries for information to put with the picture, the media in Cyra stayed quiet and just watched as I passed.

We moved into an enclosed corridor, the sandstone walls rising high on each side to an arching ceiling of beautiful sandstone filigree craftsmanship. The Glacial glass roof showed the frozen sky above while remaining untouched by the deepest cold.

"The connecting corridor," Wolfe educated me. "The original palats was half the size of the palats today. The King who ruled Cyra during the expansion didn't want to open any existing rooms to the elements. So he built the extensions as a separate building and had the filigree arched ceiling created to show a connection. The glass additions to the palats were installed two centuries past."

Hildebrand opened the door to the right, and we stepped into the receiving room, where Luther stood talking to his father by the fireplace. Admittedly, he looked the most relaxed I'd ever seen him outside our bed. He stood there with a glass of dark hot liquid in his hand with a Cyran smile on his lips.

Hartwin left my side to remove his cloak. While Wolfe helped me out of mine, Hartwin went to Luther's side, bowed his head, and murmured something. Luther's smile disappeared, and the straight line of his shoulders returned as he nodded to Hartwin and allowed his eyes to meet mine for the tiniest of heartbeats.

Taking my elbow, Didrika steered me towards one of the couches. "I think Hart was kind enough to snitch on us just now. Let's leave the boys to work out how they want to deal with their stupidity, shall we."

"Usually, Luther reacts by locking me in my room for a week and telling me to stop acting selfish, childish, or both," I grumbled.

Didrika growled. "Yes, the Prince has a talent for making people feel as if they are the ones misbehaving when they aren't reacting how he wants them to. Especially females. It has caused the occasional disagreement between us."

"Occasional?" Wolfe raised an eyebrow, taking the seat on my other side. "You and the Prince can barely be in the room without starting a fight. Been like that since you were children."

"That's because he's a sexist rövhål, and I'm a female ahead of my time." Didrika laughed.

"And yet, without those altercations, you would never have made elite, Rika." Chas smiled as he joined us.

"True." Didrika turned her attention to me again. "I nearly bested the Prince in tryouts. He was the best fighter amongst the Elite, screening those who had completed the five-year testing. I made directly for him. Had I fought anyone else, they probably still could have shrugged off my skill and refused to promote me. Nearly beating the Prince, they couldn't ignore that."

"You weren't scared of getting hurt?" I asked, my eyes a little wide, having seen how the Royal Guard and Elite fight for fun.

Didrika scoffed. "The Prince and I have been getting into physical fights since we were kids. He has always been in complete control. Luther knows when to stop. We can fight full out with each other, but he will always pull back to prevent from doing permanent damage to any of his fellow Elite. Now, if I was a Meta." Didrika blew out a breath and shook her head. "Then I would hike my skirt and fast tail it out of there before he found out if he could put his fist through my head in one punch."

The outer doors opened, and the Queen entered with her entourage. And it was an entourage. With her six Elite and four handmaids, the Queen's party suffocated the remaining space in the receiving room.

At the Queen's arrival, the King strode towards one of the two openings across the room. The page opened the door and bowed as the King walked into the dining room, his Elite going to the other door.

The Queen rolled her eyes at her companion's lack of acknowl-edgment of her presence. "Luther, please tell me you are not treating Zira so poorly already? Your father and I have been joined for over forty years and are currently fighting. You are newly married and have no reason to dislike your companion yet."

The Queen moved towards the dining room before glaring at her son. "Unless you blame Zira for the loss of that self-important älskarinna?"

"Mother." Luther shook his head. He stepped forward and placed a kiss on her cheek.

"Don't be a fool, Luther. She carries your child. Treat her like the Queen she was born to be." The Queen entered the dining room while her entourage filed into the other.

My Elite stood, Didrika giving my hand a squeeze before she joined the others, leaving Luther and me alone in the room. Luther stepped in front of me and held out his arm. "Let's get some dinner, Zira."

I stood but kept my distance from Luther. "Yes, my Prince."

"Zira?"

"Yes?" I stopped walking towards the dining room but didn't turn to face him.

"I offered you my arm."

Glancing over my shoulder at Luther, I schooled my features to show no emotion. "I offered you my bed, and you chose another's.

Even after what I'd been through. Even knowing your children needed you."

"You're unreasonable. I-"

"Luther!" The King called from just inside the door of the dining room. "The food is growing cold while we wait for you."

Not waiting, I strode through the door into the dining room, where the King and Queen waited patiently by the chairs at either end of a rectangular table. The size was adequate but not so big that people seated at the four places would need to raise their voices to converse.

"Princess, if you please?" The page pulled out a chair on the far side of the table. Moving to my chair, I stood and waited as Luther took up his place opposite me. Once we were all in place, we stepped sideways and lowered into our seats in unison.

Chapter Six

While the first course was being brought out from a side door, I looked over the modestly furnished room. The walls were sandstone on three sides; the fourth had sheer black curtains hanging in front. When I focused, I could see our Elite on the other side sitting down to eat their meals. They were laughing and talking, but I couldn't hear them. I assumed that meant there was a glass wall behind the curtain.

Returning my focus to the room, a bowl of soup was placed in front of me. I noticed that, other than the dining table, the only other furnishing was a side table with a silver and a black stone pitcher.

The page picked up the stone pitcher and topped up the King's steaming glass before refilling Luther's and then the Queen's. "None for the Princess," Luther stated firmly as the page took a step towards my empty glass.

When the page looked dumbfounded, the King gave a slight cough encouraging Luther to instruct the page further. "The Princess is Avalonian. They don't drink spiced wine. She will take water instead."

"Of course." The page recovered and returned the black stone pitcher to the side table. "Would the Princess prefer her water cold or hot?"

"She'll have it hot," Luther answered as I opened my mouth to reply. The page nodded and left via the side door. "Cold water in this weather would make you ill, Zira. Your body is going through enough as it is."

I was ready to shoot a cutting remark about how much healthier my body would be if my companion hadn't spent the last day away from it. Still, I held my tongue when Luther shot me a stern look. "As you say, my Prince."

"Zira, we are all family in this room. We do not stand on ceremony with each other at the dinner table," the King encouraged. "You can call Luther by his name and us by ours when we are alone." He indicated Galiena and himself.

"You can also call your companion a rövhål. We'd completely understand," the Queen smirked, putting a spoon of her soup into her mouth.

"Zira is a bit more refined than that, Mother. She doesn't air her grievances away from our quarters."

"No, she just throws you across the room and breaks the walls," Galiena chuckled.

"Roof," I corrected quietly.

"I'm sorry, my dear. What was that?" The Queen asked, confused.

"I threw him into the roof. It was the roof that crumbled."

The Queen looked at me gob-smacked, and the King coughed into his soup. Galiena swallowed and returned to her meal. "Well, try not to do that here, daughter. The quarry that this castle was built from no longer exists. We wouldn't be able to get the sandstone to match."

The King stifled a laugh by taking a big gulp of his spiced wine. He stopped after placing the cup back on the table and gave Luther a worried look. "Why did you forbid Zira from drinking the wine? It would be good for her."

"She's with child."

"Your mother drank the spiced wine during the freeze she carried you."

"And look how he turned out," Galiena added sarcastically. "No, Searle, your son is right to forbid Zira the wine. God forbid they end up with a child like him."

"I think that had little to do with the wine and more with his mother," the King grumbled.

"Me? I barely got a say in his upbringing. And when I dared ask to try for a girl child..."

"Honestly, Galiena, are you still angry that I denied you a second child? It was thirty years ago."

"Cyran's do not restrict ourselves to a particular number of children. The average Cyran family has three children."

"The royal family does not. We breed till the male heir is born. You had the heir first. That was it. Any more would have opened the potential of a second boy and a future family feud for the rule."

"You're still upset about what happened with your brother," the Queen tsked.

"Yes, I was, and I would not subject my son to have to kill his brother."

My mouth hung open in shock, and my hands covered my belly protectively. "Why would Luther have to kill his brother? Why did you have to kill yours?"

"Zira, it was a possibility, not a surety." Luther was standing calmly, sensing my sudden anxiety.

"But you demanded two. Why would you ask for two if there is a possibility they will kill each other?"

"It's different for us, Zira. When I drew up the contract, I needed a son for each throne. I wasn't expecting it to work when I took you that night. I didn't think you would allow it to."

Tears fell from my eyes. "But you asked it of me. Why would you ask if it's not what you wanted?"

The side door opened as the page entered with the glass of hot water. Luther seized it from the page's hand. "Get out!"

The page scuttled nervously back out the door. Luther moved to my side and placed the glass down before capturing my shoulders in his grasp.

"Zira, do not think for a moment that I didn't want the children growing inside you. It's my fault it happened so soon. You were raised to obey. I should have known you would open your body to my seed as soon as I asked it of you. After all, you came to my bed willingly once we joined. I was overjoyed to find you with child, Zira. Bad timing as it is. It was more than I had hoped when I forced you to join with me."

Trying to get my emotions under control, I turned my head to the side to wipe away the tears and found the other room watching intently. Inhaling a steadying breath, I didn't fight when Luther hugged my body to his and wrapped his arms around me.

"Did I hear right?" The King's voice cut in quietly. "Zira is carrying two boys?"

"Oh, wonderful! They'll have each other as playmates from day one." The Queen squealed in delight. "And with her succession requiring a female, Luther can't deny her a daughter either. I'll get a granddaughter as well. This is the best news I've had in decades."

"I think you are missing the problem here, darling. Luther has decided to change the succession of Avalonia from Uncle to Nephew to Mother to Daughter. That means they will have a son with no throne to rule."

"Father."

Despite my face pressed against his chest, I could still feel Luther shaking his head at his father.

"You're right, Luther; dinner is not the place for this discussion. I apologize. Once Zira's anxiety has dissipated, let the page know we are ready for the next dish."

Luther shifted back enough to bring my face to his. "Our children will fight together and for each other, not against one another." He stole my breath when his lips touched mine in a chaste kiss.

Luther kissed the star under my left eye, and I couldn't remember why I was upset anymore. I was with my companion, the father of the children growing inside me. I was safe in his arms. "Will you stay with me tonight?"

"Zira." Luther stroked the side of my face, then sighed, "I have a war to plan. I promise I will come to our bed tonight and be there when you wake in the morning. Will that suffice?"

I hesitated. My body was already suffering from the lack of intimacy. Luther would satisfy his promise if he didn't come to bed until the early hours, but I would pay the physical toll.

Luther saw my hesitancy and misread it. "She is dismissed, Zira. I will not be revisiting her bed."

"You hurt me when you stay away," I reminded, straightening a bit more as I recomposed myself.

Blowing out a heavy sigh, Luther took another step back. "Zira, we are on the verge of war. Cyrans always strategize all potential outcomes before taking action. That requires my time on top of ruling Praldia and being your husband. I love you, but being a husband does not supersede my other duties."

"And saying goodbye to your ánægjuhóra was one of those duties?"

"Yes!"

I bowed my head, putting my lips together on the insult I wanted to hurl at him. "As you say, my prince." My tone was cold as the weather outside.

Luther frowned as I stepped back out of his hold and sat down. If he could see them, my eyes would have told him that if there were a body of water nearby right now, he'd be finding out how well Avalonians fight in the water.

"Oh, you idiot," the Queen muttered.

Luther looked at his mother to see her shaking her head; his father was rubbing his left temple and avoiding looking at them both.

Shoving open the Kitchen door, Luther nodded to the page. Staff waiting to clear the table and set out the main dish entered and did their duty.

Taking his seat, it was clear to everyone that Luther was analyzing our conversation and the exact moment he realized what he had said wrong. Luther opened his mouth, but his father beat him to it.

"Luther," Searle caught his attention, ceasing his tongue. "I warned you last night there are some bridges burned that you will never rebuild. Let the river have this one and build another further upstream." Searle picked up his fork and started eating his meal.

Pain bloomed in my chest. Luther's father warned him not to go to Adima's bed last night, but Luther ignored him and went anyway. He'd wanted one last night with his lover before he let her go.

Suddenly my stomach rebelled. I raced out to the connecting corridor, where I puked on the floor at my feet.

As the last of my stomach contents pooled on the sandstone floor, my knees buckled, and I crumpled. Arms scooped me up before I hit the ground, and I whimpered at the sudden jolt as my body shot back in the other direction and pressed hard against a Cyran's chest.

"Shh, I got you, Princess," Hart assured. "Chas, go ahead and pour a glass of the Hälsodryck. Didrika, the Princess, will still need to eat once the sickness passes."

"I'll get the kitchen to put her dinner aside and bring it to the room," Didrika assured. She pushed past the crowd in the receiving room.

The Queen moved through the Elite and placed a cold washer on my forehead. "Here, hold this to her forehead, Hart. It will help her feel better. I remember the sickness like it was yesterday. It is horrible what a child does to the mother's body." The Queen smiled sympathetically at me, then returned to the dining room. "Let's get back to dinner. I'll have the staff bring up the Princess's Elite meals. Luther, will you be attending on your companion? Should I have meals sent for your Elite?"

I knew Luther's answer before he shook his head. "I have duties to see to before I can retire for the evening. Anberon, go with Hart and stay until the shift change, then come find me."

"As you say, my prince." Anberon bowed.

Luther looked to Hartwin and stopped whatever he was about to say. He looked over his shoulder to ensure the others had cleared away. Only Anberon, Wolfe, and Hildebrand remained. "You're angry, Hart?"

"Why would I be angry, my Prince? Why would the fact that the Princess is the first of her kind ever to suffer the sickness bother me?"

"Because you and I both know her sickness has nothing to do with the babes."

"You are wrong, my prince," Hartwin corrected respectfully. "Her sickness is the babes within her reacting to their mother's distress."

Without another word, Hartwin turned and walked back to the apartment, holding me tighter to him. "He does love you, Zira. He just forgets that he fell in love with an Avalonian. Remember, he is stressed right now. The woman he loves and his children are in danger, and he has enemies now where he never thought to find them."

Chapter Seven

The shift change came and went. Anberon left along with Wolfe, Hildebrand, and Didrika, while Hartwin and Chas stayed. Luther permanently appointed them on guard duty until further notice. After an hour of watching the Elite play Kort, I untucked my legs and put aside the book I was reading. "Elite Hartwin and Chas, I plan to retire for the evening. You will both accompany me to bed."

All of the Elite froze. "Princess?" Hartwin blinked wide eyes at me.

"You have both been awake for far too long. One of my Elite must be in the room with me, and I wish to be held while I sleep. The bed is big enough for all three of us. If two of you are in bed with me, there will be no suspicion of anything untoward happening," I justified.

Several dropped their heads or covered their mouths, but I caught the smirks on their faces as I stood. Chewing my lip, I looked at Chas. "Am I wrong?"

"No, Princess." Chas stood, took my arm, and walked me toward the bedroom while shooting the others a dark look. "It is a good suggestion."

I'd already bathed after dinner and returned to the sitting room to wait for Luther. But it was late, and I was too tired to try any longer. When Hartwin walked in and shut the door behind him, I unsealed my robe and threw it on the end of the bed. They'd seen me naked that morning; the need to be modest in front of them was passed.

Chas removed his boots as I climbed under the sheets and to the middle of the large bed. Meeting my eyes, Chas put his hand to his uniform closure. When I gave a slight nod, he removed his shirt and pants and threw them on the end of the bed.

Hartwin, standing on the other side of the bed, turned red and lost it. "What the hell do you think you're doing, Chas?!"

"The same as you're about to do, Hart. We are giving our Princess what she needs. Skin-to-skin contact." Easing back the sheets, Chas slipped into the bed with me. He moved over until he lay pressed along my side and rested his palm over my growing abdomen.

"Are you out of your mind? Luther could come in at any moment."

Unlikely. "Hart!" I snapped instead. "I am beyond tired and beyond waiting for my companion. As your Princess, I am ordering you. Get naked. Get in this bed. Hold me until I go to sleep. Both of you will stay and sleep with me until Luther comes to bed. At that time, you have my leave to return to the Elite quarters and rest until morning."

Grumbling under his breath, Hartwin removed his clothing and got into bed on the other side of me. As soon as his body pressed against my side, I felt better. Turning towards Hartwin, I snuggled my face into the nook of his shoulder.

Chas cuddled up against my back, one of his hands brushing against my rear as he cupped his junk so that it wasn't touching me and the other draping over my waist to cup my slight belly. The nourishment of intimacy was almost immediate. It wasn't the same as what sex with my companion would provide, but it was better than starving.

In contrast, Hartwin tensed as his body reacted to my proximity, his hardening length pressing into me. With a sigh, I took Hartwin's hand and moved it between us to mimic what Chas was doing. Hartwin gasped when my hand brushed his hardness.

"You could take a few lessons on how to be a gentleman from Chas. Now, relax and go to sleep, Hart. That's all we are doing here," I murmured to his shoulder, already slipping into my dreams.

The door opened some hours later. While I heard it, it didn't wake me. But Hartwin and Chas lifting their heads in unison to look at who entered alerted me enough to listen to my surroundings if I needed to wake quickly.

Dozing, I didn't move until both men moved away from me and climbed out of bed in unison, taking their warmth and support for my body.

"Explain?" Luther's voice seemed tense in the darkness.

Even though I knew Luther wasn't asking me, I decided I should answer anyway. With a sigh, I sat up, tucking the sheet around me, allowing Luther to see I was naked with the men. Let's see how he handled that idea.

"My Elite required a rest. I needed comforting, and you weren't to be disturbed as usual. I found a solution mutually beneficial to everyone," I told Luther, enjoying the way his jaw clenched before I turned my attention to my guards. "Thank you, Elite Chas and Hartwin. The Prince will send someone to wake you both when he leaves in the morning. Go rest until then."

Rolling away from Luther, I snuggled back down to sleep. I'd seen the time. We were only hours out from daybreak. He was cutting it fine to keep his promise.

"We held her while she slept, Luther. Nothing more," Hartwin assured quietly. Sealing his uniform, Hartwin grabbed up his boots.

"And you needed to be naked for that?" Luther's voice was even, but I recognized his anger.

"Are you jealous?" Chas dared.

There was a moment's silence. Cyrans weren't meant to suffer jealousy, but I'd been counting on that not being the case with Luther. Chas was clever enough to work out my game, it seems.

"If you don't like finding another man naked with your companion, you should not neglect her physical needs while she carries your child." Chas bowed his head to Luther. "Goodnight, my Prince." Chas marched out of the room, and Hartwin shut the door as he followed him.

Climbing into the bed, Luther rolled me onto my back as he maneuvered between my thighs. He pressed into me without preparation, thrusting as if desperate for his release. The roughness of Luther's kisses and the aggressive way he claimed me portrayed how Luther felt about finding me naked in bed with two other men. I hoped that meant coming to me might become more of a priority. Still, I also wanted to ensure Luther knew better going forward.

As I regained my breath after my release, I felt Luther ready to finish. Grabbing his ear, I pulled away from his body. Luther's eyes went wide with surprise but rolled like I wanted to stay with his ear. I followed Luther over and straddled him as soon as he was on his back.

My air ribbons lashed out, wrapping around Luther's wrists and binding our arms together. Luther's eyes shone angrily in the darkness as I ground my pelvis against his. "You didn't like it did you?" I asked gently. "Finding me in bed with another man?"

"No!" Luther grunted.

Dropping my face to his neck to hide my smirk, I kissed his jaw. "I don't want anybody else, Luther, but I won't put my health or our children's at risk. We are on the eve of war. I refuse to let your stubbornness weaken me before we face our enemies."

I stilled and met Luther's eyes so he could see how angry I was with him. "My mind is made up. If you do not make the time for my well-being, Luther, I will take what I need from someone else."

Releasing the ribbons biding us, I rolled away from him, moving to the bath, leaving him unsatisfied on purpose.

The bath started pouring as soon as my feet hit the bottom step. At the same time, a large hand grabbed a handful of my hair. "Are you threatening me, Zira?"

Without conscious thought, a symbol flash-burned on my spine, and the water filling the tub rose up and crashed into Luther with force. He released me as he was thrown against the steps, sputtering with the wave washing over him.

Warily, I stepped into the bathtub, fresh water spilling around me, my power ready and waiting to protect me.

Finding his feet, Luther glared at me. He blinked. He frowned, then looked to the side and took a deep breath. "That was my fault. You warned me never to grab your hair like that."

Luther swallowed and took another breath, but when his eyes returned to mine, he was my guardian, my prince, and not my companion. "We've discussed this. I am a ruler of one country and the son of another. I don't have time for tantrums."

"I'm asking you to make time for my health and well-being, Luther!" I snapped, exasperated, slapping my hands on the water and getting little satisfaction when he backed up a step. "If you aren't willing to do that, don't bother with this war because I'll die before I can take the throne."

Luther stepped forward, his frustration highlighted in the way his hands clenched into fists. "Wars take strategy, Zira. I'm risking my companion and children, so I need to get this right."

"You are risking us by staying away!"

"I'm here now, and you chose to pick a fight."

Angrier than I had ever been, I stood up in the water, so he didn't have the satisfaction of talking down to me. "Once a day isn't enough! Ravid told you what was needed. He warned you, and you chose to ignore him. Just like you ignored your father when he warned you not to choose your älskarinna over me last night."

"I couldn't just cast her out, Zira."

"No. You chose to make me suffer. To punish me. You made your preference clear, Luther, when you decided you needed one more roll with your mistress and dumped me with your Elite for them to take care of me. Did you forget why we are here so quickly? You use the children I carry as your reasoning, but I fought off one of your Elite when he tried to kill them. If you keep neglecting me, I will be too weak to protect them next time."

Glaring at me, Luther ground his jaw but held his tongue. I got the sense that he was not used to being yelled at. Let alone by a woman. What was clear to me was that my words weren't sinking into his thick Cyran skull while I continued to raise my voice at him. It was a waste of my precious energy.

The bathwater stopped running. Dropping into the tub, I turned my tear-streaked face away from Luther and took a breath to calm down. "I've let you know how I feel, Luther. It is up to you what you do with it, but know the safety and well-being of my children are my priority."

Luther stayed quiet for another moment. "It's obvious we have reached an impasse that won't be solved in our current moods. Maybe the morning light will find you more reasonable." Luther turned his back on me and strode towards the bed.

Reasonable?! How dare he!

With a screech, I picked up the carafe of fragrant oil beside the bath and threw it at him. The glass smashed against the bedpost, just a few inches from Luther's head, covering his torso, the bed, and the floor with rose-scented oil.

Turning back to me with his mouth hanging open, Luther glared at me like I was a commoner who threw their feces at him instead of oil. "I am your prince. You dare to attack me?"

"You are a jävla rövhål, and you are not worthy of me!" I screamed at him.

Luther's eyes flared. Clenching his jaw and fists so tight the veins of his neck and arms looked ready to explode, Luther grabbed his clothes from the chair in the corner and stormed out of the room naked.

"Call someone to clean up the mess in there," Luther ordered to the Elite on watch in the outer quarters, then he turned right and shoved through the door into the Elite's quarters.

Jervaise stepped into the room, worry etched over his face. Covering my face, I sank into the bath and started crying my heart out. "Get out," I managed to sob. With a bow of his head, Jervaise closed the door.

Curling over my knees in the bath, I cried some more, going over every word just exchanged. I'd meant to make Luther jealous enough that he would think twice about neglecting me. While he certainly did not like finding me in bed with others, it seemed it wasn't enough to make me the priority I should be. I wasn't being unreasonable. If I wasn't carrying his children, I would not demand his attention, but he either couldn't comprehend, didn't care, or thought I was bluffing.

The anger I felt burbled to a boiling point, and I yelled my frustration into the bath water. A symbol I'd never used before flashed on my natal scale. The room started to shake, picking up in ferocity. Small bits of debris fell from the ceiling and walls. Letting out a scream of fright, I gripped the edge of the tub expecting the building to fall apart around me.

The doors flew open, and a half-dressed Chas raced across the shaking room, struggling to keep his bare feet under him. Jumping into the bathtub with me, Chas then grabbed my face and pressed his lips to mine. He didn't kiss me, just his mouth against mine as he stared into my eyes, and I read his greatest desire. To protect and care for me. The shaking slowly faded as I wished I saw the same thing in Luther's gaze.

Once the room was still again, Chas stepped back from me. He looked over his shoulder. "Jervaise, give me the Princess's robe; then we'll need food and another serving of hälsodryck that she can ingest on the move."

Relaying the order for food to one of the other Elite, Jervaise walked into the room and shut the doors on the people scurrying around outside. Collecting my robe, he walked over to the bath handing it to Chas while keeping his face turned away. "Don't you want a towel first?" Jervaise asked, quickly turning his back.

"No time. The protocol is to evacuate to a safe zone after an earthquake, just in case of an aftershock." Chas held up the robe, ready for me. "Princess?"

Stepping forward, still in shock, I met Chas's eyes. "Did I do that?"

Chas smirked. "First time?" I nodded. Chas slipped my robe on and closed it. "Let's not tell anyone else. Earthquakes are common in Cyra, though they don't normally get that large away from the fault lines. Still, no one will think to blame you," Chas assured me as he scooped my legs out from under me. "Jervaise."

Jervaise turned with his arms ready and took me from Chas. "She needs to dress quickly. Can you see to it while I grab the rest of my uniform?" Chas asked as he headed for the door.

"Of course." Jervaise carried me to the wardrobe and set me down, grabbing what I needed from the closet. "Princess." He handed me my clothes and turned around to give me privacy.

Facing him as I dropped my robe to the floor, I pulled the underslip over my head, followed by the long-sleeved dress. "Ready."

Stepping back into the wardrobe, Jervaise slipped a winter cloak over my shoulders and walked me to the door. When he opened it, my other three Elite were waiting, handing a military uniform jacket to Jervaise. He shrugged into it and checked the room. "Where's Chas and Hartwin?"

"I'm here." Chas stepped through the elite room doors, pulling his jacket on, looking every bit the soldier as the others. "Hartwin left with the Prince before the quake. They'll probably be at the marshalling area already. We're going this way." Chas pointed over his shoulder. "We're not risking taking a public pathway. The off-duty Elite will go the main way and give the illusion they are escorting the Princess to distract."

Cyra

As Jervaise took my arm, my Elite closed in around us. We made our way through the Elite chambers and into the former älskarinna chambers, already converted to house my Elite, to the hidden pathways. Tancred handed me a glass of hälsodryck along the way, and I swallowed it down, then I was passed a bowl of berries to nibble on.

We meandered through the pathways for what felt like hours before we finally exited into an alcove. Tancred poked his head through a door, making sure the coast was clear, then waved us into another corridor. A few meters down the hallway, he pushed the doors open into a large room full of soldiers and royal staff.

Wolfe and Hildebrand were just inside the doors. When they saw us enter, they stepped in to join our group. "We were getting worried. You're the last ones here," Hildebrand grumbled.

"Zira was in the bath when the quake hit, and the Prince's rooms are the furthest from the compound," Jervaise defended.

"The Prince has been here almost fifteen minutes," Hildebrand argued.

"The Prince wasn't in his rooms with his companion," Chas growled. Placing his hand on the small of my back, Chas stepped forward to end the conversation.

My group moved through the press of bodies that cleared out of the way to stop and stare. For most, it was the first time they'd seen me.

At the far end of the hall, Luther stood with his parents and the captains of their guards. Didrika stood off to the side, scanning the room. Her shoulders relaxed, and she exhaled hard when she caught sight of us approaching.

When we reached the royal family, my guard opened a path for me to join them. Luther turned to watch me, his eyes blank with absolutely no emotion. Stepping out of the circle of my guard, I met his eyes for a moment, letting him see my anger had not cooled, and then I moved to the side to join Didrika. Luther frowned and murmured something to Hartwin.

"Morning, Princess." Didrika grinned. "Not relieved to see your husband still alive?"

"About as much as he is that I am," I grumbled, holding my half-eaten bowl of berries out to the female Elite in offering.

Didrika raised a brow and took a handful. "You two still fighting?"

"He's calling my bluff."

"Will he win?" Didrika queried before popping a few berries in her mouth.

Huffing, I thought about his palpable anger at finding Chas and Hartwin naked in my bed. "He won't like it if he does."

Didrika assessed me and then grinned. "I knew I liked you for a reason." She looked over to where the royal family was talking animatedly. "You should go and talk to them. They are waiting on the damage assessment."

"I think Luther and I have said all we will say to each other for a while."

Didrika cocked a brow. "Giving him the silent treatment?"

"Will it work?"

"Oh, yeah. The Prince hates being ignored."

When I looked at Didrika, the hummer in her eyes made me smirk, and we laughed together. The royal family all turned to assess us, but it was the King who made his way over to us. "Ladies. Should I ask?"

"We were just discussing girl stuff, my King. You know, hair braiding and the likes." Didrika winked.

King Saboa shook his head, a playful smile covering his face. "Be careful, Rika. If Luther thinks you are teaching his companion your way of thinking, he will forbid you to spend time with her. I'd hate you to lose a kindred spirit."

Didrika beamed at the idea. "Kindred spirits. That would make sense. The Princess certainly is a fiery and determined one."

"It would seem so," King Saboa agreed. The King turned his eyes to my lips. "Tell me, Zira, did your plan to make the Prince jealous tonight work in your favor?"

I swallowed. "You know?"

"There isn't much I don't know, my dear. Answer my question?"

"No, my King. It appears jealousy only makes your son angrier and more distant."

Saboa nodded. "It is an emotion Cyrans do not deal well with. Are you hatching another plan to manipulate Luther with Didrika?"

"No, my King. I am not the manipulative type. I prefer honesty. I've told my husband my expectations and what I need. He's told me what I request is too much. As such, I've decided on a different approach."

"Oh?" The King's brows raised. "May I be given a clue?"

Bowing my head politely, I kept my voice soft as I said, "Not yet, my King. Though I'm sure, if you already know about tonight, you'll see the next one coming, a long-distance out."

"Ah!" The King touched his finger to his nose and turned back to his family. Before he reached them, he spoke quietly to Elite Penrod, the captain of his guard. Penrod's eyes came to me. He smiled, shaking his head, and nodded to whatever the King instructed.

"You told him your plan, didn't you?" Didrika looked confused. "I couldn't get a thing out of what you just said, but he understood exactly what you meant."

I swallowed, glad the King caught on. "I believe he did."

Chapter Eight

Wandering around the bedroom room aimlessly, I rubbed my belly as I sang an Avalonian lullaby. It was more to calm myself than the fetuses growing inside me. Twelve hours ago, we'd been given the all-clear to leave the safe room. Luther and I hadn't spoken since our fight.

When I arrived at lunch to find him missing, I was informed he'd returned to Praldia an hour before, resigning Galiena and me to eat alone. It appeared that I lost Luther's affection by leaving Praldia to seek protection from the King.

As I turned to cross the room again, Hartwin sat in the bedroom chair, eyes closed as he listened to me sing. Chas was asleep on the bed. That was the arrangement we'd made. While I was in my room, one would sleep, the other watch, except Hartwin wasn't watching.

A breeze caressed my ankles when I walked by the far corner of the room. I stopped to assess the wall and noticed the subtle tell of a hidden door. Checking back over the silent room, no one stirred when I stopped singing, suggesting that Chas and Hartwin were both sound asleep. Well, as much as the Elite gets.

Moving to the wall, I gave it a gentle push. The door released back into the room. Glancing over my shoulder once more, I stepped into the tunnel between walls, entering the same hidden pathway we'd been using to get around the castle.

It made sense for an escape route from the Prince's chambers. I also understood I wasn't shown this doorway for precisely this reason. So that I couldn't try and sneak off without my guard. I hesitated in the corridor. This wasn't like the palats in Praldia. I felt somewhat safe there; I'd spent half my life there. This was a strange place full of strangers.

Choosing not to explore the tunnels, I decided to discover where the breeze was coming from. Fresh air was something I'd been craving for months. Leaving the door open, so the Elite knew I wasn't trying to hide, I stepped lightly down the turret steps next to the Prince's chamber.

As I rounded the last turn on the stairs, the breeze and cold increased. Peering around the corner, bleak light entered the stairwell through an open doorway. No movement or sound came from outside the door. Sensing precisely what this was, I took the last few steps to the ground hesitantly. My curiosity overrode my sense.

Outside the doorway was an undercover area that looked out over a private garden. A Cyran woman dressed in finery with short blonde hair sat by a pond. Watching the rest of the courtyard, I moved behind the pillars supporting the wall above. The garden looked empty of anyone else, but that meant nothing.

When I reached the steps down to the garden, Adima lifted her head and smiled at me. "Finally. I was hoping to get to talk to you alone. I wasn't sure if Luther would show you his private garden, but I expected it would be the only freedom they allowed you."

Standing, Adima huffed and brushed down her dress, avoiding looking at me. "I find I'm experiencing an emotion I wasn't aware I felt. Sympathy. For you, for the situation you've been placed in, for what you've already been through." Satisfied with her dress, of wanting to get a reaction, Adima looked me over. "I have always manipulated people to get what I want, but it seems I can't manipulate this situation."

Meandering her way to the bottom of the steps, Adima admired some night-blooming flowers. "I have planned to be Queen since I was a small child. When I was old enough, I realized that even if I didn't become Queen, I could become the prince's permanent älskarinna. I hoped for more. I still do."

Turning her hazel eyes on me, Adima didn't try to hide her viciousness. "You messed everything up coming here. I would never have been put aside. He may have been your companion, but when Luther took the throne, he would have left you behind in Praldia, and I would sit by his side. He loves me!" Adima shouted, watching for a reaction.

Remaining still, I studied her quietly. Growing frustrated, Adima turned side-on and breathed deeply to control her emotions. "I shouldn't blame you. You wanted this even less than he did." Adima took a whistle from her dress pocket and blew it. The slightest sound reached my ears, telling me it was made for animals.

Adima put the whistle away as two quigs emerged from the camouflage of the garden and started moving forward. "You have suffered loss after loss. It isn't fair that you suffer for something you have no say in, but that is where we are. Sadly, removing you means I get my plans back on track. I'm sorry, Princess."

Air flash burned on my spine, and my ribbon snapped as the razor activated. It whipped across Adima's abdomen, and I pulled it back without her noticing my hand twitching. Her eyes blinked, registering the sting of pain she felt, but her attention was too focused on the approaching danger. The blood slowly oozed over the front of her dress.

Adima cocked her head, watching me. "Luther said you were strong, but I expected you to run or scream when you saw your death coming." She started backing away, probably giving herself space so that when the carnage began, she wouldn't wear any of it. "You're very composed. I hope when death comes for me, I am just as digni-fied and able to hold my head proudly."

When I stayed quiet and still, it got the better of Adima just as the quigs came even with her. "Say something!" she yelled at me fero-ciously.

The quigs heads both turned towards Adima. With her focus on me, she didn't notice. They lifted their noses in unison, and feral grins broke across their hideous faces as they caught the whiff of blood. Now, I was safe.

"I'm sorry too," I sympathized quietly, my tone soft and neutral. "I'm sorry you didn't research your mercenaries better before you hired them. Quigs don't hunt and kill on sight. They rely on sound and smell. If I screamed or yelled, they would target me. Luckily, the smell of blood will override their primitive brains with the need to kill and feed."

Adima's face was full of anger. She looked at her mercenaries and realized they were closing in on her. Confusion shuttered her rage. Her eyes turned, searching mine. Fear masked her face when I indi-cated her dress, and she looked down. Her hands tentatively touched the blood-soaked cloth. Tears streaked her face as she halted her retreat and gaped at me as if just realizing now I was actually a monster.

"I'm a peaceable person, Adima. Killing will always be my last option, and only in defense. I'm sorry your hunger for power drove you to this."

Finally realizing her mistake, Adima tried to run for the steps. The quigs gave chase. Not needing to witness the carnage, I left her to her death.

Shutting the door to the garden, I had one foot on the spiral stairs of the secret passage when her screams echoed through the silent night. The noise of the quigs growls joined with the tearing of cloth and flesh, and Adima's screams changed in pitch and intensity as they tore her apart.

Moving up the stairs quickly, I re-entered the bedroom and shut the hidden door quietly. Everything was as I left it. Both men were still asleep. Swiping the tears from my face, I went to bed and lay down, keeping my back to the door.

Chas's eyes sprang open and filled with worry as he observed my tears. Uncurling a finger, I put it to my lips. Chas scanned the room and then gave me a subtle nod.

A moment later, the door burst open, and my Elite piled into the room along with members of the royal guard. Hartwin was on his feet immediately; Chas sat up, pulling me behind him, watching as my Elite moved to form a wall between the bed and the guard.

"See, the Princess is safe," Wolfe declared to the head guard.

The guard nodded and then continued through the room to the hidden door. Twenty men followed him into the tunnel.

"What's going on?" Hartwin stepped forward to meet Wolfe.

"A woman was heard screaming in the Prince's private garden just now. They were sent to ensure the Princess was safe and investigate if the Prince's apartments had been compromised," Wolfe explained.

Wolfe turned to address me and noticed the tears still falling down my face. Frowning, Wolfe dropped his gaze to my mouth and spoke to the Elite instead. "Hildebrand, go down and see what happened."

Hildebrand nodded and disappeared into the tunnel. At the same time, Wolfe analyzed my appearance, his eyes pausing for a moment on my feet. Following his gaze, I noticed the splash of green Cyran blood across the bottom of my dress and foot. Probably, from when my ribbons snapped back after cutting Adima.

Shifting casually, I tucked my feet under my skirts and adjusted the fold of the material to hide the blood splatter. Wolfe opened his mouth, narrowing his gaze, but the weapons firing outside stole his attention.

Rushing back into the room, Hildebrand slammed the door with a curse before meeting Wolfe's eyes. "There are quigs in the garden. They've attacked and killed a woman, but that's all I saw. We must move the Princess until we are sure there are no more within the castle."

Grabbing my arm, Wolfe dragged me from the bed and towards the outer quarters. My Elite closed around us as we moved through the elite quarters, into the hidden tunnels, and down to the King's meeting room. Once we were safely ensconced, Hartwin started barking orders. Chas disappeared and returned with a drink and food, handing it to me.

Moving me away from the others, Wolfe kept his voice low as he asked, "Something I should know, Princess?" His eyes drifted down to the blood splatter on my dress.

Looking down, I purposefully spilled my drink over the blood, covering the stain with a darker fresh one, then cussed and dropped the cup. Stepping back from Wolfe, I pretended to make a fuss over the spilled dark liquid.

Grumbling under his breath, Wolfe grabbed a cloth from a cupboard and squatted to help me clean the floor. "Were the mercenaries yours, Princess?"

I lifted my head insulted. "If I was going to kill someone, Elite Wolfe, I have the means and capabilities to do it without engaging such vile creatures as quigs."

Sitting back on his haunches, Wolfe studied me. "Were they here to kill you?"

Meeting his eyes, I gave a slow blink and then busied myself, wiping my dress.

Wolfe cursed. "And you don't want anyone to know you weren't where you were meant to be, which means your Elite weren't with you." Wolfe ran a hand through his hair, looking over to where Hartwin was talking to one of the Kings' Elite. "They both fell asleep, didn't they?"

"Chas was meant to be sleeping. Hartwin was on watch."

Glancing across the room to where Chas stood watching us, Wolfe huffed. "Chas knows, though, doesn't he?"

"No, Elite Wolfe. Like you, he suspects. I'm sure he will ask exactly what you just did once he has the chance." Rising, I moved away to the corner of the room where I ate the food I'd been given.

The King and Queen arrived minutes apart, their Elite filling the room entirely. Searle made his way to me immediately. "I've decided you should have your own apartments while staying here, Zira. Somewhere former lovers of the Prince are not familiar with."

"Former lovers?" I asked, concerned.

"Yes." Searle swallowed. "The woman murdered was Adima, Luther's älskarinna. It is believed she hired the quigs to kill you, but they turned on her first."

"Oh."

Chas had moved up beside Wolfe, both listening to the conversation.

"As such, I believe it's for the best you be given new accommodations."

"As you wish, my King."

Searle nodded and went to step away. His eyes fell on the bottom of my dress. "What happened to your dress?"

"Oh, I was shaking so badly when we got here that I spilled my drink before I managed to take a sip. Elite Wolfe, I'm afraid, was also marred by my clumsiness."

Searle turned his eyes to look at Wolfe, who bowed slightly. "It is as the Princess states, my King. Her dress was not so stained when we moved her here."

The King hesitated over Wolfe's wording. "And where was the Princess when the attack occurred?"

"In bed with me, my King," Chas answered. When Searle cocked a brow at him, Chas extended his explanation. "While we did not go to bed together, the Princess was there when I woke. Elite Hartwin was on watch. I'm sure he'll confirm that after pacing the room for some time, the Princess laid down to rest also."

"I see." Searle turned his focus back to me. "And yet, you were not surprised nor concerned to find out Adima was the victim."

When I met the King's look evenly, despite his focus being on my lips, Searle gave a slight shake of his head as if he was uncertain how I knew before him it was Adima. "Now I see fully what it was about you that bewitched my son, Zira."

"I bewitched nobody," I murmured unhappily.

"I didn't mean that as the insult you took it, Zira," Searle assured. "But I am learning very quickly you are nowhere near as frail and submissive as you seem." Turning on his heel, Searle marched across the room to his Elite.

"And I'm learning very quickly why Avalonians are the Boogie men of assassins," Wolfe grumbled quietly.

"Try growing up with them," Chas muttered.

Wolfe nodded. "Explains how you climbed the ranks so quickly, Chas, and why you scare the skit out of the Queen." Wolfe turned his eyes to me. "You know he's the only Elite the Queen has ever refused her fitta."

I blushed at the vulgar term Wolfe used. "Well, the Queen and I stand opposed to that then."

Wolfe's brows jumped into his hairline in shock. "Has things changed so much since you arrived here three days ago, Princess?"

"Not in that way, Wolfe." I swallowed. "Not yet, anyway. But a lot will need to change if the Prince remains absent."

Hartwin stepped into our small gathering. "Princess, we've been given the all-clear. The King has sent ahead for your new apartments to be readied. They should be done by the time we get there."

Giving Hartwin a nod, I gestured he led the way. My Elite closed in around me as everyone departed the safe room in different directions.

Chapter Nine

My new rooms were further along the upper floor and not far from the King's residence. "Why do I feel these new rooms allow the King to keep a closer eye on me?" I whispered to Chas, who was holding my arm.

"Just be glad they aren't so he can keep you company in his son's absence," Chas whispered back. When I looked at Chas slightly terrified. Chas simpered. "Don't worry, the King has a type, and you're not it."

"Best words I've heard all week," I murmured.

Chas smiled and patted my arm before stepping away from me inside the outer quarters. The living quarters were significantly more significant than the Prince's. "Do my Elite have rooms here?"

"Yes, Princess. Those doors there are your Elite's quarters." The Queen's Steward, who greeted us, pointed to large double doors to the right. "They also have direct access to your room if needed in a hurry." The steward walked toward the two large doors on the left, throwing them open. "Your inner quarters."

He walked into a stunningly decorated secondary living area, slightly smaller than the one off the main corridor, but it made it more intimate. The steward turned to the right and opened a single door walking into a light-filled bedroom. The massive bed stood in the center of the room, with the Cyran-style sunken bathroom a side feature.

"Your bedroom. The door on the right leads to your Elite's quarters, and then there is your private balcony." The steward walked to the wall-to-ceiling glass doors and opened them onto a large balcony covered by a slanted roof which kept it free of the snow.

This was much better. "Thank you. I'd like to make one addition, if I may?" The steward bobbed his head. "I require a small kitchenette in my inner living area. Just enough to house a cooler and a decent supply of food for me to snack on."

"Of course, Avalonians do require more frequent meals. I'll see to it immediately." The steward left the room.

"Why didn't you ask for that in Praldia?" Hartwin raised a brow at me.

"They were Luther's rooms. These are mine," I answered shortly. Leaning on the rail of the balcony, I enjoyed the fresh air. The balcony was almost the size of the outer living area. There were sofas and a little corner garden with grass and a water feature.

Taking it all in, I was relieved. I could handle being locked in my room all day with this amount of space. The balcony had a fantastic view of the plains surrounding the castle, the enormous river that wrapped around two sides, and beyond that, the city of Herald, the capital of this planet.

For the first time in weeks, I didn't feel claustrophobic. The thought reminded me of my companion and how he didn't even share with me his private garden that I could have used. And thinking of that beautiful green space reminded me of how I discovered it.

Keeping my eyes on the fast-flowing river outside the castle walls, I felt my joy wilt away again. "Has someone told the Prince about Adima?"

Hartwin paused in my peripheral vision. "I called him while you were talking with the King. I wanted him to know why you'd been moved."

Sure, that's why he called him. "You shouldn't bother the Prince with such trivialities, Hart. He's a busy man."

"Zira..." Hartwin warned, lowering his voice and stepping closer.

"In fact, we shouldn't disturb the Prince for anything unless it concerns the upcoming war from now on."

Hartwin tensed beside me. "Are you ordering me to break communications with my Prince?"

Finally turning to face him, I stepped closer to Hartwin. He immediately dropped his eyes to my lips. "Would you?"

"No." Stern, short, with no hesitation. Hartwin's loyalty was to his prince.

I expected that would be his answer. After all, he gave me up because he discovered Luther wanted me. Giving Hartwin my back, I made my way inside. "Chas, gather my Elite in the outer quarters, please."

Chas bowed and moved into the elite quarters through the side door while I continued via my private quarters to reach the main living area.

"Zira, whatever you are playing at won't work," Hartwin warned, grabbing my arm to stop me as I entered the outer quarters.

Wolfe stood from where he sat, observing how Hartwin gripped my arm.

Yanking my arm from Hartwin's grasp, I stepped back from him as the twelve Elite assigned to me by Luther filed into the room, joining us. "You don't have my trust anymore, Hart. I don't believe you have my best interest at heart."

The silence in the room was palpable as Hartwin stared at me, his eyes blinking as if my words hurt him.

Ignoring Hartwin, I focused on the gathered Elite. "Elite Hartwin is no longer the captain of my guard. Until final replacements are made, Elite Wolfe, will you act as my captain?"

Wolfe bowed his head. "It would be my honor, Princess."

Giving him a nod, I gazed at my Elite and their wide eyes flicking between Hartwin and me. "The Prince has impressed upon me that he is too busy running Praldia and planning a war to be disturbed by my day-to-day needs. As such, you will not report my private business to anyone except the King unless it is related to the war. You will instead direct any and all inquiries to Elite Wolfe. Does anyone have a problem with that?"

Tancred stepped forward. "Please don't take offense, Princess, but I don't wish to be caught in a war between you and our prince."

"I understand, Elite Tancred. You can grab your stuff and report, with Elite Hartwin, to the King that you are returning to Praldia and the Prince's personal guard. Thank you for your service these past few weeks."

Tancred stepped back into the elite quarters to gather his belongings.

"Anyone else?"

When everyone stayed where they were, I turned and looked at Hartwin. "Get your stuff together, Elite Hartwin. I wish to meet with my personal guard, of which you are not one."

Hartwin stepped closer. "The Prince will overrule you on this. He is still your guardian."

"The Prince is not here, Elite Hartwin. When he is, he can try forcing you back on me, but I assure you, it would be a mistake for him to do so. Now, I've asked you to report to your King."

The Elite held their breath while Hartwin and I faced off. Tancred came out of the Elite quarters and took Hartwin's arm, stepping him back before putting one of the two military-issued bags in his hands. "I got your stuff for you, Hartwin. Let's go." Tancred walked over to the door and stepped out.

"You won't win this, Zira," Hartwin warned.

Wolfe stepped forward. "That's twice you've addressed the Princess informally in open company, Hartwin. To do so shows disrespect for her and her position. I believe the Princess is right to dismiss you."

"Stay out of this, Wolfe. She's using you to play a game," Hartwin growled.

Wolfe went to respond, but I stepped forward and touched Hartwin's chin, bringing his volatile eyes back to me. I kept my voice soft, keeping what I said for the two of us. "When I was brought to the palats in Praldia, you made a request, Hartwin. I am doing what you asked. Take your honor and go, Hartwin. You made your choice between Luther and me years ago. For you to stay now would be detrimental to my contract with the Prince."

Hartwin swallowed. His eyes filled with the same emotion I remembered that day by the river when he shattered my heart. With a quick nod, he turned and walked out, slamming the door behind him. I closed my eyes for a moment, then started getting organized. "Elite Wolfe, I need you to arrange for me to have a personal comms device, please?"

"Yes, Princess."

"We are down two Elite. That will be remedied, but in the meantime, I'll need you to organize my guard to compensate. Since I only leave my room for the main meals, we can cope with the shortage."

"Of course."

When I gazed at my Elite, concerned faces looked back at me. "I have no intentions of causing trouble with Prince Saboa, so you can all relax. I must know that my guard will have my best interests at heart. That means, when the Prince's behavior puts my health at risk, you don't tell me I'm acting like a spoiled brat."

Jervaise stepped forward. "Princess, if I may ask? Are you planning on taking one or more of us as your lover in the prince's absence?"

"Taking care of me when the Prince ignores me will not be what you think. Elite Chas will explain why."

Chas stepped forward and looked over his fellow guard. "Avalonians are monogamous. Still, it is acceptable when a woman is with child, and her needs are greater than her companion's ability to meet them, that the companion's brother assists. However, no seed but that of the chosen companion may soil the royal womb."

"For that reason, I won't be taking any of you as a replacement lover," I assured. "Whoever meets my needs will need to be relieved of duty afterward so they may sate themselves elsewhere. We can't afford that. My personal guard ranks have dwindled too much as it is. If something were to happen, I would put you all at risk by making your numbers so few. I won't risk your lives any more than I will mine."

"You've thought this through." Jervaise tilted his head, eyes assessing me as if I wasn't what he first thought.

"Yes, Elite Jervaise. The Prince is not the only strategist in the system." When that response earned a snicker from a few guards, I nodded at Wolfe. "I will leave you to your men, Elite Wolfe. I'd like my comms device within the hour."

Slumping down on the couch in my private quarters, I cuddled a pillow to my chest and bowed my head. The tears I'd been holding in from when I'd decided to turn on Hartwin started to spill forward. It was the right thing to do. He would take Luther's side no matter what, and I didn't need someone else making me second-guess my instinct. Still, it hurt to have to do it. More so to see that look in his eyes again after all this time.

After the initial impact, my tears ran dry. My brain was determined. It was time to retake control. Walking to the table, I poured and drank a glass of water.

A quick rap preceded Wolfe stepping into my smaller space and closing the door behind him. "Thank you for putting your trust in me, Princess."

Raising a brow, I prompted the rest with, "But?"

"But I wanted to ask, why didn't you choose elite Chas?"

Again I found myself finishing his words. "Because he outranks all of my Elite except Hartwin?"

"Did he tell you that?" Wolfe considered.

Elite rank was overarching, but despite never being revealed to outsiders, there was a ranking system. Only the King, Prince, and other Elite were supposed to know the actual ranks.

"No. It's the way they so easily defer to him. Just like everyone defers to Hartwin and you." I poured another glass and handed it to Wolfe, indicating he should sit then I sat opposite him. "Chas won't be my captain because I need him on the night shift right now. He was raised part Avalonian, even if he is full-blooded Cyran. He knows the boundaries and treats me as a Princess of his own blood."

"You just told the men none of them will be your lover."

"And they won't. Chas and I have grown quite close while in quarters. I don't have that with any of the others."

"But you are being honest with me?"

"I was honest with the others. Chas and I will not be lovers, and I will not be taking a lover. Cyrans cannot grasp the concept of affection the way Avalonians do." I considered Wolfe. "If I asked you to join me in bed and provide intimacy, what would you expect?"

"I would be rolling around in that bed with you till both of us see stars," Wolfe answered honestly.

I smiled kindly. "To an Avalonian, that is passionate sex. Intimacy is not the same thing. Intimacy does not require one or both parties to have an orgasm, and it does not require sexual penetration. When I asked for intimacy from Chas last night, he climbed into my bed, pressed his naked body against mine, and caressed my children through my abdomen. Hartwin climbed into my bed and instantly got an erection."

Wolfe assessed me. "I would hazard a guess that Hartwin's reaction was from previous exposure."

When I lifted a brow at Wolfe, he continued. "You two have history. The way he addressed you and felt comfortable manhandling you..."

Focusing over Wolfe's shoulder, I swallowed. "When I was young, a boy lived near me. We were close friends. When I came of age, we became lovers. I loved him and wanted no other in my life. Two years ago, Hartwin and Commander Stark removed him from my life. I've never gotten over him, and I'll never forgive them."

With a sigh of disapproval, Wolfe pushed a comms unit across the table. "As you requested, Princess. What happens now?"

Collecting the comms unit, I typed in a message before sending it. "Now, I play catch up."

Chapter Ten

"Goodnight, Princess," Jervaise farewelled as he escorted me back into my quarters after dinner. The other Elite finishing their shift echoed the greeting.

"Goodnight." I moved towards the inner quarter's door, Wolfe close behind me.

"I'll wait for Chas to come in, then I'll bid you goodnight also," Wolfe informed as he shut the internal doors.

"Actually, if you wouldn't mind waiting a little longer, Wolfe, I have a guest coming in an hour," I informed him. "Can you notify security we expect a long-range teleport directly into my inner quarters?"

Wolfe let his eyes hesitate only for a moment before he took a seat on the lounge and typed something into his comms. "Of course, Princess. I'm gathering your guest will be coming in from Praldia?"

"You would be correct, Wolfe," I confirmed, pouring myself a drink of the Hälsodryck.

"Whose name will the teleport link connect under?" Wolfe asked carefully as he typed.

I smirked. "It will be unlisted."

"And will your guest be requiring quarters during their stay?"

"No. He will return to Praldia after a few hours." I took the seat opposite Wolfe. "Don't fret, Wolfe. He is an old friend, and the person who helped me escape Praldia to seek the King's protection."

Wolfe's face eased, and I could see he was happy to find out who managed to teleport me directly into the King's chambers when it was a locked location.

"You may tell the King," I assured, "But not the Prince."

Wolfe nodded. "I can accept that, Princess, though the King may inform the Prince later."

"I would ask that he didn't." I levelled Wolfe with my eyes, and he quickly dropped his gaze to my mouth.

"I will ask the King's confidence," Wolfe confirmed.

"Thank you." I settled myself down and closed my eyes to rest until Ethelred arrived.

The lightning cracking through my inner quarters brought me out of my doze. I opened my eyes to see Wolfe and Chas standing, watching the space between the lounges and the outer quarter doors. They both had weapons drawn and held ready at their sides. I stood up, and a moment later, Ethelred disembarked the teleportation channel. He dropped to one knee before me.

"Princess." Ethelred stood, and I stepped into his strong arms. "To hear your voice is to hear the sunrise," Ethelred murmured. I tensed at the warning we were being listened to. Ethelred hugged me firmly until I took a deep breath and stepped back from him.

"Thank you for coming," I greeted and gestured for him to join me on the sofa.

Ethelred took the seat opposite where I stood while I focused on Chas and Wolfe. "Thank you, Elite Wolfe. You can get some rest now."

"Princess." Wolfe bowed his head and walked out.

Meeting Chas's eyes, I tilted my head towards my bedroom door. Without a word, he stepped into my room and closed the door.

Ethelred smirked. "Taking a leaf out of the Queen's book, are you?"

I shook my head. "The Prince has called my bluff that I will take a lover in his absence. I'm not willing to put my health at risk for him."

"Nor should you," Ethelred agreed. "Is that why you summoned me?"

I smirked, sitting down. "Would you like to be my lover, Ethel?"

"I wouldn't say no, Zira." He grinned.

"Maybe later." I blushed. "Right now, I have another job for you."

Ethelred considered me. "Am I going to like this job, Princess?"

"Perhaps not," I admitted as I picked up a media viewer, opened a blank window, and wrote what I wanted from him. "The Prince is unreasonable and unwilling to take care of my health needs," I stated clearly while I typed.

I NEED to know his strategy for the upcoming war against Avalonia.

"I NEED a plant that only grows in the ocean in Avalonia. Here is what it looks like." I held the device out to him to read.

"This could be very difficult to get. Could you not just take a lover here to care for your needs?" Ethelred advised.

"I will be doing that. The plant will benefit me in another way." I advised him and saw the unhappiness on his face grow as I held the tablet back to him.

HE WILL BE TAKING me with him. It's the only way to end the war quickly and with the most minor casualties. Therefore, I need to know what he is planning and when.

. . .

ETHELRED TOOK a deep breath and stood. "What you require is inaccessible. I don't know if I can get this for you."

"Could you try?" I asked.

I watched him pace back and forth, deciding if he could do it. I didn't interrupt his thinking process. Ethelred was intelligent and good, but I'd discovered he was brilliant at being bad. He had a great mind for strategy and mischief, which I found to be shared among the Elite Cyran guard. While Ethel was a well-respected trader, he'd also developed networks with smugglers, black market traders, and mercenaries. This had undoubtedly entrenched him as the go-to man when even the Prince wanted something nobody could get. It's how we'd met. I wanted something nobody else could give me; it just so happened that I had something Ethelred needed.

Ethelred stopped pacing and looked at me. I saw the smile slowly form on his face. "Okay, Princess, I can get you what you want."

"And the cost?" I asked. I wasn't stupid. Ethelred was a trader. I may be his Princess and friend, but that did not mean his services came free of charge.

"And there we have our problem, Princess, because your money belongs to your husband now. You have nothing to pay me with." Ethelred retook his seat and sat forward to meet my gaze. Well, he looked at my lips.

I tilted my head, assessing him. "That's not true, or you wouldn't be looking at me like that." Ethelred's eyes told me he'd already decided on his price.

"You were on the native council when they bargained with Skog for the Crystalstar mine on behalf of the Prince. Rumor among the smugglers is that the council struck their own deal with the natives and hid a certain ore from the Prince. The rumor suggests that Skog was rich in Crystalstar and kilocycles. The council has been dividing that score and selling it off on the black market."

I assessed Ethelred. "I've heard that rumor. Why would you think the native council would do such a thing?"

Ethelred's smile grew when I hadn't denied it. "Because you sell it and give the natives of Skog a percentage. It's been bugging the Prince how wealthy a land Skog has become from the dismal earning they receive from mining the Crystalstar for him."

"If you discovered this rumor is true. What would you do with that information?" I asked carefully.

"Two things," Ethelred admitted. "First, that's how you would pay me. Secondly, I would take that information to the Prince."

I shook my head. "Use something else to gain favoritism with the Prince." I was not having him take that from me.

Ethelred's eyebrows jumped. "So it is true?"

"You are wrong about the native council." It was my turn to sit forward. "Some members of the native council are greedy little squirrels. They would strip Skog barren if they thought for even a second it was an ore-rich land." I admitted. "I was the negotiator on the contract. I oversaw the geological testing and the report that went before the native council and the prince. I assure you, the native council has no agreement with the Skog natives," I promised sincerely. And they didn't. On the other hand, I had made myself a tidy fortune from my twenty-five percent cut of the profits. It was well hidden, my earnings deposited into a Cyran bank here on Cyra itself.

Ethelred's eyebrows lowered. "I was sure the native council were the klockglas smugglers?"

"No," I confirmed. "Not klockglas and not from Skog." I assured. I sat back casually. "If you were asking about ruter out of Massor..."

Ethelred's mouth fell open, and he was so surprised that he met my eyes for a moment. "The native council is mining in Massor?"

I smirked. "For five years now." I took a deep breath. "The Prince never looked there, and as such, certain members of the native council decided not to inform him of how plentiful its land was. Four council members have lined their pockets very well from the high-grade ruter buried there."

Ethelred studied me. "I want the name of the smuggler."

"And that's all you want as payment for what I ask?"

"And the name of the council members," Ethelred clarified.

"Blackness, Ethel," I grumbled, standing up. "They'll know I told you. That could get me on the wrong side of some people."

Ethelred stood up and moved towards me casually. "You are the Princess. You are about to go to war. What makes you think it could be worse than it already is for you?"

I swallowed as Ethelred closed the proximity between us, his hand caressing my cheek. I nodded and stepped back. "You have a deal. What would you like as a down payment?"

Ethelred smirked, remembering the first time I'd hired his services, and I'd refused to pay an advance. "The dagger," he stated clearly.

Confusion took over as I wondered what dagger he was referring to.

"The one Elite Utz had buried in his chest before you took it." Ethelred leaned into me, his lips mere millimeters from mine. "You took his hand off and stabbed him to protect yourself. You wouldn't have taken the weapon unless it was dangerous."

I assessed Ethelred for a moment before I stepped back, shaking my head. "I lost it in the channel. It's probably washed out to sea by now," I lied. I was a good liar; I had to be. I wasn't going to ask why he wanted a weapon he thought could be used against me. He was a trader. Anything of value was worth having.

Ethelred's face dropped in disappointment. "Then it will have to be an 'I owe you', won't it, Princess?"

Taking a stabilizing breath, I opened my mouth and betrayed people I never thought I would. "Dali D'ver is the smuggler running the Massor operation," I informed Ethelred.

"Dali?" Ethelred laughed. "I would never have suspected him. I thought for sure you were going to say Singh."

I frowned. "Blackness, no. The council would never do delicate business with such an animal."

Ethelred smiled and looked towards my bedroom door. "You are starved of nutrition, Zira. You need to take your rest now." He bowed as he stepped back. "I will contact you when I have what you need."

Bowing my head, I waited while Ethelred activated his teleportation chip and left. I felt the betrayal of those I'd worked with for years, but they'd turned on me first, forgetting the secrets I carried. I'd do nothing to hurt the natives, but those smuggling the ruter did not give back to the land or people.

With a deep breath, I opened the door to my bedroom and walked in, closing the door behind me. Chas was in the reading chair reading a book. "Your guest has left?" he asked. He would have been listening for the teleportation channel sounds.

"He has. I need intimacy and rest now." I advised as I walked towards the bed, releasing the clasp on my dress.

Chas stood and started to disrobe. I kept my slip-on as I climbed into bed, Chas climbing in beside me and cuddling me to him. He lifted my slip enough to place his hand over my womb and sang a Cyran lullaby to my unborn children as I relaxed in his arms.

"Prince Saboa will be waking soon to find you have dismissed Hartwin and cut him off," Chas reminded me quietly. "You may not get much sleep before he wants to discuss that move with you."

"Then let the guard know I am exhausted and am not to be disturbed until morning," I murmured.

"That will not keep the Prince out, Princess."

"If he bothers to come in person, he can do his husbandly duties while he vents his unhappiness. If he calls, he can crawl into a worm-hole," I sighed.

I fell asleep while Chas typed a quick order into his comms for the two Elite on duty in the outer quarters.

Chapter Eleven

The doors to my room flew open as Luther stormed in, his face filled with his ire as he approached where I lay. Chas slipped from the bed behind me, drawing Luther's gaze to his naked body for a moment before it returned to me. His jaw clenched as he yanked the bedding back and took in my slip, then his eyes scanned the sheets as if looking for evidence of more before he stepped past the bed to the windows.

My eyes went to the window and groaned at the darkness outside. "Chas, I'll need food if the prince wishes to converse with me in the middle of the night."

Bowing his head, Chas went out to the inner quarters and shut the doors to the bedroom. Getting up, I put my arms through my robe, pressed the closure at my waist, and dropped into one of the comfy chairs by the fireplace. Opening the little cooler the steward arranged for me in my room, I took out the Hälsodryck, poured myself a serving, and then sat back and watched Luther while I sipped it.

The sky outside was dark, but the lighting around the palats still provided a view of an evening landscape. Luther stood with his hands clasped in his lower back, much like I saw soldiers on guard duty do. Only the crackling of the fire filled the space between us.

A knock at the door. Chas came in, fully dressed, and placed a plate with some berries, cured meats, and ost on the small table before me, then left again. Picking up a handful of food, I tucked my legs beneath me and sat back, watching my companion's back as he breathed. The silence continued, so I got comfortable and grazed.

"Did you fuck him?" The question broke the silence without warning.

"He held me and sang Cyran lullabies to our children. His cock has never come near me," I answered casually before popping another berry between my lips.

The silence gathered around the words and swallowed them again. The fire crackled. I finished the plate of food and poured two glasses of water. Picking mine up, I sipped it.

Luther took the glass I'd set aside for him and sank into the other seat. The flames reflected in his eyes as he drank the water. Luther set the glass on the table again and sat back, his eyes on my lips. I decided to get this over with. I was tired. Both physically and emotionally.

"Hartwin became a risk when you abandoned me. Cyrans may not be monogamous, but I am. I can accept intimacy from another and not risk my morals. That's not the case with him. Hartwin also didn't make my health a priority. He sided with you. I couldn't trust him, and you couldn't trust me with him. He had to go," I justified.

Luther shifted his eyes to the fire, the midnight blue of his irises glowing orange as flames danced in them. His olive skin glowed in the light, giving shadows to the contours of his body. His strength was hidden by his uniform, but my body experienced it enough times that I already knew it by heart. Heat and need slithered and pooled between my legs.

Setting my cup down, I uncurled my legs and rose to stand, deciding that I should offer him some relief since Luther didn't come in here yelling and screaming at me. "You're welcome to take your pleasure from me since you've taken the time to come and discuss my reasoning with me in person. But I also understand if you need to get back to the things that are actually important to you."

Ignoring how Luther's face snapped in my direction, I moved to the bed, removed my robe and chemise, and climbed up on the mattress. Lying on my side so I could stare at the snow floating down from the sky in the darkness, I gripped the sheet in my hand, waiting. So far, Luther hadn't said a word. That was unlike him and probably more terrifying than when he yelled at me.

Rough fingers touched just above my knee, making me flinch with surprise since I hadn't heard Luther approach. They skimmed up the outside of my thigh, over my hip, dipped to follow my waist, and then climbed my upper arm to my shoulder, where they circled once before making the return journey.

The mattress jostled as Luther climbed on behind me. Still, instead of curling in behind me or climbing on top like I expected, he stayed on his knees and kissed my hip as he shoved a pillow in front of my pelvis. "Roll to your stomach."

Rolling forward, I pressed my forehead to the bed while the pillow he placed lifted my hips into the air for him. Before I even got comfortable, he forced my legs apart and licked through my middle. The shock made me jolt and gasp. Tightening his grip on my thighs, Luther kept my legs open as he started to feast on me, tasting my hunger for him, licking and sucking my readiness from my flesh.

Luther sipped at my lust like a man deprived. The more my body readied for him, the more fervently he drank. I clawed at the bed sheets and begged for release, but that only caused Luther's grip on my thighs to bruise and his tongue to drill me until he'd unearthed a river of need. Only then did he give me two of his fingers while he sucked at the crown of my passion and spilled me into the stars.

While I panted and prayed, Luther covered me, thrusting into me. Crying out, I gripped the sheet, my knuckles turning white with the strain of holding on for dear life as Luther pounded my body. He kept me pinned down with a hand on my hip and the other on my shoulder. Our bodies were apart except where he buried inside me, bringing me to repeated climax but never hinting at his own.

If he had given me words of endearment, touches of affection, and kisses as he changed positions, I would have believed he missed, desired, and wanted me. But he gave me nothing but his cock and his bruising grip. Sweat coated my body, and my fingers ached from holding it so tight for so long. The room grew lighter as the night dwindled to morning, and Luther chased the darkness from the sky through my body.

Just before the sun won the sky, Luther shoved deep one last time, yelled a curse, and spilled into me. He pulled out of me, climbed off the bed, dressed, and left without a word. It was then that I understood the very definition of hate sex.

Gone were the passion and desire that had drowned me our first night together. Or the affection and possession that had built in the weeks that followed. I understood as I watched the sun lighten the sky and let my tears hide amongst the sweat-drenched sheets that I lost him when one of his Elite betrayed him because of me.

Utz's blade severed more than just my air ribbon. It cut Luther's adoration for me at the root. In the days that followed, his actions towards me had withered the growing bloom of affection I'd been nurturing for him. My companion, the father of my unborn children, hated me, and I think I was relieved.

Eventually, finding the energy to get off the bed, I moved slowly to the bath. I fell into the heated waters that filled around me. Floating there until the water cut off, I sank beneath the water. I lay on the bottom of the tub, staring at the beautiful, intricately carved sandstone ceiling from the stillness.

No one came looking for me. I had no doubt my Elite on duty had heard their Prince with me for hours on end and assumed I'd be resting to recover. Thankfully, I had enough supplies in the cooler to cover my nutritional needs for the morning. I probably should have sent for breakfast, but I wanted to be alone. Chas hadn't returned to the room when Luther left, nor did anyone come in with the shift change. It was weird to have this solitude again for the first time in months, and I welcomed it.

Taking my tablet, I went out on the balcony, wrapped myself in the King's fur coat, and browsed the broadcaster feeds. Praldia was speculating on why I was taken to Cyra and left there when the Prince returned. The Cyran news was all coverage of Adima, the royal Älskarinna's funeral. Apparently, it was held this morning. And there was Luther. Standing front row, only meters from Adima's parents as they lowered the torch to the covered pyre.

With a finger, I traced Luther's angry eyes, his jaw tense and clenched. The broadcaster talked about the Prince's grief at losing his most favored Älskarinna while the footage showed the funeral. They speculated whether the quig attack was meant for the Prince and they got Adima by mistake while she waited in his garden for him to join her, or if I was the target and Adima was killed by accident. None of them suggested she hired the mercenaries, that she shouldn't have been in the garden, or even that she had been dismissed.

"His most favored älskarinna," I murmured to myself as I saw that line pop up again and again. The broadcaster showed old videos of the two dancing and flirting at previous balls and festivals.

My body ached. Setting aside the tablet, I walked to the balcony edge, looking out across the river and the city beyond. "You didn't come back last night to talk to me. You came back for her."

Bowing my head, the real reason Luther even bothered to come planet-side was realized. I clenched my face to prevent crying, to prevent letting how much that stung impact me. When I refused to shed any more tears, my back twinged, and the resulting seizing of muscles freed dribbles of Luther's seed from between my legs.

Sickened to my stomach, literally. I lifted my skirt and swiped the drips inside my thighs. Turning to wash my hands, I slowed my steps when I noticed the fluid wasn't opaque as expected but black.

Swallowing with difficulty, I continued to stare at the blood on my fingers as another cramp released another flow down my inner thighs. Going to the door for the inner quarters, I slid it open to find

Wolfe and Didrika sitting there discussing a report they were reading.

"Princess, you're awake?" Wolfe greeted with a smile. "Did you wish to eat lunch in your room today? The royal family is at an event."

"The funeral. Yes, I saw it on the news," I answered.

"Princess, is something wrong?" Didrika was on her feet, her eyes on mine, on the tears tracking down my cheeks.

"Could you find Elite Jervaise, please? He needs to return to Praldia immediately and fetch my doctor, Medic Nyla. And after he's left, I'd like to ask the King if he'd grant me a divorce."

"A divorce?" Wolfe was on his feet, both the Elite looking very concerned now. "Princess, did the prince hurt you last night?"

Didrika was typing into her comms. "We can fetch the medic, but the King will not give you a divorce, Princess. Not while you carry his grandchildren."

"Well, I think that won't be an issue now," I muttered to Didrika as I showed her my hand.

"What-?"

The outer doors opened, and Jervaise stepped in. "You need Medic Nyla? How bad is it?"

Blinking more tears free, I lifted my dress to show my feet and the small pool of blood that had collected in the minute I'd been standing there. "Pretty bad."

"Blackness!" Wolfe cursed.

Jervaise's face drained of color as he looked over his shoulder to the Elite in the other room. "Wake Chas right now and report I'm doing a long-range teleport, and when I come back, I'll have a medic with me." He touched his wrist as he said the last, and lightning cracked before he spiralled away.

"Princess, I'm-" Didrika's eyes were filling with tears, her hands clenching as if she wasn't sure whether to hug or let me go.

I eyed my blood-smeared fingers again, too numb to get upset beyond the tears cascading down my face. A violent cramp ripped through my inside, curling me over myself, and I cried out. The doorway filled with worried Elite and pushing through them, Chas. His eyes found my feet, his mouth opened, and then his eyes met mine. "No, Princess. No, no, no-"

My eyes rolled up into the back of my head as he bolted forward, but he was too late as the blackness stole me away.

Chapter Twelve

Luther

I was still angry. Never in my life had a woman infuriated me like Zira could in one look. When I returned to the palats to discover her Elite unconscious and Zira gone, I was sick with worry that I'd lost her and that my sons would be lost by the time I found her. But that wasn't the case.

Once again, my wife proved strong and capable and dispatched her adversary. It was what came after that cut me. When she hid from me, escaped to my home, and begged my father for his protection. By doing so, she declared I was incapable of keeping my wife safe. She all but told me I'd failed to do my duty to her and our sons and that she didn't trust me.

Nothing about our relationship had been easy. I don't know why I expected it to be smooth sailing once I made Zira mine. I knew it wasn't going to be. I forced her to join with me, and I knew Zira was passionate and driven. She had no issue calling me names in open court, so she certainly wasn't going to hold back in private.

Zira's passion and drive to protect those who couldn't defend themselves was half of her appeal. As I expected, the sex was phenomenal. Stubborn, intelligent, and dangerous, but when she submitted to me? Stars! It was the hottest thing I'd ever experienced.

But I went from being the Prince who forced her to marry him to the inept companion when Utz betrayed me. She went to my father. Trusted him and not me. I'd never failed anything in my life, but I let her down when it mattered. It was in her eyes when she looked at me now. I had to deal with this war, get it over with, and then I could go back to trying to prove I was worthy of her.

That last night together, when she'd taken her pleasure from me and left me unsatisfied, angered me beyond reason. It angered me that the woman I adored didn't want me for me but because of her biology. Zira wanted my cock to nurture the babies growing inside her, not because she desired me. I felt used and replaceable. The way she spoke to me, threatened me, and blackness, how much I hated finding her naked in bed with other men. No other had seen her naked before me. Not even her previous lovers. Yet, she'd bared herself to Chas and Hartwin. I'd never felt such fury as I did that evening.

"Prince Saboa," Anberon called my attention back to the room. Commander Stark and Ravid were still strategizing, but I was too consumed in my thoughts. Zira hated me. When she told me what she thought of me the last night we spoke, the venom in her voice kept playing over and over in my head.

'You are a jävla rövhål, and you are not worthy of me!'

"What is it?" I kept my back to the others. I didn't want them to see how angry I was and think it was their doing.

"Hartwin and Tancred are on their way back to Praldia," Anberon conveyed.

That made me pause and turn to meet my captain's eyes. "Why?"

"I wasn't told. They are reporting back to you and returning to your guard."

"On whose orders?"

"The King's."

What the hell was my father doing, dismissing Zira's guard? He knew Hartwin was like a brother to me. There was no chance he'd betray me. I looked to Commander Stark. He'd been close with my father. Maybe he had some insight.

"I don't know, my Prince, but the King wouldn't make this decision without reason," Stark counseled. "Could it be because of the Älskarinna?"

"Unlikely," I answered. Annoyed at this unexpected issue, I huffed. "Commander Stark, Ravid, take a break."

Waiting while they bowed and left, I indicated Anberon should stay and shut the doors. "Who replaced Hartwin as captain?"

"Wolfe."

That made me pause. I expected Chas. "Wolfe will give me the King's answer. Who would you call for honesty?"

"Jervaise. He can't hold his tongue to save his life," Anberon smirked.

Pressing my comms, I called Jervaise.

"My Prince," he answered. I guess that meant he's on the night shift still.

"Why are Hartwin and Tancred returning?" I asked straight out.

"The Princess gave the option for us to stay or return to your service if we felt we couldn't choose her well-being over our loyalty to you," Jervaise answered. "It was a good move on her part. She needs to know her Elite are hers. She hasn't trusted us since we were appointed, especially since Utz betrayed us."

And there was my failure like an open seeping wound. One of my Elite tried to kill my companion and unborn children. "I would argue that the Princess's well-being and loyalty to me go hand in hand."

"When the Princess was in Praldia," Jervaise answered, his shoulders tensing. He agreed with me but defined there was a limit to my argument.

"Are you implying that has changed, Elite Jervaise?"

"I'm not implying anything, my prince. The Elite are trained to pick up on the smallest nuances in behavior. All of us have noticed the shift in your attitude."

My eyes flicked to Anberon, but he stood staring at the floor. He agreed with Jervaise's assessment. Gritting my teeth, I turned back to Jervaise. "Hartwin chose to leave?"

"No. I'm unsure how it started, but I witnessed Hartwin manhandling the Princess, and he disrespected her twice in front of us. The Princess dismissed him as her Captain and appointed Wolfe in his place."

"Why Wolfe?" I tried to tease out the truth here. Chas was the highest rank after Hartwin, and I wasn't blind to how close he'd become with Zira.

"Elite Wolfe was never your Elite, my Prince. He was your father's. The choice made it clear again that the Princess's trust in her Elite is shaky at best, both because of Utz and because we were your Elite for years before we became hers."

My fist clenched on my desk. "I see."

"When Elite Hartwin was dismissed, the Princess's exact words were, 'You don't have my trust anymore. I don't believe you have my best interest at heart'," Jervaise reported. "It was obvious words had been exchanged before the rest of us were summoned, but I believe those words are at the core of everything."

Taking a moment to absorb those words, I felt like they were not just meant for Hartwin but also for me. "How was the Princess after the news of Adima broke? I heard she was moved to a new suite and that the quigs were meant to kill my companion." And that Adima had hired them.

Jervaise's face turned to look over his shoulder, then came back to meet mine, his posture tense. "We've been ordered that no one is to be informed about anything to do with the Princess. Any inquiries about her or her well-being need to be funnelled through Wolfe. He's currently sleeping, but I could wake him if you want to ask about your companion?"

"And who gave this order?"

"The Princess. She understands you are quite stressed and busy preparing for war and doing your duty as the prince. She does not wish to add to your burden."

She doesn't want her Elite telling on her to me. She's testing if she can trust them to put her first. It was a smart move, one I appreciated. When I'd chosen my Elite, I did so from the newly graduating cohort to ensure their loyalty was to me, not my father. Commander Stark was the only member who had ever served the King.

"Should I wake Elite Wolfe for you, my Prince?" Jervaise pressed.

"No. I'll be planet-side this evening. I will speak to my companion myself. Thank you, Elite Jervaise." I cut the comms and turned my eyes to Anberon. "My companion instructed her Elite to cut me out of her life. Is there anyone you trust who can filter your updates?"

"Hartwin, Tancred, and Jervaise were in my platoon. They were my best source of inside information. Two are out, and Jervaise just made it clear his loyalty is to the Princess," Anberon answered.

"Even if it was you asking?" I tried.

"Especially since it's me asking. He's not stupid."

"It was a good move on her part," I acknowledged.

"You don't give your companion enough credit. She stayed and acted as always when her parents were tried as traitors when others would have run or thrown themselves at your mercy. She is intelligent and, having seen her in action, very dangerous when pushed. Don't be so surprised that she knows how to protect herself."

Nodding along with Anberon's assessment, I tapped my fingers on my desk. "Adima's funeral starts mid-Cyran-morning, but I'll return once I've finished the council meeting this afternoon."

Anberon's jaw tensed. "Your älskare was dismissed and tried to murder your companion."

"The news of her dismissal hadn't circulated, and her actions that brought her death will not be revealed to protect her family's reputation." I didn't miss Anberon's anger at my words. As Jervaise said, the Elite were trained to pick up on the nuances. I was just as much Elite as I was the prince. "That angers you that her betrayal will be hidden?"

"No, my prince. That makes sense. There have been too many betrayals since your contract with the Princess was established. That's not good optics. However, attending the funeral as if she was still your älskarinna will be detrimental to your relationship with the Princess."

"More detrimental than failing to protect her from a traitor in my own guard?"

"Yes." Anberon surprised me with his certainty. "Zira is Avalonian royalty. She was trained as a young child to expect assassins to try and kill her. It's how she saved your life. But she is a woman raised to love one man and—"

I stood, Anberon's words igniting my anger. "And that one man is not me. She doesn't love me. She hates me!"

Anberon stepped closer. "You took a terrified woman who had accepted death and forced her to be your companion without wooing her first. Despite that, she was warming to you. Your fraternization with Adima in front of her humiliated her. If you haven't noticed already, your companion believes your actions over your words. Suppose you attend that funeral as if Adima was still your lover, and you mourn her even after she attempted to kill your companion. In that case, it will hurt Zira in a way you will never be able to repair."

Swallowing the truth of Anberon's words, I sat back in my chair. "I've been ordered to attend. My family must save face."

Anberon shook his head slightly but took a step back and regained his composure. "You claim you failed to protect her from Utz. Don't fail to protect her from this. Ask your bloodstones if you don't believe me about the harm it will cause her. Let their wisdom be the voice you listen to."

Bowing his head, Anberon moved to the door. "I'll organize your travel back to Cyra."

When the door shut behind him, I sighed. Taking out my pouch, I held the Bloodstones in my hand and focused on my relationship with Zira. When the stones warmed, I discarded them on my desk and read the markings. Conflicting messages. There was love, hate, acceptance, rejection, gain, and loss. The future was always hard to see because the slightest action or inaction could shift it dramatically.

Taking up the stones again, I asked if Zira would hate me for attending the funeral. The same markings appeared but in a different order which put more emphasis on the loss and made it grief.

Trying again, I asked the stones if Zira could ever love me. Once again, the order changed the focus to be on love. Still, this order again suggested that immense grief was attached to those emotions.

One last time, I cast the stones, asking about the past. Had Zira loved me before Utz attacked her? The dies were more explicit in their answer now. Acceptance, with the hope of love in the future.

Bowing my head, I scooped the stones back into their pouch. Standing, I readied for the meeting with the council. As I stepped out, my Elite prepared to follow. "Anberon, when we get planet-side, I want the Princess's Elite to be clear that no one is to mention Adima's funeral to her. What she doesn't know can't hurt her."

"How will they explain the royal family being absent for lunch?" Commander Stark queried.

"If I do my duties to my companion, she should be too tired to bother with breakfast or lunch." Some of my Elite snickered, but Anberon didn't look as convinced. "Let's go. The sooner this meeting is over, the sooner I can exhaust my companion."

HOURS LATER, I stood in the large courtyard of Adima's family estate. The other mourners ate, drank, and droned on about how wonderful she was. I wasn't ignorant of the kind of person Adima really was. My arrangement with her had been a political move. Not that I hadn't enjoyed watching her do anything to impress me and earn my favor. Blackness! Her saving grace was that she was beautiful and eager to please because her personality was not charming.

"Is that Hildrebrand?" Anberon asked beside me.

Glancing across the attendees, I spotted a familiar figure cutting through the crowd to reach my father, the King.

"Wasn't he on duty when we left Zira's suite?" I checked.

"Yes."

"Is he my father's snitch, do you think?" I asked Anberon.

"If he was, he would surely wait until he's off duty to seek the King out to report," Anberon muttered. "Could it be another kidnap attempt?"

"Let's go find out." I'd taken only a few steps in my father's direction when Hildrebrand reached him and exchanged words quickly. My father's head snapped up, scanned the crowd, and landed on me, and the stricken look made my heart quicken as he turned and walked away.

"Get onto comms. I want to know of any transmissions or happenings around my companion or her rooms."

Chapter Thirteen

The clinic room I'd been placed in was comfortable in a sterile way. The machine beside me hummed soothingly, with a regular ping to let the medics know it was working as it should. It provided them comfort while it added to my trauma.

Curled on my side, I ignored the medics behind me while they murmured to each other in a way that kept my brain from interpreting their words. My abdomen cramped again, making me whimper and curl a little tighter. Squeezing my eyes closed, the crystal blue tears I'd been shedding for the last hour escaped in a fresh release.

A cool hand felt my forehead disguised as tucking my loose hair back from my face. Nyla had done it enough times now that I knew the move for what it was.

The Avalonian skin could pick up even the slightest temperature changes. It was born by picking up thermal shifts in the water as an alert system.

Lifting the sheet, Nyla checked the bed pad they'd put under me to catch the blood and detritus. Folding it over on itself, Nyla removed it. She placed another before covering me again and moving to the prep area. "That's the second," she told Medic Ellery with a weary sigh.

Ellery had been here when I regained consciousness in the clinic. I hadn't asked why. He'd been charged with learning from Nyla how to care for me. Plus, he would report truthfully to Luther, something Nyla was not honor-bound to do.

In the corner I was facing, Chas cupped his hand over his mouth and closed his eyes. He'd refused to leave my side, citing an Elite had to stay with me at all times. The rest of my day shift was outside. One in the waiting area and the rest lining the corridor.

There was a knock at the door, and then Didrika stuck her head in. Her eyes watered as she took me in, flicked to Chas, then hardened her gaze before meeting the eyes of my Medics. "The King is here and would like to see the Princess."

"We'll talk to him outside first," Nyla responded.

"I'll stay with Zira while you do?" Didrika replied. "Two must be in the room with her."

Nyla's tiny cool hand squeezed my shoulder, then she followed Ellery out into the waiting room to greet the King. Didrika came to my side and took my slender hand in hers. "I'm sorry, Princess."

Using my hand in hers to show my acceptance of her sympathy, I closed my eyes, causing more tears to escape. "If Luther comes-"

"Of course, he'll come. You're his companion," Chas assured.

More tears escaped. Didrika rubbed my shoulder with her free hand. "Chas... let her finish," Didrika schooled. "It's okay, Princess. What do you need when Luther comes?"

Another cramp radiated through my abdomen, causing me to swallow a whimper before I could answer Didrika. I had to take my hand back to apply pressure to the outside of where my body was hurting.

"I don't want to see him," I rushed out with a sob. One hand gripping my waist, the other my pillow, I turned my face into the softness to hide from the room as best I could.

Didrika rubbed and squeezed my shoulder gently, then stepped back as the door opened. I expected the King but was surprised by the soft hands that touched my upper arm before starting to rub my back through the sheet. "Oh, Child," the Queen soothed. "Missfall, while common, is so devastating. I'm so sorry for your loss."

Taking the hand from my pillow, I gripped hers as another cramp surged through my body.

"Has she not been given pain relief?" The Queen asked.

"The Princess refused," Chas advised from the corner.

Tsk'ing me under her breath, the Queen leaned close. "You've suffered through the worst of it already. You need to rest and recover. Please, accept what the medics offer to help you through this."

With a sob, I nodded into the pillow. The Queen tucked my hair back behind my ear again. "Good girl. You need your strength to recover. Trust me, I was a midwife before I became queen. Didrika, inform the medic the Princess is ready."

Bowing her head, Didrika stepped out into the waiting area. A moment later, Nyla came back into the room with Didrika. "You're ready to accept pain relief?"

Forcing myself to pull it together and not blubber everywhere, I sucked in a breath, turned to meet Nyla's eyes, and wiped the tears from mine. "Yes, please. I'm exhausted."

Going to the prep area, Nyla checked a vial, then brought it to the machine beside the bed. She inserted it into one of the compartments next to the fluids they were pumping into me. "This will help the pain. We'll keep you here to monitor the bleeding and ensure nothing surprises us."

Already I could feel the medication seeping through me, easing the pain in my abdomen. Taking a breath, I relaxed my muscles.

"Will she need a procedure?" The Queen asked Nyla.

"Not necessarily. We'll monitor the Princess's temperature overnight and do a scan tomorrow to check that everything is clear. If some debris is still attached to the endometrial lining, then yes. We don't want to risk an infection that could kill her."

The door opened and closed as the King entered the room. "This space is looking crowded. Chas, I hear you should be on the night shift. Go rest so you can relieve Wolfe in a few hours."

Chas looked like he wanted to argue, but the order came from the King, so he got to his feet, took my hand, and squeezed it before he left. Searle waited for the door to shut, met Didrika's eyes, and tilted his head towards the door. With a bow, Didrika exited as well.

Sighing, Searle pulled over the chair Chas had used to sit in front of me and took my hand. "I'm sorry, Zira. The timing of this pregnancy was terrible. The chances of an Avalonian carrying twins to term are already meager. Add assassination and back-to-back abduction attempts, and I'm surprised you managed to get this far through the pregnancy."

When I tried to take my hand back, Searle refused to relinquish his hold, adding his second hand so that he didn't have to hurt me to keep hold. "I mourn the loss of my grandsons, Zira. Please, don't think any of us would rejoice at your grief for one second.

"I look forward to being a grandfather, and I hope to the stars that at least one of them has your strength and gumption because they will give their father just as hard a time as he gave me."

Tears spilled down my cheeks. Still holding my hand, Searle swept a few strands of hair back from my face. "No one blames you for this loss, Zira. You have no need to fear or to feel shame. Luther will stand by you."

Easing my hand free from Searle's, I gripped my pillow. "Thank you for your kind words. But I now know that Luther and I are incompatible, so I need a divorce."

Searle sat back, hands on his thighs as he considered me, then flicked his eyes over the room. "Medic Nyla, was there a biological reason for my daughter's loss?"

"A combination of stress and malnutrition, my King. Not from a lack of food, but of the heart," Nyla answered. "You must remember that Avalonians are an emotional species and require more than food and water to sustain our bodies' needs. Especially during pregnancy."

Searle gritted his teeth but gave her a nod. "Thank you. If you could excuse us," he requested.

Before his attention came back to me, the King waited for Nyla to slip from the room and the door to close. Blowing out a breath, Searle used his thumb the wipe away my tears. "I will not agree to a dissolution, Zira. As your companion, Luther has made some questionable decisions, but I know my son. He does love you. You are both stressed about the upcoming war. I think you should wait until after things have settled and you have peace to try again."

Too tired to argue, I cuddled into the pillow again. "As you say, my King," I responded, then turned my gaze to the wall and refused to look his way again.

"Ah, you may not agree with me now, my dear daughter, but I am right."

A commotion broke out outside. Voices rose in volume until they were yelling. "For the falling stars," Searle grumbled and stormed to the door, throwing it open and stepping into the waiting room. "What is going on?"

"Elite Didrika is refusing to let me see my wife," Luther boomed.

"The Princess pointedly ordered that she did not want to see you," Didrika responded venomously. "And I can't blame her."

"Watch yourself, Elite. Fucking the King doesn't make you better than me," Luther snarled.

"Enough!" Searle snapped, and everything fell quiet. "Luther, now is not the time. Zira needs to rest, and I fear your presence will only agitate her."

"Why? What happened to her? Is she okay? Are my sons safe? Will everyone stop staring at me and tell me what happened to my wife!"

There was a beat of silence.

"No," Luther breathed. "What happened?"

"The stress of the last few weeks, combined with malnutrition from a lack of companionship, was more than her body could endure," Nyla answered.

"We believe the Princess saw the broadcast of the älskarinna's funeral, and it was the last insult she could bear," Jervaise added.

Another beat of silence, and then in a croaky voice. "I didn't want to go. I wanted Adina declared a traitor, but you insisted we cover Adina's machinations, and I attend that star-condemned farce!"

Covering my face, the pain came back tenfold, making me curl in on myself and fresh tears to surge free.

"I never told you to avoid your companion or her bed," Searle refuted. "If you were taking care of her, reinforcing her emotional needs, the funeral would have been inconsequential! I told you. Warned you repeatedly to be careful what bridges you burn with your companion. How many times did she tell you what she needed from you? How often did she beg you to love her, Luther? By the stars!"

Gripping the pillow, I almost screamed as it felt like something was tearing me apart inside.

Snarling, the Queen stormed to the door. "Shut it, both of you! The damage is done, and your carry-on out here is making it worse for your companion. Medics, the Princess needs you. Searle, take your son elsewhere to ream."

Nyla and Ellery were back fussing as I screamed from the next agonizing cramp, the absorbent pad beneath me suddenly seeming saturated.

Through blurry eyes, I saw the Queen step back in and shut the door, her face pale as she watched me.

"She's hemorrhaging," Ellery announced. "We need to scan and see what's causing it."

"She's in too much pain to lie still," Nyla decided before grabbing another drip pack from the counter and connecting it to the machine. "Princess, we're going to put you. We need to find the source of the bleeding and stop it."

As the anaesthetic took me in its grip, I considered I already knew what was causing it. I'd had my heart torn open one too many times.

Cyra

"Are we going to lose her?" The Queen asked as I was dragged into the starless night.

"We can't lose her," Nyla replied calmly. "I won't allow it to end like this for her. She deserves to live, to have the life denied all our Princesses before her."

Chapter Fourteen

It was a black-and-white landscape. Only the security lights remained lit this late at night, but beyond the castle walls, there was just the pitch black of night and the snow-covered land.

During my week of convalescence, I'd taken to walking to the lookout tower's upper deck and sitting here to admire the beauty of the nothingness of the east bank. In spring, the fields would bloom with the autumn-sewn seeds. But for now, they were just snow as far as the eye could see.

"Princess," Kylar called my attention.

Looking to the North, where Kylar was posted on sentry, Luther strode across the castle rampart, Anberon by his side, Luther's gaze fixed on the tower.

Blowing out a huff, I stood and walked to where my Elite waited patiently. "Let's go meet him. I can't avoid him forever, and I don't want him disturbing my peace here."

Moving down the stairs to the mid-level, we crossed the bridge that connected the northern rampart and met Luther just as he reached the other end. "My prince," I curtseyed as I always did before we were joined, ensuring I avoided looking at his face. Not that I did the last previously, but I couldn't look at him now. My heart ached with what was lost, and I blamed him for all that pain.

"Zira," Luther said my name as if it cut him deep. "Rise up. You are my wife, not my subject."

Flinching at that cursed word, I stood to my full height, shoulders back and eyes set on the badge of Elite on the epaulets of his uniform.

"I think it's time we talked," Luther pressed as our Elite stood around us, waiting for direction.

He was right, I couldn't avoid him forever, and he'd at least given me a week. Whether that was his father's ruling or because his duties retook priority, I didn't know or care. If I'd had my way, I'd have left this palace and gone somewhere he could never find me again.

That was probably why the King ordered my Elite so I would not be out of their sight. Chas had also been relieved of duty and told to take leave. According to Wolfe, the King felt we had become too attached and was concerned that Chas might take advantage of my emotional state.

Offering me his arm, Luther gestured the rampart. "Shall we walk?"

We strode away in silence, the Elite allowing a safe privacy gap to form as they followed behind us.

"Firstly, I'd like to tell you how sorry I am, Zira. For your loss, for not being there for you. After a week of retrospect, I acknowledge I handled your coming here badly. My anger over Utz's betrayal. My failure to protect you. How you ran to my father for help. The continued threat to both of us from your enemy. All of it negatively impacted my behavior toward you. I shouldn't have let it eat at me like that."

Clenching my jaw as tingles sparked several symbols down my spine, but I withheld my power. I tamed it rather than letting my emotions control me.

Licking his lips, Luther filled his lungs only for his shoulders to slump forward and his head to bow like a scolded child. "When you refused to see me, denied me the right to comfort you, or share in the grief of losing our sons, I felt completely betrayed. I'd spent the night loving you–"

"Loving me?" I stopped and turned to glare up at the Prince. "You didn't love me that night. You fucked me, and you did it with anger and loathing."

"Zira, that's not–"

"There wasn't any intimacy between us. You didn't touch me except with your cock. You came to me angrily. You fucked me the same. You poured your loathing into me, and that is what your sons absorbed. That is what they took from you. You poisoned us with your rage and reinforced it by betraying us, and you have the gall to demand I share my grief with you? Jävla rövhål!" My palm burned, and it took me a moment to realize that it was connected to the shocked appearance and blooming heat on the side of Luther's face.

The Elite glanced from me to their prince, then to Anberon. Blinking, the Prince's captain turned his attention back to watching for other threats. The rest of the Elite followed his example. Jaw tight, Luther avoided my eyes, but he stood there and waited to see if I would strike again. Instead, I composed myself.

"You cost me my sons. You killed your heirs. I'm done trying to make this marriage work," I told Luther. "Since I am no longer with child, I no longer require your affection or your attention. Go plan your war, Luther. I will not distract you any further from your priorities."

Storming off, I made it only a few meters. "Zira, you are still my wife. There is still a contract."

It took everything in me not to give in to the itch of the symbol for sonic on my spine and see how well the prince could fly. But killing him would seal my fate as well.

"You forget that I control the ability to conceive, my Prince. You have proven you cannot take care of me when needed once already," I spat at him instead, tears forming along my lash line. "There is not a chance in this galaxy that I would trust you with my health in such a way ever again."

"Zira—"

"If you tell me to be reasonable, I swear to the stars I will murder you and throw myself from the battlements and be done with this!" I snapped, causing Luther's jaw to drop open.

Taking a step closer, I glared at the Prince. "Unless you can convince your father to see the merit in a divorce, I suggest you find another ánægjuhóra and breed bastard heirs with her. Because you have 'noll chans' of me fulfilling that contract now," I answered using the Cyran term. "I will act my part as your companion for formal appearances. I will be your bleeding heart for the people of Praldia, but you are not welcome in my bed. I want nothing to do with you on a personal level ever again."

Grinding his jaw, the Prince just glared at me. When he said nothing in reply, I curtseyed again. "Good evening, Prince Saboa."

Striding to the next set of stairs, I didn't look back. My Elite caught up to me, silent as always. The night shift is always more solemn than the day. If Jervaise had been here, he would have said something. What? I don't know, but his tongue always shared his thoughts, even when unwanted.

I made it to my inner quarters, safely tucked away from most of my Elite before the first tear fell. I wasn't entirely alone. The King had ordered me not to be left alone, even to bathe. That Elite must be in the same room at all times. They didn't have to watch me as long as they could hear me. To that length, Kylar and Erhaird turned their backs as soon as the doors to the inner quarters shut behind them, giving me the illusion of privacy.

Before I could fall into my grief, there were raised voices in the outer quarters. Then the doors burst open, and Prince Saboa stormed in, his Elite forming a barricade to prevent mine from interfering.

"Get the King," Kylar told Erhaird as he came to my side. Saboa glared at the Elite, but when all he did was stay at my side, Saboa's eyes returned to me.

"You can relax. I won't hurt her," the Prince told Kylar, even though his eyes tracked the path of my tears.

"I have seen the Princess take down an invisible assassin even with a knife in her back. She has dismembered her would-be attackers, dove off a cliff, killed Utz and thrown you into a ceiling hard enough to crack the stone. It is not the Princess I worry will be injured if you push your luck, Prince Saboa."

I could have kissed Kylar for that answer, but he also admitted he was ready to protect his prince, or maybe he was worried I'd do something I'd regret in my grief. Obviously, the King did, considering his edict.

Returning his furious gaze to me, Luther cupped my cheek in his palm. When I tried to jerk away, Luther gripped his fingers almost painfully and held me until I stayed still to wipe my tears away with his thumb.

"You are my wife. There will be no end to that until death."

"Don't tempt me," I hissed.

Adding his second hand to the other side of my face, Luther gently made me stare into his eyes. "Read my desires, Zira. I give you access to my deepest passions. Read me and tell me I don't love you. That I don't ache for you, for our sons."

Snarling, I tried again to jerk away, but Luther didn't release me or back up. He stepped closer instead, making Kylar and Anberon shift nervously. Ignoring the Elite, Luther stared into my eyes. "Do it!"

Staring into Luther's eyes, the glyph for desire burned near the base of my spine. I fell into Luther's gaze, funneling through his wants to find his needs and the passions that made his heart beat, only to see my face staring back at me. It shifted from different moments he encountered me throughout the years until it stopped on the vision of me the day I told him I carried his child.

That image swelled his heart and filled every sense of me. It was his everything, that moment. The moment his love told him that they created a life together. A piece of both of them would come into the world and forever join them as one.

Digging deeper, I sought a specific memory now, a particular emotion, and when I found it, my heart broke again. The pain as he realized our sons were lost, his guilt and grief, and the rejection when I refused to let him be with me.

"No," I whispered as the glyph for sonic flash burned. Blinking the flood of tears from my eyes, I hugged myself, sobbing to my chest as his pain joined with mine. It was easier to hate him when I could tell myself he didn't care, that he didn't love me and wanted her. But I caught his emotions around Adima, and now the blinkers were off.

Across the room, Anberon was helping Luther to his feet from where he'd landed. The sofa was on its back, having broken Luther's trajectory, and went to the floor with him.

"You think that changes anything?" I snapped at him. "You think I will forgive you the lonely nights, the abandonment? You left me alone when I needed you. You weakened me, starved your sons and me, and your actions killed them. I don't care that you are hurt. You deserve to suffer for what you did to us!" I yelled at him between sobs.

"I do," Luther agreed, his eyes still locked on me. "But I hope one day, knowing my true desires, my true intentions, you may find it in you to forgive me." Brushing himself off, Luther came closer to me but kept a respectable distance this time.

"My desire will not change. It was you from the first time you called me a selfish ass before the entire court. You are not just my bleeding heart, Zira. You are my heart. Now that I have you, I will not release you." Luther waited for me to meet his eyes. "My wife until death."

When Luther's gaze went to the door, mine followed to find the King and all our Elite observing from the outer quarters. Searle watched but remained silent.

Straightening, Luther focused back on me. "I will respect your wishes concerning intimacy and hope that you may forgive me enough to grant me a chance to win your heart again. However long I have to wait, Zira."

"The contract states three in five. It will be void long before I forgive you," I warned.

"You're not hearing me, Zira. I don't give a starless existence what a piece of paper says. My wife until death."

"Yours or mine?" I asked, glaring at my husband.

The side of Luther's mouth twitched as if he found the question humorous. "Zira, we both know you would be the victor of any physical altercation between us. I will never lay a hand on you to hurt you physically." He stepped closer and dropped his voice. "But I will sacrifice my life on the altar of your grief if it means you will one day forgive me. I earned your distrust and hate. I don't deny it, but I am not infallible just because I wear a crown. I make mistakes, and I have an ego that sometimes makes it hard to see past my nose. That is the curse of growing to adulthood with a crown. Was your brother free of his ego?"

When I continued to glare at him, Luther gently wiped away a tear that escaped at the mention of my brother. "I am not perfect, Zira, but I will strive to be worthy of you since you have declared I am not."

I didn't react to him calling me out for the words that I'd screamed at him in anger because, since that night, I had believed it. None of his actions have proven otherwise since.

"I meant what I said. I will not risk my life to give you a second chance," I threatened, hoping it would be the thread that unwound this bind.

"Then there will be no children," Luther replied without hesitation. Bowing low, Luther held it for a breath, then turned and strode from my room. He exchanged quiet words with his father and then continued to leave, his elite bowing to show me the honor of my position before following their prince.

The King waited and raised a brow at me. Clearing my throat, I straightened my spine. "I will not waiver. If you force me to stay with him, there will be no heirs."

Searle took a breath, blew it out, and shook his head. "That is your choice. We have laws in place if such an unfortunate outcome befalls the throne. There is a line of succession in reserve outside my immediate bloodline." With a slight head bow, the King turned and left.

Dropping my head, I closed my eyes while Erhaird gave orders to the Elite and Kylar righted the furniture. I took a deep breath when the room was quiet and still again.

"Princess, can we get you something?" Erhaird offered.

"Something to drink that will have me rusig quickly," I answered. "I think I've earned the right to drown my sorrows."

Erhaird looked to Kylar. Kylar jutted his head towards the doors. "Raid Jervaise's stash. He's got the best stuff."

Waiting for Erhaird to leave the room, Kylar firmed his eyes on my mouth. "There will be rules to this, Princess. We will cut you off when we think you've had enough. You will not be allowed on the balcony–"

"In case I get loud?"

"In case you fall off," Kylar corrected. "I'm performing a risk assessment in my head. You should have a bath now. I'm not letting you in a tub full of water while rusig."

"It's impossible for Avalonians to drown, Elite Kylar."

"It is not impossible for one who can vanish in water to think pulling the plug and escaping down the drain is a good idea while drunk," Kylar countered. "This is not Praldia. There are creatures living in our sewers that won't care what crown you balance. You're a snack to them, and they'll only leave your bones for us to find."

Blinking at Kylar, I blew out a breath. "Bath while sober it is." Turning on my heel, I headed into my room, unsure if Kylar was telling me fables and unwilling to take the chance he wasn't. He was right; once I was rusig, I'd probably try and escape, so taking the dangerous options off the cards was smart. The truth was, I was probably going to curl up by the fire and cry my heart out like I had every night since I was released from the medic bay.

But I didn't want to do that tonight.

"Elite Kylar, after my bath, I'd like to play Kort with my Elite on duty."

"While you drink?"

"While I drink myself into a stupor. I need to hear laughter. I need to remember how to laugh."

"I'll happily deal you in, Princess." With that, Kylar went to the fire and turned his back. Once I'd washed and gotten ready for bed, he escorted me to the outer quarters and joined the game of Kort until the early morning hours. Just before shift change, they helped me to bed, and I passed out and slept undisturbed nearly the entire day.

Chapter Fifteen

"*Then there will be no children.*"

Luther's words played over in my head. He didn't even hesitate.

"Princess," Wolfe called my attention to him as he took the couch across from where I was eating my breakfast. I'd refused to join the King and Queen for meals since the missfall, choosing to eat alone in my rooms. "That was quite an eventful night. How is your head this morning?"

Did they really think I'd never been rusig before, or that I didn't know my limits and to alternate having water between drinks to prevent dehydration?

"I'd like to go out this morning," I told Wolfe instead of answering.

To give him credit, Wolfe didn't flinch or react in any way other than to ask, "Anywhere specific, Princess?"

"I'd like to visit Elite Chas and meet his aunt and cousins. He's told me so much about them, and I think it would do me good to get out and socialize with like-minded people."

At that, Wolfe frowned. "Another Avalonian?"

"An Avalonian who lost their child and is far from their home planet."

Considering my request, Wolfe sighed. "Princess, Chas's aunt, was a mercenary when she met his uncle. While I understand she left that life behind, if she still is in contact with those people, this could be dangerous for you."

"No more than returning to Praldia would be, and you wouldn't think twice about making those arrangements for me," I challenged. "At least you know this city, these people. I'd like to call on Didrika on the way home."

"I'll need a few hours to work a risk assessment and plan. Going tomorrow would give me more time," Wolfe suggested.

Meeting Wolfe's eyes, I smiled. "Going tomorrow is not spontaneous. If you have time to plan, my enemies also have time." Setting aside my breakfast, I stood up. "Trust me, Captain. I am not new to this. I know what I'm doing. I haven't left the palats since arriving here. I've basically been on lockdown since my joining. No one will suspect this, and by the time they get wind of it and start to formulate some spur-of-the-moment plan, we'll be back in the palats walls."

Striding towards my bedroom, I didn't look back. "I'll expect to leave in an hour."

The two shadows for the day shift followed me back into my room and turned to face the door to give me privacy when I headed straight for the bath.

Once I was clean, I sat in the warm scented water and replayed everything that happened last night. The prince should know better. I wasn't the submissive Princess everyone thought me to be. The Princess that my uncle raised and abused died in the Avalonian throne room alongside her brother.

Since I escaped to Praldia, my life, and mindset had shifted significantly. I'd maintained the first rule of being a royal, to serve the good of the people. Praldians may not be my people, but they were who I was able to help in my exile.

As I grew up, I knew I needed to be self-sufficient. My parents wouldn't live forever, and I had no hope of returning to Avalonia. My work with the lemmings of Praldia led me to make connections and earn the favor of some unsavory people. Merchants and smugglers who would help me not only help the natives but also deliver me a nest egg that could easily support me if I ever chose to leave Praldia or needed to disappear.

Then Hartwin and I became lovers, and everything shifted again. I devoted myself to him, to being his mistress, forgoing marriage and possibly children. In all honesty, I didn't want to subject another Avalonian Princess to my upbringing anyway. Ten years ago, I was convinced it was best for the Avalonian royal bloodline to cease with me. Still, if Hartwin had asked me for a son, even illegitimate, I would have given him one. I loved him that much.

When Hartwin gave me up, I all but died inside. There was no other man for me but he, and if Hartwin did not love me, then children would never be a factor again. I dismissed the interest of other men. I did my duty to the people and made peace with the fact that I would die alone and the Avalonians would slowly lose their magic in the generations that followed my return to the stars.

The demise of my parents only made me believe my death would come sooner than I had planned. I wasn't scared. I accepted my fate. Dare I say, when I kneeled before Prince Saboa and offered my neck, I felt relief. The heartache of Hartwin's dismissal would come to an abrupt end, and I wouldn't have to live with the pain anymore.

Then everything shifted again. The Prince took control of my life. At first, I wasn't sure it could be any good, primarily when Hartwin was assigned as my guard. But Luther confessed his feelings, how he'd protected me, and ignited a tiny spark of hope in my heart. An ember that he smothered quickly and surely after I arrived in Cyra. Now it was just a cold dark lump of nothing.

Rubbing my chest, I massaged where the love I lost and where the hope that died both ached behind my chest bones. There was a third pain there now, but it was sharp and filled me with an emotion I'd never felt for anyone. I wanted to hate Saboa like I loathed

Abaddon for stealing my brother from me, but I'd seen his grief. The contempt he now felt for himself because of his actions was vengeance enough.

Saboa may still have me as his wife, but it was only in name. He knew he'd lost me and had no one to blame but himself. That sort of guilt and self-hate was punishment enough.

"Princess? Are you still with us?" Elite Hamlin called over his shoulder. I must have sat too still for too long.

"Yes. Just thinking," I assured.

"Then there will be no children."

Luther's words echoed the pain in my soul because they were true. But they also broke my heart. Luther wanted children. He longed to be a father. He dreamed of holding his sons, teaching them, and playing with them. When I'd read his desire, I'd even seen him adoring his daughter.

Saboa should give me up and move on with another. Have the family he dreamed for us with someone else and let me vanish into the darkness of his memories. His guilt would always be there, but plenty of guilt-ridden hearts had learned from their mistakes and moved on. I could live with being the lesson upon which he became a better husband for someone else.

Wiping the tear that escaped my eye away, I cleared my throat of the sob caught there and then splashed my face to wash it clean. Pressing the button to empty the tub, I wrapped my robe around my body and made my way to the wardrobe.

I got ready for the day by selecting one of the dresses sent over from Praldia. My belly had vanished, and so those dresses fit me with ease. That alone would have reduced me to tears since the missfall, but today I was focused, my mind shifting pieces and making plans.

"I'd like to eat again before I go out," I told the Elite.

Hamlin tapped his comms and notified one of the Elite in the outer quarters. "Shouldn't be too long, Princess."

"Thank you. I'm going to sit by the fire to dry my hair. You are free to move around." Crossing the room, I lowered onto the ottoman that sat before the fireplace and brushed my hair out, helping it dry faster. It was still snowing outside, so I didn't want to leave it damp.

Wolfe brought the food tray in and sat in the chair facing me while I ate.

"Since you prefer notice, Captain, tomorrow, I'd like to go clothes shopping," I informed him. "Do you think that will be possible?"

Bowing his head, Wolfe pulled out his comms unit. "I'll work up a risk assessment and plan while you call on your friends today."

"Thank you."

"Princess, you're not going to cause me any trouble today, are you?" Wolfe queried.

Smirking, I picked up another mouthful and ate it slowly before answering. "I promise you, Captain, I merely want to check on my friends. The two being punished because they stood up for me against the man who should have been there for me and failed to."

"Didrika's suspension is warranted. If we disagree with our charge, we either keep it to ourselves or express our concerns privately. Rika was out of line in how she addressed the prince that night."

"I heard her words. And while I agree with what you just shared, I also believe she was acting according to my wishes. Therefore, she shouldn't be punished for following orders," I countered. I hadn't had the brain power to consider the ripple effect of everything that happened that night. Still, now that I was starting to plan, I had to view all the implications.

Not disagreeing with me, Wolfe bobbed his head. "In Rika's case, you are correct, but there has always been a dissonance between her and the prince. I believe her suspension was merely the prince taking his frustration out on those he could. People always lash out when grieving. Chas is not so defensible."

"The prince's jealousy is the cause of that one, not his grief. I assure you, Chas and I are not lovers and never will be. Yes, we became close, and I turned to him for comfort since he understood my ways. What did the prince expect us to do with the forced proximity and isolation from everything I once knew?"

Frowning, Wolfe sighed. "Princess, Elite Chas wasn't suspended because he offered you comfort or stayed by your side in the clinic. The King sent him home because he attacked his prince."

This was new information. "What?"

"When the shift changed, I reported your turn for the worse to Elite Chas to make him aware of your precarious situation. Moments later, the prince arrived to get an update on your condition from the medics. Elite Chas punched the prince in the face, called him inappropriate words, and then launched another flurry of attacks at his sovereign."

"By the stars!" I covered my mouth, eyes wide at this unexpected situation. Telling your prince, you think they are a jackass for treating their wife ill was one thing. Physically attacking them was treason. "What happened?" I gathered myself enough to ask.

"Saboa responded in kind, and the altercation became quite violent, to the point they endangered other patients and themselves. The Elite had to separate them, and Chas was charged and taken to a holding cell. When the King asked the Prince if he wanted him charged, Luther declined, citing he was obviously distressed over his concern for you and needed an outlet just as much as he did. The King and Prince agreed, however, that Chas needed time out to cool down and to remember where the line between an elite and his charge should be drawn."

Taking that all in, I pressed my lips together and gazed at the fire for a moment. "Is that why you didn't want me to go today? Do you think I will cause Chas distress by visiting him?"

Scratching his chin, Wolfe considered the other two Elite in the room. Chas was well-respected by his peers. He was one of the highest-ranked Elite. "Actually, I think seeing you will ease his worry. Since he was suspended, he's not been allowed to contact anyone to ask about your health—that's not a personal restriction. It is the case with any Elite on suspension that they are cut off from any information of duty. So I think visiting him and Rika will put them both at ease."

Blinking at Wolfe, I took a moment to double-check my thinking. "Do they at least know I lived?" Wolfe looked disheartened when he gave a slight shake of his head. "Stars! They have probably been quite stressed waiting for news."

"The only relief they probably have had is that your death has not made the news, but neither has your recuperation. The broadcasters are in the dark about everything that has happened this last week."

Finishing my snack, I drank the water with it and stood up. "Well, let's not leave them wondering. When you're ready."

Chapter Sixteen

Arriving at the Royal Soldiers motor pool, several platoons were loaded onto troop transports. What surprised me was when Wolfe and Hildebrand marched me over to one of them, the royal guards stepping back to let us board first before following us onboard.

"How is this subtle?" I hissed at Wolfe.

Lowering his mouth to my ear, he kept his voice low. "Royal troops regularly do unannounced training maneuvers all over Gyra. Lucky for Chas, they are about to have one in their area."

"You say that like there is a joke I'm missing," I muttered.

"Well, his area doesn't often see troop transports land without a raid in progress, so this could prove interesting." Standing straight, Wolfe wrapped his wrist around one of the hanging handholds; his other arm went around my waist to hold me as the door closed. Not that I was going anywhere, tightly packed in by my Elite as I was.

"Lucky I'm okay with confined spaces," I said under my breath.

A tremor passed through the ship, the engine spooled, followed by that moment of weightlessness that accompanied the sudden shift

against gravity. Spreading his feet a little wider, Wolfe gripped me as the instant acceleration knocked my center of gravity off-balance.

I'd never traveled in a Cyran battleship before. Still, it had much the same effect as the lift-pads in the Prince's palats on Praldia. Groaning, I covered my stomach, feeling suddenly hollowed out and nauseous. "Why do all forms of Cyran transport have to make me feel like I left my innards behind?"

Wolfe chuckled as the ship carrying us cornered, and the only thing that stopped me from toppling through the guards was his hold on me and the wall of Elite surrounding me. Still, the speed and sharpness of the turn meant Hamlin had to quickly catch himself on Wolfe's shoulders to prevent crushing me between them.

We immediately turned the other way, and Jervaise had to do the same thing. "By the stars! Does the driver know the Princess is along for the ride?" Jervaise complained to Hildebrand. "Is he trying to get her crushed?"

Wolfe lifted his chin at Hildebrand. "Tell the driver to stop show-boating. We're trying to go unnoticed."

Just as those words left his mouth, the lights went out and came back on red, and then a voice came over the comms. "Evasive manoeuvres in five."

"What in the blackness is going on?" Hildebrand shouted into his comms as Wolfe and the other Elite were suddenly pushing through the crowd with me to reach the side wall, where I was strapped into a harness.

That's it. That's all the warning we got, then the nose of the transport lifted steeply, and we were climbing and turning quickly. My Elite struggling to get their harnesses on, several of the royal guards who hadn't moved fast enough lost their footing. They slid and collided with each other and the door, their grunts of pain barely audible from the noise of the engines.

The ship banked hard to the side, and then we were plummeting. My breakfast turned in my stomach. Covering my mouth, I focused on not puking everywhere. Whatever was happening, I didn't want to be too busy being sick if my Elite needed me to move quickly.

"Hild, have you got an answer to your question?" Wolfe snapped.

"The transport is being followed. They think it's Skvaller"—the tabloid broadcasters—"but can't be sure," Hildebrand answered.

Cursing in a way I'd never heard the Elite do around me before, Wolfe touched the teleportation band at his wrist. "Tell the pilot to even out and give us enough time to jump ship."

"I'm sorry, what?" I asked, not enthused by the idea of that as Hildebrand relayed the command. My Elite were already unstrapping themselves from their harnesses, stumbling as they did but using their massive arms to keep hold of the straps as they surrounded me again.

As Wolfe unbuckled me, the ship banked hard again, and he lost his footing. Hamlin wrapped an arm around me before I could fall. "I'll take her," he called to Wolfe as the transport evened out suddenly.

Before I could ask what was happening, teleportation rings surrounded us. Then the ship was gone from under my feet, replaced moments later by the cold crunch of snow as Hamlin and I fell to the ground. At the last second, Hamlin twisted, pulling me around, so I landed on top of him, a snow bank exploding around us from the force.

The air rushed out of me. Several other grunts and impacts sounded around us for the next ten seconds.

"That son of a-," Hamlin called the driver several words not appropriate for me to understand, let alone hear. "Are you okay, Princess?" He finally asked, looking down his nose where I was sprawled across him.

"I would prefer to long-range teleport between planets or ride the Prince's lift-pad a hundred times a day, then get back on one of those transports again."

Hamlin dropped his head back to the ground. "Me too!" He blew out a breath, then started helping me up. Another pair of hands lifted me off my knees and held me aloft long enough to get my feet under me, then let me go to offer Hamlin an arm up.

Finally able to take in our surroundings, I realized we were outside a lovely home on what appeared to be a farm if the ground wasn't covered in huge drifts of snow. I could barely see around us from where we now stood on the road, the snow banks had piled so high, but I could make out the roof of other farmlike buildings further back from the house.

"We aimed as best we could," Jervaise explained as I shivered. Wrapping an arm around me, he led me down the road after the other Elite making our way toward the building.

When we reached the path cleared to the front door, Wolfe brought us to a stop. The snow was as tall as him on each side, and I got the sense it was purposely done. "Nice way to ambush visitors," I murmured.

Wolfe turned his gaze from assessing the path to me. "What do you suggest?"

Blowing out a breath, I gently pinched the gash on his head. Reaching my other hand out, I touched the edge of the snow and felt a tingle in the water and heat symbols on my spine. The snow shifted, melting, and some water funnelled up and washed against Wolfe's brow, clearing away the green Cyran blood.

"Take an Avalonian with you," I muttered, enjoying the way Wolfe's eyes were wide with surprise. Taking my hand back, I visually assessed the injury. "Does anyone have any suture gel on them?" I asked and stepped out of the way as Rylan came forward, swinging the pack from his back around and digging in one of the pockets.

"I'm the trained trauma responder on this shift, Princess," Rylan informed me.

Jervaise stepped in beside me as the snow continued to melt away from the path, causing a cascade of water to start flooding around us instead. The Elite stood very still, watching as the run-off washed around us, but didn't even come near their boots. "Nice trick," Jervaise murmured.

As the surroundings freed up, it exposed the booby trap lying in wait. One of the Elite moved forward and assessed it. "Looks like it's a manual trigger. Someone on the inside controls it."

"This is ridiculous. Can someone just use their comms to call Chas and tell him we are here already?" I huffed in frustration.

"Comms get monitored. If we use them to communicate with Elite Chas, it could get picked up that you're here," Wolfe educated.

Lifting a brow, I stared at him. "Then don't say I'm here."

Chuckling, Jervaise lifted his comms, pressed a few buttons, then waited for a beat before saying, "Go outside. I sent you a surprise to cheer you up." Jervaise's eyebrows lifted at the response, glanced my way, and cleared his throat. "It'll be worth it. Hurray up. Just, ah, put your pants on first." Then he disconnected.

"Do I want to know?"

"Ah, he was very warm where he was and didn't want to leave it to come out in the cold," Jervaise told us.

A few seconds later, the front door opened, and Chas emerged, pants on but not entirely sealed yet. I averted my eyes. Not that I hadn't seen Chas naked, but I'd never seen him hard and, um, slick. Spotting the small group back by the road, Chas quickly sealed his trousers and cursed. Then he rushed down the stairs and swept me into his arms as he hugged me. "Princess."

"This shit is why you got suspended," Hildebrand grumbled. "Is anyone else home? We need to clear the house."

"Cora's in my bed, but everyone else is out right now," Chas informed me as he set me down and stepped back.

Bruising still marred his chest and the left side of his face. Luther hadn't looked as banged up, but then he'd been fully dressed, so maybe he hid the evidence of their brawl easier. He was also shiny with perspiration and surrounded by a cloud of florals that could only be a woman's perfume.

"Do you need to take care of her before we speak?" I asked, suddenly aware of what he must have been doing to look the way he did coming outside. "I can wait."

"Preferably inside," Wolfe added, scanning the sky. "We had some fun getting here."

Chas bowed his head and led the way into the house, directing us to the sitting room for guests while he went to freshen up. "I'll get you a drink, Princess," Jervaise excused and headed through another doorway.

Wolfe and Hildebrand stayed by me while the rest of the Elite went to clear the house and secure it. Standing by the window, I focused on the path to the house outside, my spine tingling.

"What are you doing?" Wolfe inquired.

"Putting it back how it was. If we get discovered here, that could help us," I justified. Eyeing me, Wolfe glanced over my head to Hildebrand but stayed silent.

"Here we are, Princess," Jervaise called for my attention as he set a tray on the low table with a clear pot and matching cups. As I sat on the couch, I noted the purple bloom in the bottom of the pot and smiled. Jervaise noticed what had my attention and gave me a wink. "Ammita says it's a taste of home."

"It's true. We always had the Kudai blooming tea flowers at the estate." Sighing, I fidgeted with my dress for a moment. "I know it's only been a couple of months, but it feels like forever since Captain Stark dragged me before the Prince and took everything from me, including this small indulgence."

Jervaise's face fell, but before he could comment, a woman's cry of pleasure sounded further into the house. The three Elite turned my way, possibly looking for a reaction. I did my best not to be affected, but I'm sure they caught how embarrassed I was to be aware that Chas had finished what he was doing when we arrived.

"After all the times we've heard you and your companion together, you still get flustered by the basic need for pleasure, Princess?" Jervaise teased.

"It's bad enough knowing you've heard me, let alone sitting here waiting for someone to wrap it up so you can visit with them," I answered. "Chas mentioned her as if you all know her. Is Cora a regular acquaintance of his?"

Lifting a brow, Jervaise stared at my lips. "He's not mentioned Cora to you?"

The way Hildebrand and Wolfe shifted made me uneasy. "No." Jervaise's mouth thinned as he studied me.

"Wait, is Chas joined?" Please don't tell me I've had a married man in my bed. Ignoring that we've never done anything, he has been naked with me, comforted me, and kissed me.

"No," Jervaise answered. "Not anymore. But he was before he became elite. Cora is Chas's ex."

Hushed voices reached us out in the hall as they moved to the front door. It opened, and a few more words were exchanged. Then it closed briefly before the buzz of the teleportation system engaged outside.

Clearing his throat, Chas came back into the sitting room, freshly showered and fully dressed in civilian clothes. "So, Princess. To what do I owe the pleasure?" Chas asked.

Chapter Seventeen

"Wolfe, you have a shopping trip to plan. Hildebrand, I'd like to know what that hullabaloo getting here was about and confirm the threat, please. Jervaise-" I looked his way and had nothing. "Make yourself scarce," I dismissed everyone.

"Princess-"Wolfe began.

"I'm visiting with a friend and would like some privacy. You can protect me outside of this room, and Chas is unlikely to allow me to kill myself, is he? So the King's concern need not apply right this minute," I justified.

Wolfe's harsh mouth frowned deeply, but he bowed his head, and they all left the room, sliding the doors closed.

Chas cocked his head. "Suicide?"

"The King hasn't outright suggested it, but I've not been permitted a moment's peace even in the bath since the loss," I revealed.

Face falling, Chas bowed his head. "I grieve for your sons, Princess. I should not have left you alone with him, left you alone-"

"You think you would have fared better denying your prince

private time with his companion than you did attacking him with your fists?"

Grimacing, Chas rounded his broad shoulders forward. "I am not proud of my behavior that day. I was wretched with worry for my Princess, and I knew who was to blame."

Rolling my tongue against the back of my teeth, I held my grief at bay. Just. Instead, I picked up the tea and took a sip.

"May I ask if the grief of that day will have a long-term impact?" Chas inquired gently.

"If you mean will I be able to breed again, I could if I choose. However, my marriage did not survive the loss of the heirs."

Chas's entire bearing changed. Not to joy but horror and fear. "The King granted you a divorce?"

Huffing, I set my cup down before I broke it by accident. "Don't be daft. Luther is a spoilt man-child with his father wrapped around his little finger."

Chas nearly spat out his own sip of tea. "Princess-"

"I've been told the marriage will remain whether I abide by the contract or not. When I threatened no heirs, neither the Prince nor the King flinched. They would rather sacrifice the throne to distant kin than let me go. But that is their choice to make."

Chas's face softened as he put his cup down. "We make those sacrifices for love. Luther never really cared about the heirs. He just wanted you. The King insisted on having them in the contract."

I knew that. I'd gone deep enough into Luther's desires to know his love for me was as genuine as they came. It didn't change the hurt and betrayal. Sitting straight, I met Chas's eyes. Desire flash burned on my spine, and it took everything to blink away before I saw more than that beautiful Cyran woman's face. Her long pale hair was decorated with spring flowers as she signed her marriage contract to another man.

Clearing my throat and avoiding Chas's eyes, I didn't pry. "Well, Luther got me, and now he is stuck with a companion who wants nothing to do with him. The prince and I are done for all intents and purposes and will only be an act we perform for the public from now on."

Chas deflated back in his sofa chair, looking exhausted. Not the joyous sated I expected after bedding a woman I knew he longed for. "I'm sorry to hear that. As angry as I am at the Prince for how he treated you, risked you, and caused you grief, he is still my prince, and I know how much he adores you."

Refusing to meet his sympathetic gaze, I collected my cup and sipped more tea.

"Why did you come here, Princess?" Chas asked softly.

Smirking, I stood and roamed the room. "I needed to get out of that palats. Breathe some fresh air for a minute. I needed to let the two guards who stood against their beloved prince in my honor know that I was okay. That I lived and appreciated their loyalty."

"I don't think Luther is beloved by Didrika," Chas snickered. "She already hated him. You've just given her decades worth of ammunition against him."

"Why?"

"For the same reason you do. You both blame the prince for losing the men you love." When I blinked at Chas, waiting, he shook his head and sat straight again. "It's not my story, and you'll never get the full story because it was a classified mission. I think the reason Didrika became Elite was purely to get the full story that she couldn't be told without that level of rank."

"And you?" I asked of him, having already gleamed the answer but wanting him to be the one to offer it to me. "Why did you become Elite?"

Chas stared at his cup. "Heartbreak. Don't pretend Jervaise didn't gossip about Cara to you. He can't help himself."

Lifting a brow at Chas, I joined him on the couch, sitting next to him. "Actually, I had to ask, and all he gave me was she was once your wife."

Chuckle snorting, Chas turned away to prevent offending me. "That's very unlike Jervaise. His tongue is usually very loose."

I sighed and replied, "Not around me." Waiting a bit, I placed my hand on Chas's thigh. Automatically, he covered it with his giant paw. There was nothing there but the affection of friends. "You don't have to tell me. I know enough about heartbreak to know that sometimes the only way to endure it is to paint over it and ignore the unsightly crack in the wall when you walk past."

"Thank you."

Leaning my head on his shoulder, I stared at the same wall as Chas, both of us easily near each other. "Can I ask why she was here today, though, if she's the one who ended things?"

Chas took a beat, a deep breath, and poured more tea. "Cara wants a baby."

"Oh." There were a hundred questions, but I wouldn't ask them. Chas had never mentioned Cara to me. He talked about all his family, aunt, and cousins, but never his older brother or the woman he loved so much that his heartbreak drove him to train for Elite just to distract himself.

Chas swirled his drink, watching the violet water steam and swirl. "It's hard to resent her when I ended up here. The Elite are my new brothers, and I have a beautiful ethereal Princess who calls me her friend." He squeezed my hand on mine. "Did you really come to ensure I knew you were alive?"

"Well, no," I said, picking up the tea. "I came to meet your aunt, who I heard so much about, but now I'll be coming daily for the Kudai tea."

Giving me a Cyran smile, Chas gave me a little shoulder bump. "You're welcome any time. If you give me heads up next time, I'll ensure my aunt is here and my ex is not."

"Sort of ruins the element of surprise then, doesn't it?"

Chas chuckled. "I'll work out a code with Jervaise for next time."

Finishing my tea, I stood up. "I should go. We still need to visit with Didrika."

Chas rose to see me out.

"Chas, as much as I appreciate the loyalty, you should not have struck your prince like you did. You certainly should not have started a brawl when he acted in kind. Would you have hit me if our positions were reversed?"

Bowing his head, Chas licked the corner of his mouth. "With respect, Princess. If your actions endangered the prince's life, you wouldn't have been allowed to stalk his medical bay. The King would have had you locked in a cell to wait to hear if the prince forgave you or condemned you."

Inhaling at the truth of his words, I stepped into him, gripped the back of his head to make him bow it to meet me, and kissed his left brow. If the wide-eyed stare he shot my way as I backed up was any indication, he had not expected that. Clearing my throat, I felt myself become shy at the action. "In Avalonia-"

"I know what it means," Chas cut in. "Thank you. You honor me greatly."

The door slid open, and Hildebrand stepped in with Wolfe and Jervaise. "Princess, I have that information you wanted. The pursuer was a Skvaller bloodhound. He was lurking around the palats hoping for juicy gossip about the Queen or prince and spotted you boarding the ship. Captures of you are worth a fortune in the tabloids right now, so he followed, just hoping to get some stills."

"Are you sure?" I asked.

"We're sure," Wolfe answered, handing me a tablet. I watched one of the broadcasters showing footage of me boarding the troop carrier with a caption of 'Princess tags along with Royal guard on training maneuvers.'

Breathing a sigh of annoyance, I handed the tablet back. "Which means we must go back to the ship so they can capture some stills of me with the troops."

"It would be a good idea, Princess," Wolfe answered. "I'll message Rika and invite her to attend the palats to discuss her behavior. It'll just so happen to coincide with dinner."

"I think you missed the reason the Princess came to me, Captain," Chas told him. "She hates to be cooped up for too long. The Princess likes long walks every day, swimming, getting out in the fresh air, and being surrounded by nature. She felt imprisoned in Praldia. I dare say she's faring worse here."

"Well, I have the balcony for fresh air, and I've been making nightly treks to the watch tower. So, I'd say it's better than Praldia. Doubly so since I don't even share a suite, let alone a bed with my guardian."

All the Elite exchanged looks at how I referred to the prince but bit their tongues.

"Right, well, Jervaise, you will be in contact with Chas about the next time you'll drop by to pick up some of the Kudai tea for me. Wolfe, you're going to invite Rika to the palats and arrange for us to be served dinner privately in the winter garden. Let's go watch the royal guards raid something."

"A raid?" Chas gasped, eyes wide and looking to the others.

"Well, at least make it something interesting. I'm used to regular kidnapping and assassination attempts at this point. Watching a bunch of shoulders line up seems rather droll in comparison."

Jervaise and Chas snickered, getting my humor immediately. Wolfe and Hildebrand took a little longer, and even then, they didn't look too sure.

Meeting Wolfe's eyes, I tilted my head despite his gaze dropping to my lips. "Something interesting, Captain. Make it worth my time."

"Yes, Princess."

Thirty minutes later, I was standing well out of danger while the royal guards—minus the few who needed medical attention after being crushed in the flight—raided a business connected to the quig mercenaries Adima hired to kill me.

The royal guard was a well-oiled machine. They flowed and worked together beautifully and controlled everything around them from the moment they landed.

"We don't really have anything to charge them with," Jervaise revealed as the Cyran employees were dragged from the location and made to lay on the road outside while the royal guard searched the premises. "But we can trash the place and see if anything shakes loose to implicate their direct involvement."

"But you are sure they organized the hit?"

"They received the payment, were who Adima contacted," Jervaise confirmed.

Thinking about it, I looked between the detained employees, my eyes locking on the Cyran, who apparently owned the business. "Is the Skvaller here?"

"Yes, Princess."

"Good. Open up a path to the owner. I want to ask him a question."

"Princess?"

"Cyra is going to war with Avalonia, and the prince hopes to change the line of succession. But our people are traditionalists, and it's hard to effect change. I'm about to make the first bid for my crown and make this interruption to my day count. Get me to the owner. I'll take it from there."

Chapter Eighteen

T wo of the King's Elite were waiting for us when we returned to the palats. Wolfe cursed under his breath, then went to speak with them.

"How much trouble am I in," I asked Jervaise.

He watched Wolfe's tense shoulders as the Elite spoke with him and didn't look as concerned. "All depends on what we are busted for. There is the leaving the palats with little planning, the teleporting from a moving vessel, visiting an Elite on suspension, or the public interrogation you pulled on a Cyran citizen."

"It's not like I disemboweled and tortured him on the street," I huffed. "Since when have Cyrans had problems with a little breath play?"

The side of Jervaise's mouth twitched. "True. Thankfully, the Skvaller didn't catch your words while performing that trick, or I wouldn't be the only one having nightmares tonight."

Wolfe returned, looking disgruntled. "The King wishes to see you immediately." Wolfe took my arm without any fanfare, my Elite fell in around me, and we followed the two sent to collect us to the King's private audience room.

The King was waiting when we arrived, along with a small contingent of his Elite. Unfortunately, the Prince was also there. I cursed under my breath. Still, I made my way to the dais, stopped at the bottom, and lowered into a curtsey as I had every time I'd seen either of them since the missfall.

"Enough of that!" The King snapped. "You are family. You do not bow to us in an informal setting." Sighing, he looked me over as he stood. "Your visit today was unsanctioned. When I suspend an Elite, it is punishment. You cannot override my rule."

"I was not overriding anything, my King," I humbled. "I merely wished to visit with someone who showed loyalty to me when they defended my honor and let them know that I am well and grateful."

"You're grateful that he attacked me?" Luther huffed.

"As Elite Chas pointed out to me, if the situation was reversed—if my actions had endangered the Prince's life and caused him to need medical intervention—I would have been locked away until either forgiveness or condemnation had been handed down. Instead, my abuser was permitted to lurk outside my room and subsequently caused my condition to deteriorate, further endangering my life."

If it was possible for two men to suddenly become statues, I would have believed it of the King and Prince at that moment.

"While I did not support Elite Chas's actions in attacking his prince aggressively, I appreciated his loyalty and willingness to defend me. It is more than what my companion has shown in recent weeks." The tension in the room was thick enough to suffocate a woman, so I decided to lighten it. "Plus, there was the tea."

Eyebrows flattening, the King tilted his head. "Tea?"

"Yes. As an Avalonian lives with Elite Chas, they served Kudai Flower tea. A staple in every Avalonian household. It was a taste of home I'd sorely missed since I was forced into the joining."

Raising his brows, King Saboa considered me, then looked to his son. "And the public torture of one of my citizens?"

"A step towards gaining the Avalonian throne," I replied without hesitation. "Ribboning is an ancient power on my planet. No one has been able to do it for centuries. Not only can I do it, but to control them with such finesse as to use them for breath play..." I opened my arms to indicate the obvious, a sinister smile on my lips.

Now the King's eyebrows were in his hairline. "Breath play? Is that what you call choking someone to get your desired answers?"

The evil smile remains on my face. "Something I've found most Cyran's to enjoy. The citizen I questioned certainly did. And the humiliation of enjoying it publicly made him very keen to cooperate with our questioning to prevent embarrassment."

Grabbing up his tablet, the King waved the video of the questioning at me. "It didn't look like he was enjoying himself to me."

"Then you were looking at the wrong area of his body." I turned my eyes to Wolfe. "My Elite, who was around me, can support my claim. At no time did I threaten your citizen's life. Violent torture is such an uncivilized way to interrogate someone."

Mouth hanging open, the King looked at the screen and, this time, seemed to consider the questioning in the right light. When he realized I spoke the truth, his mouth snapped shut, and he swallowed with difficulty.

Sashaying a step closer, I tilted my head coyly. "Your people value strength. They watch that video and see a Princess willing to get her hands dirty, standing over a man twice her size and bringing him to his knees and to tears. My people see their Princess holds an ancient power long thought lost, employing the ways of her people to punish those who wronged her."

Taking a breath, the King set the tablet aside with a final look at the screen. "To what end?"

"It makes your planet and mine see me differently. Not as the shy and submissive Princess they think I should be-"

"But the potential Queen they need," Luther cut in. His eyes were glazed with desire and longing for a second, then they cleared to focus on his father. "It was a smart move."

"I don't disagree," Searle replied. "Very well. Will we see you at dinner tonight, Zira?"

"Forgive me; I have already arranged to share my evening meal with a friend." Bowing my head, I backed up a step. "With your leave?"

Glancing at Luther momentarily, the King sighed, nodded, and waved his hand to indicate I go. And go, I did. I wanted to clean up before dinner after a rough day of flying and everything that came after.

SNOW WAS FALLING AGAIN, making the night like a movie picture on the other side of the glass walls and ceiling of the winter garden. Little lights weaved around every post and rafter as if the area were lit by mini stars.

The staff had set up a table for me by the fire pit in the middle of the biome. A jug of spiced wine and bowls of soup for our first course was already waiting, kept warm with lids. My Elite secured the exits, leaving me to wait by the window.

"Why are we meeting in the winter garden?" Rika's voice reached me as the door opened.

Moving out of the darkness, I entered the circle around the fire pit when Didrika and Wolfe did. I enjoyed the surprise and relief that filled the female Elite's face. "Princess," Rika gasped, then bowed her head. "I thought I was meeting with the King." Accusing eyes fell on her father.

"Did I say the King wanted to meet with you?" Wolfe cocked his brow at his spawn, then headed off to give us the illusion of privacy.

When her father was out of sight, Didrika wrapped me in a fierce hug that made my bones creak. "Oh, thank the stars. You scared the blackness out of me, Princess." Releasing me, she stepped back and looked me over. "I'm so sorry-"

Holding my hand up, I waved her words away. Whether it was sympathy or apology, I didn't want either from her. "The stars decide our fate. We are helpless but to accept it," I replied, moving to the table and taking my seat.

Didrika raised her father's brow at me and asked, "Did you accept it so easily?"

"I'm Avalonian. We are emotional creatures. We cry when hurt. We strike when angry. I have yelled and grieved and cursed the stars for what they spun for me, but there is no undoing what is done. Eventually, we must accept that we are still here, still living, and burying yourself in grief serves no justice to those who are not."

Picking up the stone jug, I poured two glasses of spiced wine, setting the pitcher on the heating plate before collecting my glass and sitting back.

"I grieve my loss. I am still angry enough that I battle with it daily. But curling in a ball and crying, refusing to live, will only hurt those who care about me. Killing those who I blame for it won't do anyone any good, either. Though, it's a war all of its own every time the Prince is in the same room as me."

"I understand entirely, Princess," Rika sympathized, or maybe, it was empathy.

Taking a sip of the wine, I waited while Rika drank quite a bit more, then set my glass aside as I sat straight again. Refilling her now empty glass, I met her eyes, catching a glimpse of a handsome Cyran with the cheekiest of smiles before she dropped her gaze, cutting the connection.

"Will you tell me, one day, why you hate the Prince?" I requested gently, aware her heartache, while old, was something she was never going to move on from.

Didrika shifted her eyes to the fire, the pain of her loss floating in her gaze. "I don't hate him," she confessed. "I did, for a long time, but eventually, I found the truth and knew it wasn't his fault." She fidgeted with her soup spoon. "Honestly, I hated the Prince for so long that I don't know how to be other towards him anymore, even knowing it's unfair."

A little hit of a smile touched Rika's lips. "That hate for him got me through the Elite trials, so I'm never going to apologize for it. Being Elite is much better than where I would have ended up if I didn't let my rage control me."

A scoff left my mouth. Picking up my spoon, I lifted the lid from the soup and stirred it as it steamed. "If I let my grief control me, the Prince would have been missing a vital part of his anatomy and taken a flying lesson off the battlements by now."

That made Didrika chuckle darkly. "You would regret the loss of said anatomy sooner than the rest, I think."

Meeting her dark humor, I sighed. "I believe you are right. Let's eat before it gets cold."

For the rest of our meal, we chatted about Rika's life as an Elite, where she lived in Cyra. There was some whispered naughtiness about the King and his brilliant bed manner. Spoken low enough that none of my Elite should have heard, of course.

As the last plates were taken away and the final drops of spiced wine filled out cups, Didrika's smile faded. "Wolfe told me this meeting was about my actions and suspension."

Grabbing my cup, I stood from the table. "Join me by the fire?"

There were a couple of cozy seats set around the pit. I lowered myself into one, the base cushion big enough for Cyran's legs, allowing me to curl my legs under me and face the spot Didrika took next to me.

"Initially, I just wanted to visit and thank you for the loyalty you showed me that night when you enforced my wishes," I answered. "Plus, I needed to get out and do something. Sitting around in your rooms with nothing to do is not how you overcome grief."

Giving me a nod of understanding, Didrika tilted her head. "You said initially?"

"Did you catch the news today?"

"Where you questioned that Cyran with your ribbons until he shot his load in his pants?" Didrika snickered.

"Something I didn't share with the others was what he whispered back to me right before he came and blacked out," I revealed. "As much as I'm sure my Elites are loyal, they also report to the King, and I'm not sure I'm ready to hand this tidbit over just yet."

Rika didn't so much as squirm. "I am still loyal to my King, Princess."

"I know, but you are also currently on suspension, which means out of contact, yes? No contact in either direction?" I checked.

Frowning, Rika leaned closer. "What are you thinking, Princess? If you conspire against-"

"No. Nothing like that," I assured, waving away Rika's worry. "The threat is to me, not the King or Prince. I need a lead followed up, and you and Chas are in a perfect position to do it for me without it getting back to the prince prematurely. They will not consider it a viable threat, but when I take the Avalonian throne, I need to know what wolves are at my feet."

Didrika widened her eyes, then leaned closer until our whispers were nearly lost in the crackling of the fire. "What lead?"

"The man I questioned today admitted Utz was one of his employees."

"Blackness!" Didrika's head swung around, ensuring we were still alone. "He hired Utz to abduct you?"

"He's the middle man. He only connects clients to those who can do the job they need. But if what he told me is true, he connected my would-be Avalonian abductor with Elite Utz. Someone who was not the Barbarian, but hoped to use my womb to take the power of the throne for themselves." I waited for Rika to take that in, then added.

"I need to know who it was, and I'd also like to know how they planned to do it. Utz admitted to me it was not one of the Barbarians. And that my abductor would be a better choice for my companion, as he would keep the bloodlines pure. Avalonian women born of our magic have built-in birth control. No herb or spell can override it."

Because the Barbarians were born without magic, it didn't exist for them, so the Barbarian never considered that issue.

"He armed Utz with a way to negate my ability to ribbon, so he must have planned how to bypass my natal scale. I need to know what it was before I go home."

"And you want me to look into this for you?"

"I'd like to take advantage of your suspension and have you and Elite Chas look into this for me. At the very least, question the man to find out who the client is. I'll pay you."

Sitting back, Rika considered me. "I'm not a mercenary. But I have been deathly bored, and hanging out with Chas during our suspension sounds like a good idea. I'll call him tomorrow and organize it."

"Thank you."

"Please. I love a bit of mischief." Rika shot me a wink, then finished her wine and stood. "This was fun. Let's do it again soon, Princess," she stated loud enough for the others to hear.

After she left, I stared at the fire for a little longer. That raid today was kismet. I would never have known where to start looking for my betrayers at home, but being forced to make a show for the Skvaller opened that door. I was not stupid enough to ignore such a blatant invitation from the stars.

Chapter Nineteen

After the day's events, I'd forgone the nightly walk to the watch tower, choosing to soak in the bath and soothe some of my strained muscles from the insane trip on the troop carrier. I didn't dissipate. Part of me wanted to, but I worried my Elite would freak out and forbid me from using the bath and only allow me the shower from now on.

If the water would have stayed hot all night, I'd probably have slept in the bath. But it was already cooling, and my Elite would probably have words about sleeping in water. They still found the Avalonian ways quite too much for them to fathom.

Not that Avalonians slept in water—though, our mattresses were usually large water bladders, giving a similar sensation. It was more that my kind preferred to be near or in water, and we couldn't drown, so falling asleep in a bath or pool was never a problem.

A heavy sigh left my lips as I pulled myself from the water. Wrapping the thick robe around me, I moved to the sitting area by the fire and curled up on the sofa closest. A tray of snacks, a pitcher of spiced wine, and another of water were on the table. Collecting the tablet, I scanned the news from the broadcasters for Cyra and Praldia while I ate.

A quick knock on the door preceded its opening. There was a brief exchange before Erhaird turned my way. "Princess, Prince Saboa would like a word."

"Is he already here?" I asked.

"Yes, Princess."

"Do I have the option of saying no?"

Erhaird eyed the door. "We will turn him away if that is what you want, but it relates to your shopping trip tomorrow, so I recommend giving him a few minutes."

Huffing, already having an idea the trip was about to get ixnayed after today's events, I set the tablet aside and gave Erhaird a nod as I collected my wine. "Kylar, if this goes the way my visits from the Prince usually do, we'll be raiding Jervaise's stash and playing Kort all night again."

Smiling before he could stop himself, Kylar quickly schooled his face and did the slow blink of confirmation.

The doors opened, and the prince stepped in, Anberon visible in my inner quarters but not following. Luther eyed me, then looked at my two Elite. "Some privacy, please." When Kylar hesitated, looking to me for approval, Luther huffed out a breath. "We are not going to fight. We need to be capable of being civil occasionally."

"Just leave the door ajar," I suggested. "Would you like some wine?" I asked Luther as he approached.

"Yes, thank you."

"Kylar, can you please grab a cup for the prince?" I requested, then turned my attention to my guardian.

He stood by the fire, considering the flames, while the Elite grabbed a cup from the little kitchenette they'd put together in my inner quarters for him. Once we had the room and a modicum of privacy, Luther turned his gaze to me. "Thank you for seeing me. I know you don't want anything to do with me, but we will need to interact on some level."

Cyra

"Are you denying me the trip tomorrow or the funds to buy myself clothes?" I asked instead of acknowledging his words. I didn't want to chat with him. While I didn't deny that interacting would be necessary for several reasons, I preferred we get to the point and make it as short as possible.

"Neither," Luther answered, surprising me. "I think it will be good for you to be seen doing something normal." Moving to the sofa opposite me, Luther poured himself a cup of wine, then sat down. "I came to talk to you because I'd like to attend the trip with you."

"You want to shop for clothes with me?" I raised an eyebrow questioning the validity of that statement.

Luther chuckled. "The broadcasters know I'm on planet tonight. You were seen twice today without me. Our advisors feel your outing tomorrow would raise questions if it's known I'm here and am not seen with you."

"You want to use it as a photo op?" I checked.

Tapping the cup with a finger as if he was choosing his words carefully before replying, Luther stared at the dark liquid. "You agreed to play your part in public."

The only reason I didn't get hostile was that his tone was casual and not accusing. "I was thinking of more formal events we had no choice but to attend together."

"We have not been seen together since you arrived in Cyra. People are talking. Staff who work in the castle gossip. I am planetside and sleeping in a different suite. That we have not been seen together since Adima's funeral is causing widespread speculation about the state of our joining."

"Is it speculation when it's true?"

"It is until it's proven or a broadcaster reports it," Luther replied. Setting his cup on the table, Luther leaned his elbows on his knees, hands clenching together. "The King would like us to alleviate some rumors with a public showing. I'll shop with you in the morning and enjoy a meal at the eatery Wolfe has cleared for your lunch. I will then excuse myself, explaining I need to return

165

to business in Praldia, where some of the public can overhear. We will kiss goodbye, and you can enjoy the rest of the day without me."

Swirling the wine in my cup, I considered. "What level of affection is expected?"

"We will hold hands occasionally, and, of course, the goodbye kiss should be more than a peck but publicly appropriate," Luther explained. He picked up his cup and sat back in his seat. "Everyone knows you were forced to be my companion, Zira. You can be distant but respectful. Polite and cooperative. No one will criticize you for it."

"Yes, they will," I scoffed.

"But it is excusable. Our publicity team has never tried to present our joining as a love match. It was as much a political move to our people as they think my parent's marriage was."

"Your mother was a politician's daughter, but she revealed to me she was a midwife before they wed," I queried.

The prince smiled. "My father fell in love with a mid-wife but couldn't get approval to marry a commoner. When he made it clear he was only interested in her, my grandfather raised her father's status, honoring him with an ambassadorship. The move allowed my mother to be forced into my father's social circle while getting her father out of the way for my father to seduce his youngest child. After a year of flirtations and whispers of them having an affair running rampant, grandfather organized their nuptials."

"So it's a common move for the men in your family to stalk and entrap the objects of your desire, not giving them an option of saying no," I accused.

Instead of being offended, Luther shrugged. "I tried to woo you for years before your parents opened another avenue to get you where I wanted you, Zira. Being opportunistic is not a crime."

"But you took away my choice in the manner. I will always hate you for forcing my hand."

Sighing, Luther stood. "I know. Just another in the list of sins you

166

will always hold against me." He drank the rest of his wine and set the cup down. "Can I confirm my attendance with you tomorrow?"

"Do I really have a choice?"

"Of course. You can refuse to go out. Remove the public eye from our relationship."

Considering the choices, I blew out a breath of frustration. "If we do this, I don't want to see you for at least a month."

"Two weeks," Luther countered. "My mother's birthday party is two weeks away. I'll need you on my arm for the event." Luther watched me grit my teeth and bowed quickly before he headed for the door. As he pushed it open, he turned back. "We should shop for a dress for the ball tomorrow, and you'll want one for the garden party during the day."

"I wasn't informed of these events. Is there any other I should be aware of coming up?" I scowled at my guardian.

I swear Luther smirked. "Several. My parents are normally very social. They canceled several events on your arrival, citing the need to readdress security after the multiple abduction attempts. I'll have Councilman Aldous liaise with you for our schedule."

Before I could respond or possibly throw my cup at his head, Luther fled. His steps were too quick, and his gesture to Anberon too hurried to be considered casual. The fact Anberon chuckled at his Prince's back also gave it away.

Kylar stepped back into the room, the flicker of humor in his eyes. "Should I have Erhaird raid Jervaise's stash, Princess?"

Dropping back to stare at the ceiling, I groaned, "No. But we will be playing Kort. And someone better be telling me funny stories of whatever gossip is to be had because I need an escape from my drama."

"Yes, Princess."

"And I need some safe conversation starters so I can interact with the prince tomorrow and not escalate, but safe for any public member to overhear."

"We can do that, Princess," Kylar assured. "Should I call the kitchen for another snack for you while we deal the cards? Your eyes are looking different from normal."

The suggestion to watch my eyes to know what I needed must have gotten around, but not the exact details.

"Are they bright blue as if glowing from the inside?" I checked as I moved closer.

"Yes. Does that mean hungry or tired?"

"Neither. But it explains why the prince ran out of here," I grumbled. "Let's play some Kort."

WHILE EATING breakfast the following day, I received a request on my tablet from Councilman Aldous to grant him access to my calendar. Along with the message came the suggestion that I may wish to hire an assistant to liaise with him on my behalf and take care of my incidentals now that I was more settled in my new role. Aldous offered to set up some interviews, inquiring if I'd prefer candidates from Praldia or Cyra, and what my requirements were.

Deciding to think about it, I left the message unanswered but granted him access to my calendar. Due to the assassination attempts, I wouldn't have a public one. Luther's had also been taken offline since the first attempt.

Frustrated, I used my comms to send a message to Ethelred's encrypted inbox asking for an update on my request. Since it wasn't direct communication, I knew not to expect an immediate response. Instead, I went about getting ready for the day.

The Elite gave me some great conversation starters to deal with the Prince. Mainly around training plans and asking him about specific experiences he'd had as an Elite.

They also gave me some gossip from around the palace that would be 'safe' to discuss in a public venue without causing any issues if it was overheard and reported. Kylar told me that delivered a certain way, the gossip would suggest that Luther and I were bonding and in regular communication.

Along with the list of safe topics came suggestions of what to avoid. Adima and the funeral being the top of that list, and anything to do with the abduction attempts was a tied second, along with my move to Cyra or lack of plans to return to Praldia. A subject I was sure I would be opening the door for anytime soon.

As prepared as I could be to spend time with the prince pretending I didn't hate him as much as I did, I let Wolfe know I was ready to go. Wolfe comm'd with Anberon and told me we'd meet in the motor pool.

"We're not going in a troop carrier again, are we?" I recoiled. "I'm not sure I can do that again so soon."

Touching the wound on his head absently, Wolfe grumbled, "No, Princess. We'll be taking the King's transport this time. No kamikaze pilots for you to worry about today. A bit more luxury in his private vehicle as well."

Scoffing, I got to my feet. "I don't need luxury, just the ability to get from here to there and back again without getting beaten up or in such a way I nearly puke at my own feet."

The Elite around me all sniggered quietly.

"Don't mind them, Princess. They're all just wishing you'd landed on one of them yesterday," Jervaise teased. "It was the highlight of Hamlin's year, and they're all a little jealous."

Checking everyone's faces, I found them all giving Hamlin the evil eye while Hamlin was grinning, not the least embarrassed. "Seriously?"

"Not many of us get to claim they caught a Princess falling through space and saved her from injury with our bodies, Princess," Hamlin justified.

"Argh!" I groaned. "I miss the days when the men around me were terrified I'd bewitch them if I looked at them twice."

"Amateurs," Jervaise chuckled as he offered me his arm. "Getting bewitched by you would be bragging rights for the rest of my career and a story I'd tell my sons and grandsons about after I retire."

Shaking my head, I couldn't help the smile pulling at my lips as I placed my hand on Jervaise's forearm, and we all filed for the door. "You wish you could be so lucky."

Leaning close so that his voice didn't carry, Jervaise whispered, "Take down an invisible assassin in front of me again, and I'll get on my knees and beg."

Laughing, I leaned into him. "Then I would be the one with bragging rights. Bringing a disciplined Elite to his knees."

"You took down an assassin and kicked the Prince's butt in a throw-down. You already have lifelong bragging rights," Jervaise laughed. "Leave something for us lowly guards."

As we reached the outer doors, Wolfe came in beside me. "Enough play. Focus."

"Jealous?" I asked.

"Very," Wolfe admitted with a wry grin.

Jervaise gave me a wink, then the doors were open. Everyone was back on their best behavior as they became the fearsome soldiers everyone knew them to be. But behind the doors, they were becoming something else. Friends, almost. And the ones willing to lower their guards and joke and play with me, I appreciated greatly because I would have gone mad by now without them.

Chapter Twenty

"Where would you like to start today?" Luther asked as the transport made its way to the city center. He'd joined me in the corridor before the motor pool, so we entered together, his Elite surrounding mine just in case a Skvaller was luring around again.

"Sleepwear," I replied.

The prince frowned. "You want clothing to wear to bed?"

Staring out the window, I sighed. "Yes. I'm not allowed the privacy of having my room to myself anymore. It would alleviate some awkwardness if I toss and turn in my sleep and wake up to find I've thrown the blankets off if I'm not naked underneath."

Jaw clenching, Luther eyed me, then nodded and typed a message into his comms. "Sleepwear it is."

The transport was split into three sections. The driver's space also housed half our Elite. Luther and I sat in a chamber in the middle, sealed off from the others with privacy glass. The rest of Elite sat in the rear compartment. Luther used his comms to communicate with the teams and the driver. Still, he had explained that the privacy glass could be removed if we needed to escape through the front or rear of the vehicle in the case of an ambush.

"Did Aldous contact you?" Luther asked, putting away his comms.

"He suggested I hire an assistant to liaise with him on my behalf," I told the prince. "I don't think he likes me and doesn't want to deal with me directly."

"Typically, you should have been appointed an assistant immediately. I had planned for Padget to serve us both." Luther stopped at the mention of his sister. He didn't need to clarify. I understood he was still hurt by her betrayal.

"I haven't seen her at the Palats," I probed gently.

Luther eyed me. "Good. She's been forbidden to approach or contact you in any way."

That didn't surprise me. While I would usually be upset by that and felt terrible for the woman, I also didn't forget that she was the reason I was nearly abducted. I wouldn't be seeking her out, either.

"Would you like Medic Nyla transferred here to care for you during your stay?" Luther offered.

Blinking at the suggestion, I was about to agree, but then exhaled in refusal. "No. Nyla is finally reunited with her family. They stayed away long enough because of me. I don't want to be the reason they are separated again. I've recovered. I'm healthy. There is no need for Nyla to be sent here to care for me."

"I don't want you to feel alone."

Glancing at the prince, I took him in momentarily, then shook my head. "I've always been alone. I'm adept at it."

"Even as a child? When you had your brother with you?" Luther probed.

"Even as a child," I confirmed. "Zimri and I were close but didn't grow up together. He was the future heir. I was the toy doll to keep the Queen occupied while the King dealt with running our world. Zimri was educated separately, taught to fight and to lead."

"The vision you showed me was of a brother who loved and adored his sister," Luther pressed, his tone gentle.

"He did. He was a good brother, but our time together became less the older we got. What you saw was not just the love of a brother but of any educated man who understood that the power the Kings held was always delivered to them by the blood of their sisters."

"Would he have stood behind you and let you claim that power?"

Giving the question genuine consideration, I assessed all of my brother's words defending me and his words of arguing for better treatment of the royal womb.

"He hated how I was treated, how our mother was dismissed, and her title removed as soon as I was born. Zimri wanted the Princesses to be recognized for their blood, not just for the ability to give birth to the next heir. He wanted our titles for life, status, and importance to remain a fixture of the palace."

"What made him treat you so differently from your uncle if he knew you were more powerful?" Luther pressed.

"Like you said, he was a future king and had the ego of one. The difference between my uncle and Zimri was that my brother was not threatened by me. My uncle and the Kings before him resented their sisters for being more powerful than them and relying on their blood to claim the throne. Zimri loved me, but would never have elevated me to a queen and kneeled before me."

Taking a breath, I admitted just how different I was from the girl I was then. "He wouldn't have had to. He would have made an excellent king. I would have been content with him showing me the respect of being his beloved sister. That's all I wanted... back then."

Clasping my hand, Luther squeezed it once. It was reassurance and comfort, but I still stared at his hand on mine, caught between accepting his offering or severing his hand for touching me. Before I could decide either way, the transport stopped, and Luther removed his hand, sliding to the door. "We're here."

Swallowing my emotions, I slid across the seat and followed

Luther onto the street. He offered me his hand this time, and despite not spying any broadcasters, I accepted and let him walk hand in hand with me to the store.

An advance team of the other half of our dayshift had already cleared the store leaving us as the only customers with the staff waiting excitedly. The moment we entered, the owner introduced herself and offered Luther a beverage.

"That would be lovely, but I'll browse with the Princess first. I can relax while she tries anything she is interested in."

I finally observed the store displays and realized we were in an upmarket store dedicated to ladies' underthings, sleepwear, and robes. Far from the standard satin slips that were regular on Praldia, this store held undergarments in various materials ranging from a thicker, soft fleece for winter to a sheer, see-through gauze that revealed everything and made the reason for wearing it pointless.

Rubbing the flimsy material between my fingers, I marveled at the softness. "What is the point of a slip that covers nothing?" I asked Luther quietly.

His mouth twitched as he leaned towards me. "Seduction. If you were to remove your dress and reveal you wore that underneath, I would be inside you before you could draw your next breath."

Flinching, I recoiled from the garment as if it stung me. "No need for that, then," I muttered, moving on to the area where sleep clothes were displayed.

Again, the materials ranged from fleece with long sleeves and legs to sheer gauze. I bypassed the see-through items and ignored the full coverage since the palats was always heated. I'd probably overheat in one of those.

I picked up a set that contained a chemise and bottoms that were stretchy so they could cling to your body. I'd never seen anything like it before but was fascinated by the idea of not getting tangled in your bedclothes. It would probably cover my butt at most, but I'd try it as long as it covered my back and intimate areas.

What I really got excited about was the Avalonian-style sleep-wear. Much like the slips we wore beneath our clothes, the Avalonian style joined together at the crutch. So, it was still loose and flowy, but added a layer of protection to a woman's core. Growing up, this style was used as underthings, made of satin and cotton for sleeping.

I gathered a few items and headed for the fitting room, my Elite following and standing guard while I tried them on. Happy with both styles, I came out to find a woman my age waiting.

"Can I find you something else to try?"

"No, I was happy with these, but I will get one of these" – I held up the Avalonian style – "in every color." Holding the little two-piece set up, I smiled. "And maybe another two or three of this one."

"Any specific colors?" The woman's smile widened at my order.

"Whatever you think will suit me."

The woman nodded, taking what was in my hand and dashing back to the sleepwear section. While she gathered my order, I headed to where the robes were and admired the different options.

"Can I assist?" Another woman appeared.

Picking up two robes in different jewel colors designed for drying after bathing, I passed them to her. Then, I gathered two for modesty before bed and put those across her outstretched arms. "What are these?" I queried, fingering what felt like a drying robe, but it was round and tapering to a point.

"Oh, that's for your hair." Handing the robes off to the first woman who had returned to help, the assistant demonstrated how to use them. "You flip your head forward after bathing like this."

She threw her head forward and put the round part over the back of her head with the taper coming over in front of her. Even though her hair was in the short style of the Queen, she gestured, tucking long hair inside the taper.

"Then twist it and wrap it on your head to stop your hair dripping everywhere," she explained. Having twisted it, she stood straight, folded the wrap back on itself, and secured it with a built-in seal at the back of her head.

Eyeing the wonderful thing, I selected two and added them with the robes in the other woman's arms. "Okay, I think that's it."

The saleswoman frowned. "But you didn't look at the undergarments. I'm sure we have a lot more variety than Praldia. Have you ever tried Twin-sun slips?"

"Ah, no, but-"

"Oh, you must! It's wonderful for hot summers. Silky feel against the skin, but airier than your regular satin, and it absorbs sweat from the skin, so you don't feel sticky and yuck." The assistant led me to a corner where she showed me the Twin-sun display, and I had to admit that the material felt lovely.

Choosing four, I handed them to her, then followed her to the counter. Luther was already there supervising the ladies folding and bagging the items I'd chosen. Once the final was tallied, he pressed his thumb to the identity reader, charging the purchases to his account.

"Thank you, ladies. If you could have this all delivered today, I'd appreciate it," Luther farewelled, his hand on the small of my back directing me out of the store.

Instead of returning to the transport, we headed further down the street full of boutique stores for everything from clothing to jewelry and shoes. Before we reached the next store, I spotted the first broadcaster taking stills of us.

Luther must have spied him because he leaned into me, his mouth to my ear, saying, "That was a good start. Let's make the next lot work a bit harder for that sale. They earn good money here. Don't make it so easy on them."

"I can't help that I know what I like and want," I replied, forcing a smile.

Looking down at me as we stopped outside the store, Luther raised a brow. "Funny, you weren't as impressed with that argument when I used it for going after you."

I'm sure my eyes became bright blue as I was forced to keep the smile in place. Luther's eyes brightened as if my sudden need to drown him thrilled him somehow.

Before I could respond, he stepped by me as Wolfe held open the door to the next destination. "Let's get you a nice dress for the garden party."

Muttering a few choice objectives defining his character as I passed, I grew angrier when Luther chuckled behind me. If I didn't hate him so much, I might have liked that he got turned on when I was irritated, which might have soothed me.

Sadly for Luther, one sweep of my hand across my flat stomach reminded me of the one reason to detest his existence. Unfortunately for me, I'd agreed to be civil and play the perfect companion in public, so I took a deep breath, composed myself, then went to work being the perfect Princess.

I didn't really need clothing. Shopping had been an excuse to get out of the palats, but interacting with Cyrans was just as crucial as in Praldia. I didn't want to be seen as standoffish, aloof, or snobbish. I was raised to care. To be the perfect balance for the heir.

So, I took the time to speak to the women who served me. Learned their names and used them. I asked about their lives, noting those who came from privilege and those who relied on a sale to survive. The latter usually saw me purchasing more than I needed as an added bonus.

By lunch, I had more clothes than necessary to cover every purpose, including two in the Avalonian style dresses, which I thought might be my new favorites.

As Luther slid into the car beside me, his eyes scanned me from head to toe, stopping at my eyes. "You need food."

"Luckily, we're heading to lunch now, right?"

"Yes." We traveled in silence for a minute. "Thank you for not taking my tease the wrong way. You had numerous opportunities to snap at me but played along."

"I promised a public face, but I hope you'll change your mind about voiding the contract. It would be easier."

Shifting in his seat, Luther didn't reply. Not to refuse or demand a second chance. He merely glanced at my hand for a moment, then pulled out his comms and sent a message. "Let's just get through lunch, and I'll leave you in peace as you requested."

Chapter Twenty-One

Every topic of conversation the Elite had suggested was used up. As we ate our mains, we conversed like two strangers getting to know each other. Over dessert, we exchanged gossip and funny stories we'd overheard from our Elite. But as our digestifs were served, I had nothing else to keep the amiable flow going. For the most part, Luther had let me direct the conversation.

"Can we discuss your return to Praldia?" Luther asked after several minutes of silence, keeping his voice low to avoid being overheard now.

Stirring the herbal liqueur, I didn't rise to the topic. "There is nothing to discuss."

"Your life is not here, Zira. The attempts on your life covered your coming here, but I've had time to ensure your safety at home now, and it's time you came back."

When I glared through my lashes at him, Luther sighed. "I have a suite on my floor cleared for you. You are not expected to share with me and can avoid me easily outside the required events. Though, I would ask that we be seen walking the rose garden or some other private time together for the sake of appearances at least once a week."

"More than proximity will need to change, Luther. I need control over my life. I want inclusion in your plans for war against my planet. And I want to be able to help the people of Praldia. There will be no more confining me to my suite unless there is an actual emergency in the Palats. I think I've proven my ability to protect myself if necessary."

Eyeing me, Luther didn't agree or disagree. His gaze was intense as if he could unearth my true motives and illuminate my hidden fears. "Anberon has liaised with Wolfe regarding the kitchenette you had installed and other needs you've requested be met while here. He is making sure everything will be ready for your return."

Huffing, I stared out the windows at the view over the city of the capital. The advanced technology of this planet was seen everywhere, but all the way to the horizon was still abundantly ancient sandstone with arched windows and remarkable details.

Even the newer structures were encased in sandstone to a height before glass emerged to complete the high rise. As if the modern had grown from the skeleton of the old. It gave the city an ambiance of mystery and romance.

"I've grown attached to my suite here," I confessed. "The large balcony especially. I like having a private space to breathe fresh air and relax."

Taking a sip of his digestif, Luther turned his gaze to the horizon. "I can build you a balcony that runs the entire ocean side of my level. Or even direct access from it to a platform on the cliff edge so you can watch the ocean crash against the rocks beneath."

That would be breathtaking. The ocean below me during the day. A star-filled sky above at night. "You would?" My voice came out breathy and awed, undermining my cold front and giving away how much I'd appreciate it.

Luther's eyes mapped my face, his eyes filling with a gentleness I rarely saw in him but knew from reading his desires was his love for me. Stars, why did he have to let his ego come between us when I came here?

"I will," Luther assured.

Silence hung between us as we stared at each other. Luther met my gaze in an open invitation for me to create a psionic link and read his desires. I didn't need to. Not with the way he looked at me. It didn't matter. The damage was done. But on top of our grief, I mourned the loss of the companionship that had started between us in Praldia. I hadn't loved him, but some affection for him had settled in my heart.

Clearing his throat, Luther turned his gaze back to the glass in his hand. "It will take some time. I'll need to have it designed and bring in the ingenjörer to ensure it is constructed with safety and security and adds to the aesthetics of the palats before I can even start building." He shot back the rest of his liquor. "We are looking at six to twelve triple moon cycles before it will be ready. You cannot stay away that long."

Wisely, I knew Luther spoke true, but that didn't stop my spine stiffening and my tongue from tingling with the need to rebel against his authority. "Maybe that time apart would benefit our joining," I challenged.

"Zira-"

'Be reasonable,' echoed in my mind, and my skin prickled, ready to go to war with Luther's ego and presumed authority over me. Yes, he was my guardian, since I legally had not reached the age of majority. Still, I wasn't a bratty child, and my opinion was valid. Especially when it came to my right to hate him.

Releasing a sigh instead of the words I was expecting, Luther focused his gaze on my lips. "There are compassionate projects that need you and cannot wait that long. The lemmings and indigenous communities of Praldia need you to be their voice in my court. I deserve your resentment and aloofness, but do they?"

Blackness! I hated when he was the reasonable one.

"Would you be happy for me to arrange your return home after my mother's birthday?" Luther pressed. "By then, I will have engaged the design teams for the upgrades, and you can liaise with them to ensure you get what you need to be comfortable."

That gave me another two weeks before I'd have to live under the same roof as Luther again. Not what I wanted, but hopefully enough time for Didrika and Chas to find some leads for me.

"I've forged bonds with some of my new Elite," I mourned, already missing Wolfe and his daughter.

Nodding as if he had perceived as much, Luther turned to the older man I'd appointed as captain. "I can seek the transfer of Wolfe and Hildebrand if they so wish to accompany you home, and Chas will rejoin your team having served his suspension. But you cannot bring Didrika with you. My father will not give her up, and I wouldn't have her there even if he would."

"Because she challenges you?"

"Because she hates me, Zira. Almost as vehemently as you do. One woman repulsed by me in my household is more than enough," Luther answered, then placed his napkin on the table and stood, raising his voice as he did. "The sun will be rising in Praldia soon. I have some busy weeks ahead of me, and I don't want to leave you lonely. Are you sure you are happy to stay here a bit longer?"

Glancing to the side, I spied the waiter nearby and understood who the performance was for. "Yes. Your parents have been so kind to me, and I'm learning more about Cyra and its people from first-hand experience."

"I'm glad you are enjoying getting to know my family. We'll talk soon," Luther said as he came closer and leaned down, cupping my cheek.

With tenderness, he brushed his mouth over mine, once, twice, then pinched my lips in a passionate yet restrained kiss. It took everything in me not to pull away, but at the same time, I leaned into that kiss, longing for the affection I'd once felt for him.

My eyes became glassy as I held back my grief about losing what had been brewing between us. Luther had potentially been my second chance at love. It was my way to discover if an Avalonian could love another. Still, he'd destroyed us before it was more than a spark.

Straightening, Luther assessed my eyes quickly before dropping his gaze, a heavy sigh leaving his body as if he knew exactly where my mind had gone. "Enjoy the rest of your day. Wolfe can sign for any more shopping on my behalf."

Bowing low, Luther left, signing the bill on his way out. Since the meal was over, I got up, my Elite immediately surrounding me as we headed outside. A second transport had arrived to collect the Prince and his Elite, leaving me the use of the King's vehicle.

"Where to now, Princess?" Wolfe queried.

"Swimwear," I declared. "I plan to use the pools when we return to the palats, but prefer not to swim naked here."

The pools at the Cyran palats were not private like the ones in Praldia. Several were joined together by shallow areas or hot zones for relaxation. Anyone living in the palats could use them, including staff. Uncomfortable with the potential for anyone to join me, I'd resisted the pools until now. Still, I was desperate for a proper swim.

Wolfe gave me a nod, told the driver our next stop, and joined me in the private area. After the car was moving, Wolfe eyed me.

"What is it?" I asked, hating the tension in him.

"I know this morning was hard for you. Holding the prince's hand, smiling, and acting like nothing happened. You did well. Even your Elite struggled to pick up the subtle tells of the tension between you, which could be explained away by the circumstances of your joining," Wolfe praised.

"But?"

"It's a pleasure serving you, Princess, and getting to know you. I will happily serve you whenever you are on Cyra-"

"You won't follow me home," I guessed the rest. I nodded in acceptance. "Hildebrand?"

"Has a family here. His eldest son just graduated from the academy. He was lucky enough to score a commission to the Royal guard here in Cyra."

"So, I will be short on Elite when I return to Praldia." I huffed. "I understand. It would always be your choice to serve me."

Wolfe bowed his head as if he was honored by my words. Then he sat back and relaxed. "I'm going to make a suggestion, but if anyone asks, I never said these words."

When I raised a brow in curiosity, Wolfe continued. "We have new graduates each year. The latest candidates will receive their commissions next week. As the royal family is usually full, they get assigned to running security for events, heading up missions, or overseeing troops elsewhere. You should take a leaf from your companion's book and attend one of the training sessions this week, then send the King a list of names of who you want on your team."

"I only need three," I frowned.

"You need three to fill in just your basic numbers. You should have another ten on rotation through the shifts to allow for rest days and holidays. Getting them fresh from graduation also ensures their loyalty is to you and not the other family members," Wolfe reminded. "They will still have to report to the King and Prince, but you will find their words are more carefully chosen when they do."

"They are more likely to cover for me than Elite loyal to Luther?" I tested.

"I merely suggest you attend a training session, see what candidates appeal, and give the King a list. How Chas arranges the shifts on his return should be to benefit you. Should you want privacy, you would do so when particular Elites are on watch rather than others."

Smiling at Wolfe, I thought about it. "I believe it would be a good idea to see what new Elites are available to fill the vacancies on my team. It would be senseless to keep taking from others and interrupting their rosters. And you are right; I'm sure several of my Elite are due for a few days off. It would be good to pad the rotation. Can you arrange something for tomorrow?"

Cyra

"I will have it done by the time you finish at the next store," Wolfe assured.

Leaning close to him, I placed a kiss on his cheek. "Thank you for your wisdom." I was rewarded with a wink.

Chapter Twenty-Two

"Oof!" Kylar winced beside me as a trainee's body slammed a guard.

They were playing a game of Capture the Flag. One flag up a center tower too high just to jump and grab. It was also surrounded by twenty trainees whose job was to stop the attackers from getting to the flag.

"It's not enough that they are good soldiers themselves," Wolfe murmured as we watched. "They have to work as a team, make sure that while protecting their charge, they aren't putting their fellow Elite or their charge in danger by making reckless moves."

Erhaird, sitting behind me, leaned over my shoulder and pointed to an older-looking guard. "That's Gallow. He's one of the trainers. Fought alongside the King many times. Gallow trained most of us, even Wolfe; that's how long he's been around."

When I lifted a brow at Wolfe, he slowly blinked. Damn, Wolfe was easily twenty years my senior, so that made the guy down there throwing trainees around left, right, and center a good ten years older again. He was taking out kids half his age and barely breaking a sweat.

"Watch how he's drawing the trainees' attention," Erhaird indicated. "He did this same thing to us many times and still kicked our asses."

"He's doing it on purpose. Drawing their focus while other members of his guard find the weak defenses to attack." I leaned forward in my seat, studying the surrounding areas. "There," I said, pointing to the shadows where another guard was lurking. "And there." Another two guards were at right angles to the rest of the attacking force.

"Very good Princess," Wolfe praised. "They're drawing attention, and then it will open a gap for these two to break through and climb the tower."

As we watched, one of the trainees left the ring to try his luck against Gallows. My Elite muttered insults while Wolfe drew a line through one of the names from the list. "Ego before duty does not make a good Elite," Kylar whispered. "He just failed."

It took a little bit longer and a few more trainees scratched from Wolfe's list for that gap in the defense to open, and the two guards ran in to take advantage. Before they could, a cry rang out, and like they were dancing, the trainees shifted, forming a second ring of defense. The attacking guards were in the open, but the gap had closed, and now they had no choice but to engage.

The battle continued until all the guards bowed out of the fight. By the time they did, only ten names remained on Wolfe's list, even though more than that remained standing.

"Team two," Gallows called as he approached where we sat.

The first team left the pitch, and the trainers reset the field. Gallows handed Wolfe another list of names. "We'll get the flag with this lot, but there are two standouts among them," Gallows told Wolfe. His eyes flicked to me, and with a slight bow of his head, he walked away again.

"He knows why we are here?" I asked.

"I always attend the assessments. Give a list of names to the King of who is good for what. That you attended with me could be your curiosity or boredom," Wolfe replied. "Though, he's seen enough royals attend and then pick the best of his graduates that if you were Cyran, he would expect you are here to recruit as well. Because you are Avalonian, he may suspect something other."

Scanning the twenty names for team two, Wolfe underlined five, crossed out three, and left the rest for judgment. Wolfe had watched them train on and off over the last year. He already had a good idea of who would be good enough, but this would be his final assessment of them.

We watched five teams battle it out on the field for the next few hours. Only two teams managed to defeat the guards. The third team held them off and prevented the capture of the flag, but suffered significant loss and made stupid mistakes that, had they worked together better, would have yielded a better outcome.

When the last team fell, Wolfe circled a few names and counted up all of those he deemed good enough from the five lists. "You have nearly fifty potential candidates. If you would like to meet and interview each of them, I can arrange that."

The field filled with all the teams, and Gallows culled the outright fails. Even then, they still had close to ninety trainees left. Still, I took Wolfe's word about their ability and that only half of those were valid candidates for my team. Frankly, my evaluation halved that number again.

"Interviews will not prove anything to me except their ability to talk. I'd like to run my own assessment," I murmured to Wolfe.

His eyebrow arched, but he didn't refute my request. Instead, he caught Gallows eye and waited for the old man to tell the trainees to get a drink while he came to see what Wolfe wanted.

"It's not unusual for Wolfe to ask for a different scenario to be run as part of the assessment. Especially when the King is looking for specific candidates for a mission," Erhaird whispered behind my ear.

Handing Gallows the list, Wolfe said, "Circled names remain behind for further assessment."

"Scenario?" Gallows asked as he checked the names, nodding as if he agreed with the choices, frowning at a few others.

When Wolfe looked over his shoulder to me, I answered for him. "Avalonian Assassin."

Gallows scoffed. "How are we meant to test that?"

Rising from my seat, I arched a brow at the old man. "Me."

"Surely not?" Gallows looked horrified. "Princess-"

"The Prince was nearly killed by an assassin of my kind already this solar cycle. It seems like the ultimate testing scenario to me. My life and the Prince's may count on their ability to recognize a threat where they wouldn't expect to find one."

"No offense, Princess, but you are no match for these men," Gallows objected with certainty that wasn't arrogance.

Smirking, I looked over the men on the field. "No offense, Elite Gallows, but I'm the only person here qualified to do this sort of testing, and while I know that those men are not good enough to stop me from taking that flag, it's whether they can even summon up enough intellect to figure out the danger they are about to be in and stay alive."

I smiled and looked at Wolfe when Gallows eyebrows drew together in a frown. "Make it happen. I'll go get ready." Turning, I started towards the exit. "Kylar, I'm going to need your help with something," I told him as he and the rest of my Elite on duty fell into step with me.

"Not to doubt your abilities, Princess, since I've seen you in action, but are you sure you want to do this? Anything you do here will get back to the King and likely the prince."

He had a point, but I shook my head. "I've shown my hand before, and it wasn't enough to make the prince fear me or even deter him from being an ass. So, making these trainees fear the Avalonian boogie man isn't going to change my guardian's perspective anytime soon."

"The prince may not fear you, but he does fear for you," Hildebrand offered. When I stopped and glared at him, the giant Elite just shrugged. "I have a family. I know what an Elite in love looks like and how fearing you could lose them can mess with your head faster than Fucqworts."

Stopping my progression, I turned to face him. "Do you think I'm being too hard on the Prince, and I should forgive him, Hildebrand?"

"No, Princess," the giant Elite didn't even hesitate. "I'm just saying I get why he's overprotective of you. Especially given your condition upon your arrival."

"All the more reason he should have taken more care of me and been present instead of avoiding me," I answered civilly. I turned to start walking, then paused and looked back at Hildebrand. "And what in the blackness is Fucqworts?"

A few of my Elite choked on a laugh before Rylan cleared his throat. "It's an infection men can get when they seek pleasure in a place where many others have been before."

Blinking at the medic, I'm sure I looked as stupid as I felt. Apparently, Hamlin felt that was a poor explanation too. "It's caused when those who entertain multiple lovers in a short time period have failed to wash between clients for some time. Man or woman. It doesn't matter. But it only infects men for some reason."

"The excretions of multiple men seem to start attacking each other and develop into a nasty infection which can reside in its host undiscovered and travel to the brain and cause decay of their clients, which leads to insanity," Rylan finished the explanation. "It can be very fast-acting depending on the severity of the infection. Not something we usually have to worry about since none of us are stupid enough to seek relief from an unregulated worker, but for Hildebrand's comparison, it works."

Lifting a brow, I blew out a breath and started back towards my suite. I needed to get changed for this testing. "And I'll take things I never needed to know about for five hundred."

When the Elite gave me a quizzical look, I huffed and waved it away. "A game the Praldian councilors regularly play. They give you the answer, and you identify the person, place, thing, or idea that the answer describes, but you have to phrase the response as a question. You win the amount of cash each topic area is considered to be worth."

"A game of knowledge rather than skill," Kylar considered. "And do you play it often with the councilors?"

"I used to. And with some other associates," I replied, as my mind turned to Ethelred. I still hadn't heard back from him. But that was a concern for another time. "Hildebrand, we must leave some props around the field to give the trainees a fighting chance. A torch, a blindfold, and something to repel water being blasted at them or strong wind. We'll probably also need a medic by the end of it."

"I'll get some supplies organized. Are you returning straight to the testing grounds from your suite?"

"We are," I assured. Enough of my Elite was with me inside the palats that we wouldn't be at risk if Hildebrand went to gather what was needed.

With a bow, he turned off down another corridor while we continued to my suite. Once we arrived, I entered my room and opened the closet. It was a lot fuller than it was yesterday. The royal attendant delivered and unpacked all the clothes for me.

Moving through the space big enough to be a child's bedroom, I searched for the training gear I'd purchased after Luther left yesterday from the same shop where I'd found swimwear.

As I scanned the racks of clothing, I noticed some of those flimsy slips I'd refused to consider in the first store after Luther suggested they were used for seduction. Rubbing the sheer material between my fingers, I couldn't deny it felt nice against my skin. However, a flame of anger ignited within me that Luther had purchased these for me even after I'd dismissed them. He knew I was never going to wear them for him. Maybe he thought I might want to wear them for another.

It made sense that if our marriage became one of show only, he would find another lover and assume that I might do the same after some time. Or entertain some of my Elite like the Queen did. It

Cyra

wasn't the Avalonian way, but neither was a female on the throne. If I planned to change one tradition, undoubtedly, another, like fidelity, could be just as quickly discarded.

Gripping the material, I closed my eyes and considered being with a man other than my husband. My mind conjured the image of another Cyran. One who knew my body well and had delivered me many moments of pleasure in his bed.

Those dark blue eyes widened as he observed me in this flimsy slip, the feel of his brown hair between my fingers as he picked me up and slammed me against the wall, ripping the sheer material away from my breasts as he took me hard and fast.

My fist closed, and I flung the garment away from me with the fantasy of Hartwin ever loving me like that again and focused on the dark clothing I needed for today's activities.

When I emerged from the wardrobe in black pants and a top that mimicked the exercise gear I'd seen the Royal guards wear when they were off duty in Praldia, it was to the wide-eyed wonderment of my Elite. They'd never seen me in anything but my dresses or robes, and this outfit did nothing to hide the lean curves of my body.

"That looks disturbingly similar to the outfit the invisible assassin wore," Kylar worried as he considered me.

"It is the standard for physical training and execution in Avalonia."

"When you say execution?" Erhard asked.

I smirked as I headed for the outer quarters. "What assassins tend to wear to execute their missions."

"Blackness!" Erhaird muttered as he opened the door for me. "We should wake Jervaise for this. He's going to be pissed that he missed it," he told Kylar.

Apparently, that made Kylar happy. "Yes. He is."

197

Chapter Twenty-Three

T he field lights were low, creating the atmosphere of dusk as I'd requested Kylar to do. The fifty trainees were lined up, waiting for Gallows to address them and explain this scenario. In the center of the field, the tower was gone, replaced with a dais and a throne, upon which Wolfe had planted his butt along with his list of names and pen.

Half of my Elite on shift were spread around the edge of the field, the other half guarding the entrances. Kylar and Erhaird went to Wolfe and took the prime guard position behind him. They'd decided they wanted in on this practice, as it was also good training for them. It's not as if they got to fend off Avalonian assassins every day. In fact, it had never been an issue until I came along.

As for me, I was already hiding. The symbol for shadow activated on my spine before I even walked out onto the field, allowing me to blend with the gloom of dusk.

Reading over the brief, Gallows blew out a huff, then eyed the trainees. "This assessment is one of the hardest. This is a real-life scenario. Protection of a royal from threat. Elite Wolfe will be playing the part of the Prince. You must not, under any circumstance, allow his life to be endangered.

"However, in saying that, you cannot use extreme force in this scenario. If you locate the threat, you are to subdue without injury. Am I understood?"

That wasn't part of my brief. Gallows was sweating about how to tell the King I got maimed on his training field if I was injured.

"Yes, Staff Master Gallows," the Elite responded as one.

"I'm going to split you into three teams. Five from each end step away. Now every second soldier take a step forward." Gallows waited for them to comply. "Front line is on throne duty. That means you stand behind the throne and watch for threats. You are the last line of defense. Take your position."

Twenty trainees jogged over to the throne and lined up behind it.

"Second line. You're on crowd duty. Sort between you which of you will take key sentry points and who will wander the crowd. You will be judged on your ability to identify the key sentry positions and crowd watch. Move out. Final ten, move closer," Gallows instructed as the next twenty moved aside and discussed their method.

"You ten are at each end of the platform. It is your job to ensure no one steps a foot up there that isn't the King, prince, or an Elite." Gallows sent them to take their places with a wave of his hand. By now, the perimeter guards had taken up their positions.

Placing his hands behind his back, Gallows let the trainees in on the final detail of the test. "Over the next two hours, shift changes will occur across the palats. The staff has been requested to pass through this field on their way to or from their shift to mimic the chaos of a courtroom. Follow the protocol of being on duty. A threat could come from anyone. As Elite Utz recently proved, the danger could be within your own ranks. This program is now active. Good luck."

Striding across the field, Gallows took the stairs to the observation area we'd utilized earlier. Staying where I was wrapped in shadows, I waited.

The thing about being raised royalty that everyone forgets is that you are made to sit still for hours from a young child while the adults do boring adult things. You act as the adorable adornment or unseen.

Stillness. Silence. Patience. Invisibility.

Do you know what I realized about those qualities of a Princess? They coincided with the same skills the invisible assassins of our world practiced. A lesson learned the hard way.

As minutes ticked by, I saw my brother's black blood pooling around my feet again and in the darkness, the eyes of a young Princess who refused to be vulnerable ever again.

Once we settled in Praldia, I told my father, a former guardian, that I wished to learn to fight and defend myself. He didn't hesitate to sharpen the weapon I had the potential to be. I didn't train to be an assassin, but when you learn to defend against them, you inadvertently gain the skills to be one.

Thirty minutes passed, and the trainees, having expected something to happen by now, started looking at each other with frowns. Voices caught their attention as Royal guards entered the field heading to their evening shift.

The guards raised brows at the trainees standing around, at Wolfe lounging in a mock throne while Kylar and Erhaird stood as perfect sentries on either side. They called hellos to a friend, but he merely gave a slight nod before keeping his eyes on his surroundings.

The landscape crew entered from the other end, loud and raucous as they discussed some silly occurrence from the day. While the trainees turned their attention that way, I casually shifted my position. Moving away from the sentry positioned only meters from me towards an unobserved area.

To be fair, it was the center side of the field, below the observation box. The likelihood a threat would approach from here was very low. It could only happen if they were inside the perimeter guard or virtually invisible at the start of the exercise. Which I was.

The shadow glyph on my spine didn't activate until I was sixteen. I'd been hanging out with Hartwin, and his father came looking for him. Hartwin told me to hide, and suddenly the glyph had flash-burned, making me invisible in the corner of Hart's closet.

Commander Stark had looked straight at the place I was hiding and still not seen me. I thought I'd been busted, but as my fear of being caught intensified, the shadows thickened around me, and I realized they were cloaking me. I never told Hartwin, but when I got home, I practiced this new power until I knew how to wield it.

Another hour passed. The foot traffic until now had been light and sporadic, but the trainees started to shift, potentially thinking this entire activity was just to see if they had the patience to withstand guarding a royal.

Fifteen minutes later, a large cohort of the royal guard entered the field on their way home from their shift. At the same time, day staff from the palats entered from another direction, and then another rowdy bunch from the opposite end. Three prominent groups of nearly fifty people chatting, laughing, and drawing the watchful eye of the trainees in every direction. As they entered the field, they broke into smaller bunches spreading out, some stopping to check out what was happening or chatting with friends from another group.

Perfect.

Keeping the shadows wrapped around me, the dark night creeping over the field aiding me, I started creeping across the pitch. Water flash-burned on my spine, and I directed groundwater to reach up beneath each of the sentries, muddying the ground beneath them, sinking their boots into the soil up to the ankle without them even noticing.

I crept up behind one of the roving sentries just as a few of the staff went to shortcut across the dais, causing the trainees at either end to politely direct them around, and for the roving sentries on that side to start doing some crowd control, keeping the area close to the stage clear.

Moving quickly, I wrapped my shadows around this trainee, a hand covering his mouth as I drew a red marker across his throat. He stiffened as I whispered, "You're dead. Wait to the count of five, then collapse quietly to the ground and don't move or make a sound."

Quickly moving on, I trailed behind a group of housekeepers who then stopped to flirt with some royal guards. One of the roving sentries approached the group to encourage them to move on or away from the dais. He, too, scored a red mark across his throat and fell into the nest of shadows I created for his body so he wouldn't be spotted by anyone unless someone tripped over him.

As I weaved closer to my target, I took out five more roving sentries. I could see Wolfe frowning and searching the crowd, his pen making marks on the page.

The next sentry I approached must have seen the shadow move in his peripheral. He spun towards me and got half a shout out before the glyph for air flash-burned on my spine, stealing the air from his throat on a gust of wind to prevent the sound from carrying. He got his hand around my throat as I slashed the marker across his throat.

Startled, he let go, eyes wide as he backed up a step, one hand checking his throat. "What."

"You're dead," I whispered. "You won't be able to talk with that wound. You have until the count of three, then you drop quietly and don't move again," I quickly hissed and moved on.

Smartly, he raised his arm to try and catch the attention of the others. Bonus for him, one of his fellow trainees behind Wolfe saw it and raised the alarm as he watched his teammate collapse. The trainees on the dais were a mix of quick-to-react and disbelieving simultaneously. But they still quickly moved closer to Wolfe as an alert was raised quietly.

One was by the body of their fallen comrade as I stepped onto the dais, forming my shadow cloak to be the silhouette of an elite. Now if someone spotted me out of the side of their eye, they'd think I was one of them.

The one who checked on his fallen teammate returned, his eyes now flitting all around. "He's dead. Throat slit, he reported to Kylar."

"Check in with the team. Is there anyone else missing?" Kylar ordered before leaning in to murmur something to Wolfe.

"Deal with it. I have too much on today," Wolfe replied, emulating Luther perfectly.

I snorted a laugh, then quickly moved as Kylar and Erhaird's heads turned, having picked out that noise amongst the cacophony of the field. Kylar gestured to Erhaird, and they both murmured orders to the trainees next to them.

Subtly, the trainees shifted formation, blocking me from getting to Wolfe from the side or behind. A smile tugged at the side of my mouth at the move.

Marching off the back of the dais, I assessed my surroundings as I moved, dropping my shadows and blending in with the crowd. Strolling amongst them. Some paused and then whispered to their friends as they looked me over. There weren't many Avalonians in the palats.

One of the roving sentries cursed when he saw me and quickly approached. "Princess?" He took in my outfit and tensed. "Who are you?"

"One of the Princess's protection detail. I only just started," I answered. "Elite Wolfe or any of her Elite can vouch for me."

Narrowing his gaze, the trainee comm'd through requesting confirmation of a female Avalonian in the Princess's guard. That brought all my Elite's attention my way. When the trainee relaxed, I could only gather that someone backed my claim.

"Apologies. You stand out, and we are currently being tested right now."

Giving him a smile, I met his eyes, and he quickly diverted his. "I'm aware. You have an assassin in your midst."

"An assassin?" he mouthed, then his eyes went over my head. He'd given me the perfect opening to his thick throat, but there were too many eyes on us right now. Though, not the eyes that should be watching me.

"Yes, I tripped over one of your sentries by the third entry."

"And you didn't raise the alarm?" he looked shocked.

Leaning in, I smiled. "This isn't my test." Leaving him gaping, I moved on. Air flash-burned, and a heavy wind blew through the field, stealing the attention of everyone as they quickly shielded themselves, their clothes blowing in the cold gust, giving me the excuse to step close to the guards at the side of the stage.

The sentries on post yelled out in alarm as they suddenly realized they were stuck in the ground, but most of it was lost to the screams of surprise by staff.

"Where did that come from?" I asked the trainees beside me to appear non-threatening. But before they could respond, I used that wind to steal the air from their lungs and stepped back into the shadows.

As the wind died and everyone calmed, muttering about it, the five guards collapsed to the ground, suffocating.

"What in the blackness?" One of the roaming sentries rushed over as they all passed out, and I quickly gave them their air back. His eyes widened as he checked their pulse. Then he ran to the bottom of the dais, and I stayed behind him.

"Elite Wolfe, we have an Avalonian attacking us," he reported. "The wind suffocated the entire watch on the left just now."

All eyes on the dais turned to the left. I slid by the trainee, smart enough to realize the threat, and lowered myself to crawl up the stairs and huddle next to the throne, which was now casting a heavy shadow.

"Clear the field," Kylar directed. "Find the threat, now. Close the protective circle."

"Shouldn't we get the prince out of here?" one of the trainees asked.

Wolfe looked at him, shook his head, and crossed the kid's name off the list.

"No. We don't know where the threat is. We've got a secure position here and a better chance of seeing it coming," Kylar lectured.

"Maybe," Erhaird added, his knee gently jabbing me in the back, letting me know he'd spotted me.

"Maybe not," Kylar chuckled, looking right at me.

A scream went up across the field as one of the play-dead trainees was discovered by a young cook. Damn, I probably just traumatized her. The royal guard was closer. They should have found that body ten minutes ago.

"Should we be concerned about how good she is at this?" Erhaird asked Kylar and Wolfe as the report of the other dead started coming back to them.

The roaming sentries remaining trying to herd off the staff was lost after the bodies started showing up. Staff raced for the exits before turning to watch what would happen next on the periphery. They all knew it was a training exercise.

"It's not like she woke up this morning and thought, 'I'd like to try being a royal assassin,'" Wolfe grumbled. His hand casually fell over the side of the throne and patted across my hair. He knew I was there. It made me smile.

"Maybe we shouldn't leave the prince alone with her anymore," Erhaird murmured.

"No. She's not stupid. That would be obvious. But the prince should reconsider public appearances with her until he's earned her forgiveness." Kylar winked at me.

Finally getting the staff clear of the field, the sentries started back to the dais, intending to close the protective barrier and make it even harder to breach.

Air flash-burned, another big gust of wind flowing through the field, hitting the Elite from the back of the stage and attacking the five trainees on the right side.

"Here, use this to shield," one of them grabbed the barricades Hildebrand organized and pulled it into place to protect them.

Using the distraction, I swung onto Wolfe's lap, wrapped my arms around his neck, and kissed his cheek as I drew the red line across his throat. Before he could latch onto me, I rolled free again.

Cyra

"What the..." A trainee dived into me as I slipped by one of his teammates, taking me to the ground.

"The prince is bleeding!" Kylar cried.

Cursing all around. Sonic flash-burned, and the Elite pinning me was thrown into the barrier of his team, opening a space.

Getting up, I raced for one of the exits. Sentries came at me. Water activated, and a wave rose from the ground, sweeping ahead of me, the groundwater crashing over them.

As I escaped, the one who had dived beneath the shelter put out there got up and gave chase. I reached where the tower had been set aside, and as I ran behind it, I pulled the shadows around me again. Ducking aside, I used the rough edges to climb above head height and further.

The trainee ducked inside and started using his hands to feel around the darkness, the only light coming from behind him, putting him at a disadvantage. Realizing this, he dropped into a crouch and fumbled at his belt. Knowing what he was looking for, I wrapped my legs around one of the support rungs and hung my body behind him.

A torch lit up in front of the trainee, and he shined it around before turning it up. My marker slashed across his throat before he could spot me. "Dead," I whispered as feet plundered toward us. Swinging back up, I climbed to the top, slipped out the opening, and eased around to the flag pole. Straddling it, still wrapped in shadow, I yanked the flag free and dropped it.

The red sheet fluttered to the ground, signaling the assassin's escape to the evaluators.

"Stop!" Gallows bellowed. "Line up."

As I looked down, Kylar and Erhaird were down there, smiling at me even though I was sure they couldn't see me. "Stay invisible," Kylar whispered. "Don't want the staff any more scared of you. Let them think it was another Avalonian or simulated."

Swinging my legs over, I lowered myself until my feet landed on each of Erhaird's shoulders. He automatically grabbed my ankles. Letting go of the pole, I bent my knees and somersaulted off, landing a few meters away in a crouch. My Elite closed around me as I straightened, and I dropped the shadows.

"Blackness, Princess. That was impressive. I saw you take down only one of them from the sidelines," Rylan praised. Which started them all comparing what they'd seen and not.

Gallows chewed out the trainees for failing to protect the prince while Wolfe came to join me and discussed some of the trainees I'd taken out. I gave points to the one who saw the shadow move before I got him. The one who approached me, the one in the tower, and the ones who used the props to defend against my attacks. Once we'd agreed on fourteen that we were happy with, Wolfe signaled for us to return to my suite.

Most of the staff had moved on, but my Elite stayed extra close as we wove through the palats halls. "You know what really sucks," Erhaird commented to the others. "Kylar, Wolfe, and I all knew the Princess was right beside the throne, but when she attacked, she was so damn quick that the Princess had marked him dead and gone again before we even realized she'd moved."

Kylar smirked. "Jervaise is going to be so pissed he missed it."

Laughing, I shoulder-knocked the cheeky Elite and shook my head. "So is the prince. Be sure to tell him I killed him right under your noses."

"I think I'll pass on that one, Princess," Erhaird snickered.

"Fitta," Wolfe muttered accusingly at Erhaird with his own smile, making the others laugh and rib Erhaird for being a wuss. Though that's not the word Wolfe used.

"You know who will hate missing this even more than Jervaise?" Hamlin asked. "Rika and Chas. That's got to be a worse punishment than suspension."

"Ooh, you're right, Elite Hamlin," I agreed excitedly. "As such, we should go get me some Kudai Flower tea tomorrow. I think I earned it. Wolfe, organize the excursion, please."

Chapter Twenty-Four

Arriving at Chas' place was a lot less dramatic this time around. We took the King's shuttle to a shopping precinct, did a spot of shopping, and then teleported from the private dining room Wolfe secured for lunch to the road outside the house.

Aware that the approach to the house was booby-trapped but safe, we didn't hesitate to take the steps to the door this time. Chas answered the door and welcomed me before leading me to the sitting room, where a steamer of Kudai tea was already waiting.

"I'll have some privacy for this visit," I told Wolfe as the other Elite took up positions inside and outside the house. "You and Kylar can help guard the door or wait in the kitchen."

Before either Elite could argue, I stepped into the sitting room, and Chas shut the doors. As soon as they closed, I was in Chas' arms, getting a hug that I sorely needed. He chuckled and cuddled me back before leading me over to the lounge.

Before I could sit, a wall panel opened, and Didrika slipped into the room with a massive smile before she rushed forward to get her own hug. "Princess. This place is a good choice for clandestine meetings. They've got secret tunnels all over the property. If this wasn't the house of one of your most trusted Elite, I'd be lecturing you on the dangers of this location."

"Chill, Rika. Only family knows those tunnels. It is for escape, not subterfuge," Chas assured.

"Because of your Aunt being a mercenary?" Didrika asked as the door to the kitchen slid open, and a tall, well-built Avalonian woman in her middle years carried a tray of steaming plates of food into the room.

"I have never acted against anyone who wears a crown," the woman answered, eyeing Didrika before her gaze came to me. "On any planet that I've aboded." Placing the tray on the table, she bowed.

"Princess Zira, my Aunt Ammita," Chas introduced.

"Welcome to my home."

"It's lovely to finally meet you." I offered my hand, but Amrita's eyes widened.

"Princess, my family are öfugt—contrare, unfavorable," Ammita explained.

Lifting a brow, I had an inkling of how she had become a mercenary now. "How many generations?"

Double blinking, Ammita kept her eyes lowered. "My mother was disgraced under your uncle's rule."

"Ah, well, not to speak ill of the dead, but the last king was a misogynist piece of pond scum. Much like the Kings before him. That's why no more kings will sit the Avalonian throne."

The woman's head snapped up, and her eyes met mine, a world of hope passing between us. Tilting my head, I kept her gaze as secret knowledge of the northern barbarian tribes passed between us. Then I offered my hand again.

"The last time I was here, I accepted Chas as kin. As my knight-brother. You are his aunt, so you are öfugt no more."

Double-blinking, Ammita took my hand and bowed to kiss it.

"You are my Princess, the blood of our people, and the source of power for Avalonia. My loyalty and blood are yours."

Smiling, I squeezed her hand. "Excellent. Now, tell me more about you, Ammita. How did you come to Cyra? Become a mercenary? Your family? I want to hear it all." Sitting, I poured the tea for everyone, scaring Ammita a little at the honor of being served by her Princess.

Ammita told me her life story while we ate the wonderful lunch she'd provided in the Avalonian style with our fingers. I prompted for details when I wanted them, but for the most part, I listened and planned. Ammita was precisely who I was hoping she would be. An outcast Avalonian who still had ties to the black market and rebel forces of Avalonia.

"It sounds like your life has been quite adventurous," I said as Ammita finished. "Even after you left the dangers of mercenary life behind to focus on being a mother."

Gifting me a smile, Ammita glanced at Chas and ruffled his hair. "They were certainly rambunctious. Being a mercenary was by far easier. Do you and the prince have plans for starting your family yet?" Chas and Didrika both turned their heads away. Sorrow etching their faces.

"The contract of our joining detailed my responsibilities to provide the prince with heirs," I answered.

But Ammita hadn't missed the shift in our company and frowned. "Are you with child now?"

"No," I mourned, my hand sweeping across my empty belly. "I was until a few weeks ago. Twins."

Ammita reached across the table, took my hand, and squeezed it. One mother who had lost a child to another. She knew twins were difficult to sustain for Avalonians, so she didn't enquire further.

"I always thought grief was universal until I lost my daughter, Leasi. My companion, sons, and Chas handled the loss differently. Cyrans struggle with such harsh emotions especially." Ammita rubbed Chas' back. "Chas ran off and married while my husband got himself killed looking for vengeance. Grief is a blackness that, once inside you, there is no getting rid of it. You must control and wield it, or it will own you and destroy you."

"Like the Salarneytandi?" I asked.

Ammita bobbed her head. "I dare say grief is the monster Salarneytandi in our folklore."

"Salarneytandi?" Didrika asked.

"An Avalonian urban legend they tell their children," Chas explained. "A demon who feeds on the soul of those who cannot control their emotions."

"But Avalonians are emotional," Didrika contested.

"We are. And we are powerful. The lesson of Salarneytandi is to ensure we can disconnect our emotions from our power. That we don't lash out and do harm because we are hurt emotionally. Those who cannot make the disconnect are said to feed the demon and eventually become one of the Andlaus—the soulless," I explained.

Chas shivered at the term but clarified, "Andlaus are believed to have had their souls devoured, and once they are soulless, their bodies become a shell the demons can use to reign pain and terror on the world. Many Avalonians believe Abaddon, the Barbarian, is Andlaus."

"I've met him. He is," Ammita and I replied simultaneously.

"That would be problematic if he is," Chas said, filling our teacups. "Andlaus are said to only be susceptible to demons and other Andlaus. They cannot be killed by mortal hand."

"'They cannot fall to the hand of man' is the correct interpretation," I corrected. "I am not a man."

The table fell silent. After a moment, Ammita took a sip of her tea and met my eyes. "If you stand against that monster, I will stand with you. I only ask that I am there to see him scream."

The side of my mouth tilted up. I thought I'd have to ask. My eyes flicked to Chas. "Do you object?"

"I dare not," Chas chuckled. "She'd kick my ass." His aunt smiled broadly.

"Then it shall be done. When Chas returns to my Elite, you will come with him."

"In what form?" Chas asked. "She cannot be one of your Elite."

"No, but Councilman Aldous insisted I hire an assistant for him to communicate with since he finds me so wholly unappealing." I focused on the two Elite in the room when no one argued. "What have you two found?"

"We got the name you were after," Didrika answered.

Chas pulled out a tablet and showed me photos of my enemy. "Lord Kaynon. Like many high-born Avalonians, his family was exiled to their country estates when the Barbarian took the throne. Lord Kaynon has managed to curry some favor with Abaddon due to his family controlling much of the farmland in the south."

"He can starve his enemy out?" I checked.

"His family always had control of their portion of the royal soldiers due to that risk. It enabled him to prevent the Barbarians from taking any control of that land. To do so meant making himself susceptible to attack from the rebel forces."

"My uncle was a fool to give one person so much power. He will use that to try and control me when I take the throne," I groused.

"Kaynon was your uncle's best friend," Ammita told me. "And the King turned a blind eye while the other farmers were assassinated one by one, and Kaynon bought up their land."

"That's a lot of farmers to kill, and no one grows suspicious," Chas said.

"He only wiped out five families before the others were scared enough for their wives and children to sell when offered." Ammita met my eyes. "The ones who sold still farm and live on the land, and are paid wages, and offered the protection of royal soldiers."

"Which means my uncle didn't turn a blind eye; he was actively involved in a hostile takeover." I kept my eyes connected with Ammita's. "But if he used assassins and they still live, then it was not a clean crime, and there will be witnesses." My gaze turned to Didrika. "Did you discover how he planned to override my natal chart?"

Blowing out a breath, Didrika dropped her shoulders. "No. I did discover that one of the plots of land he sequestered contained an ancient temple that the murdered family had protected for generations. We believe that whatever power or knowledge he has which gave him confidence that he could kidnap you and force you to his will would have come from that temple."

Just like the blade Utz used on me.

My eyes switched to the handsome Avalonian, old enough to be my father, on the screen. I thought of the map of the northern lands in my mind and where all the large food plots existed. My upbringing required me to know such things. Closing my eyes, I centered myself as I asked the following question.

"Was the temple in the eastern planes?"

"How did you know?" Didrika asked.

"The old temple of Aeron," Ammita cursed. "The god of wind and breathing."

"All the powers of wielding air fell under Aeron's domain. That temple probably had many relics to empower and quell the element." And if Kaynon knew I could ribbon, he might suspect that many of my other powers were born of the manipulation of air. Something his friend the King, as one of the few to have seen my natal scale, would have known.

Blowing out a breath, I squared my shoulders and pushed the tablet across the table to Chas. "One problem at a time. Abaddon first. Then I can worry about Kaynon."

"You have a plan?" Ammita asked.

"I have the start of one. By the time you join me in the palats, I will have the skeleton done."

Ammita smiled, understanding the old Avalonian saying. 'Áætlun er bara beinagrind. það getur ekki hreyft sig án vöðva og sina.' A plan is just a skeleton. It cannot move without muscles and tendons.

"Shortly after you enter my employ, I'll return to Praldia. Ensure you bring clothing for various climates. While it is winter here, it is summer in Praldia and is significantly warmer than Avalonia or Cyra ever gets."

Avalonia was further from the suns—one giant, Risastór sól, and Lítil sól which was a dwarf in comparison, but still larger than most planets—than both Cyra and Praldia. In fact, Avalonia sat smack-bang in the middle between the two stars that made up this system.

Some argued that Avalonia orbited the outer border of two different systems, refusing to accept a dual sun. Still, either way, Avalonia was far enough away from Risastór sól to remain cool, but close enough to Lítil sól not to freeze.

Cyra, Praldia, and Meccha all orbited Risastór sól all year round, whereas Avalonia swam figure eights around the two suns. In Summer, our planet circled Risastór sól, and in winter, Lítil sól. While all the other planets in our system considered one circle of their sun to be a year, Avalonia called it a season, with our midseason lasting mere months as our world shifted from the orbit of one sun to the next.

"I will liaise with Chas and come prepared," Ammita assured. "Should I also bring clothes for home?"

The side of my mouth tilted up as I met Ammita's eyes. She was intelligent, observant, and cunning. She understood war was upon us, and the only way to defeat the Barbarian was to go home and fight this battle on his doorstep.

"That would be wise," I agreed. Standing, I hugged Didrika, then indicated she should disappear again. "I'll see you all soon."

When Chas opened the door, it was just his aunt and him in the room for my Elite to see. Walking me to the door, Chas offered Kylar a package. "Kudai flowering tea for the Princess," he said with a grin. "I'll bring more when I return to my duties next week."

"I'll see you soon," I farewelled. Taking Chas' face in my hands, I again kissed his brow.

Chas gripped my waist, keeping our bodies at a distance. His fingers dug a little into me before releasing me slowly. When I stepped back, there was pure adoration on his face. Over his shoulder, Ammita stood with a hand over her mouth and tears of pride in her eyes.

"Soon," I murmured. Then I turned and followed my Elite out into the sun-drenched winter afternoon. Soon, I'd bring that Barbarian to his knees and take back my world and my life.

Chapter Twenty-Five

Pacing a rut on the balcony, I rubbed my hands against my upper arms and glared at the horizon. The sun was just rising. My night shift Elite would be eating a light snack, ready to turn in for the day, and my day shift would be waking and getting dressed.

More importantly, Chas and Ammita would be here soon. Chas to return to my service, and his aunt to start her role as my assistant. Double bonus, Chas promised to bring a bulk supply of the tea with him.

We were only days away from the Queen's birthday, which would see Luther return, and my need to smile and play the mild-ed Princess everyone thought me to be. Not Luther, though. Oh, no. If he hadn't been sure of my ability before now, he was very aware after Gallows informed him via the King.

Gallows had recorded his candidates' Avalonian Assassin Scenario testing and shared it with the King. Supposedly, it was to suggest a way to make that scenario a regular training feature of the Elite going forward. But I knew the actual reason. Gallows was a tattle tale.

Not that Luther or the King demanded my presence to ream me a new one. Instead, the only reason I knew was that Luther had sent me a snippet of the video—the part where I sprang up from beside the throne and killed Wolfe—along with a message of how he not only found himself looking for shadows since the first invisible assassin attack but was finding them strangely erotic since this video. Luther followed this up by sending me some outstanding quality assassin-esque fashion pieces.

Now, I could have returned those clothes along with the skimpy slips ripped to smithereens—because there was no chance I'd risk him gifting those seductive items to his mistress—but why would I turn up a gift that I'd struggle to source in my position? Luther had given me the perfect gift to become his ultimate downfall if I so chose. But I didn't.

Hate Luther as I did; I wouldn't want him or his family dead. Egos aside, they were excellent rulers. Fair and impartial in trials. Humane but firm with their people. What I learned from watching Luther rule those years in Praldia, those words of wisdom he shared with me on our walks while I petitioned him for aid for the people of Praldia, would benefit me when I took the throne of Avalonia. Luther's example of leniency would be what brought my people peace.

After thirteen years of civil war and barbarian rule, the Avalonian people deserved harmony and a throne that respected the old ways while forging a new era. One where the females of my bloodline were not treated as incubators of the next king. My daughter would hold her head high and never feel less than she was.

"Princess," Jervaise greeted gently as he stepped out to the balcony, pulling his coat against the biting cold. "The Prince has called. Will you accept the communication?"

It would be easy to say no and tell Jervaise to suggest I was still sleeping, but it wasn't like Luther to call at this time of the morning either. Maybe there was an issue I needed to be aware of urgently.

"Of course," I told Jervaise and went back inside, ignoring the widening of his eyes at my agreement.

Going to the fire, I slipped from the wrap keeping me warm, and pressed the button on the 4D comms unit. Luther's semi-transparent representation appeared before me. "My Prince."

"Zira, I really wish you wouldn't..." Luther cut off with a sigh, bowing his head. He looked exhausted. It was just about dinner time in Praldia, and Luther had no doubt been working long hours to fulfill his role as Prince while also planning a war.

Taking a breath, he rolled his shoulders back and met my eyes again. I'd already seen his greatest desire, but he was showing trust or stupidity by meeting my eyes. It was all going to count on the words he chose.

"We have our plan of attack for Avalonia. You asked to be kept in the loop. This is me informing you. We have a timeline, a location, and a strategy. I am ready to share these with you."

"Now? Via comms?" While I doubted Avalonia had the tech to hack a comms call, I wouldn't put it past some of Cyra's other enemies to have that capability.

"No. When you come home. It wouldn't be prudent to share this information this way."

"Then why even tell me?" I asked. "Just an excuse to talk to me?"

"No," Luther assured, but the word wasn't as firm this time. There was sadness behind it. "You've made your feelings clear, and I assured you I wouldn't intrude on you until our next event. But I wanted you to have time to prepare before you hear the plan."

Prepare? Prepare for what? Was the attack imminent?

"I know how much you care for your people, Zira. You were willing to go to war with me to protect those without a voice. So, I know that you will reject this plan until I can prove it is the only one that can fulfill our victory with minimal casualties."

"Luther-"

"We have worked every scenario, Zira. Multiple times with various factors for change. Hear me when I say we have exhausted all other options before settling on this plan." Luther paused for a good three breaths. "Believe me when I tell you there is no other way that does not increase the risk to innocents."

Stars above! Keeping composed, I considered what Luther was telling me. He was going to make me queen; I needed to damn well act like it and be willing to accept the responsibility of taking that damn crown. "What is the expected impact on my people?"

"We can limit the fatalities to those who are inside the palats. We've been monitoring comings and goings and determined when the least number of civilians will be present. Still, the Barbarian uses your people as shields in his war against the rebels and other would-be tyrants. We don't doubt any warm bodies that are not his own people will swim in the deep ocean of souls at the hands of his loyal followers before I can rip that crown from his head."

Yes, that sounded precisely like Abaddon. "You give him too much credit. He would bleed his own people just as easily, and will, before he submits." Inhaling, I stood tall. "So, a hundred percent casualty during the takeover. What numbers will that be?"

"At least a hundred and fifty souls."

"The very least?"

"Abaddon keeps women and children chained in the hall of his bedroom at night. By day they go to the dungeons to rest, and the fathers or men of the family are brought out to surround his throne. An ice maker always holds the chain and can supposedly turn all connected to ice before he could be killed."

Luther looked and sounded disgusted by this, but it fit with the Barbarian that beheaded my kin, had my brother slaughtered before me, and tried to rape me in their blood when I was still a child.

"The children, does he-" I couldn't say it. Even wanting to ask if he did to them what he tried to do to me blackened my soul, because if he said yes? How could I face myself if my absence had resulted in the torture and destruction of innocent kids?

Holding my bottom lip between my teeth as I forced those thoughts aside, I focused on what Luther was here to discuss. The

Queen's birthday was only three days away, so I would return to Praldia and hear the plan in four.

Luther was gifting me four days to process the worst of it before the rest, so I could ask the right questions, come to the same conclusion and get on board with his strategy without my instant emotional reaction causing an obstacle. He trusted that, given a few days to rationalize, I'd come to the same conclusion. War was never won without the blood of innocents covering the hands of the victors.

"I will take this information on board and spend the next few days processing what you have told me," I said instead.

Silence pulsed between us for a minute before Luther looked me over, seeming to notice I was already dressed for the day. "Your new Elite start in your service today?"

"Yes. Elite Chas and Didrika also return."

Luther glanced to the side as if checking something and noting I was right before nodding. "Aldous informed me that you had also hired an assistant. Was it one of the candidates he suggested?"

"I'm not a fool, Luther. Aldous must work harder than that to put one of his spies near me. No, I hired an Avalonian woman."

"Zira-"Luther growled.

"She is not a spy. She left Avalonia under the old regime and owes nothing to those involved in the civil war. In fact, she profited from it. She has a vendetta against the Barbarian and is happy to serve the Queen she hopes may deliver her enemy's head on a platter to her."

"And what's to stop her taking your head once you do?" Luther probed.

The side of my mouth pulled up. "I thought you knew why shadows turned you on?"

"Blackness, Zira!" Luther cursed. "It is late, and I am beyond exhausted. Do not tease a Cyran who desires you more than air or sleep. But say the word, and I will be there in minutes if it is not a tease but an offer."

Inhaling, I looked away. "Apologies. I cannot. I will not. My affection for you is that of a lady for the prince she respected as her ruler, not the companion you forced me to be."

That pressing silence pulsed between us again. Heartache was as intense with grief as it was with longing. For him, it was fed by desire. For me, hate. And somewhere tangled between the two, regret that this was where we ended up.

"I should let you go and greet your new staff," Luther said.

As he reached to disconnect, I stepped forward. "Thank you..." Luther paused, his eyes still locked on me like he wanted me to be the last thing he saw before falling asleep. "...for preparing me," I clarified.

Pressing his lips together, Luther bowed his head. "Of course." The call disconnected.

Closing my eyes, I stepped back, one hand gripping the fireplace mantel, the other covering my flat belly. So much lost for his pride. Giving myself a minute to roll in that grief that always floated beneath the surface of my being now, I unwrapped it like a weighted blanket of emotions over my shoulders just as quickly and shoved it out of sight.

Once composed, I glanced where Jervaise stood by the door, watching and listening to everything. Unlike the others who at least pretended I had an ounce of privacy, Jervaise looked right back at me. Not eye to eye, he wasn't an idiot. "Are they here?"

"Chas is briefing with Kylar and Wolfe in your inner quarters. The new Elite are in the outer quarters with the outgoing shift getting to know their team, and the Aunt is being shown her quarters two doors down."

"Are they adequate?" I asked. I didn't want Ammita to have left her beautiful home to live in a small cave.

"While not as grand as your suites, this is the royal wing, and that suite is nicer than the home I grew up in. She will be comfortable. So much so, we may struggle to convince her to ever leave." The small laugh in Jervaise's tone was always a giveaway to his teasing, even when his face was as fierce as an Elite in battle.

"Good, thank you. I guess I should welcome everyone and have some breakfast." When Jervaise's eyes went to the tray he'd brought me when I woke two hours ago, I waved away his silent comment. "That was just a snack to sustain me."

"Princess, your appetite puts us all to shame." This time, not only was the tease in his tone but the twitch at the side of his mouth and the glimmer in his eyes. Zimri could be like this when he had a moment to not be a prince. I liked Jervaise, even if he was the biggest gossip and, from his own admission, manwhore in my Elite.

"Come on. I must lay down the law for these new upstarts before they think I'm a pushover."

Jervaise actually laughed. "Princess, you've given them a fear of shadows. I doubt any of them will be too keen to try and be cocky in your presence any time soon."

"It hasn't stopped you." When Jervaise lifted a brow, I remembered how he reacted to me taking out Luther's would-be assassin. Cocky was definitely one word for it. "You're still miffed you missed out on watching it?"

"So, so, irate. But I have seen the video. Many Elite are very confused now if they should fear shadows or enjoy them."

"Blackness! You're all as bad as the prince," I groaned. "Well, now you're holding up my introducing Ammita to Aldous and forcing him to coordinate with her for my schedule." When I smirked and winked with a chuckle, Jervaise grinned.

"If I didn't have a lusty maid waiting to let me share her bed at the end of my shift, I'd stick around to see that."

"One of our maids?" I checked.

Jervaise's humor vanished as he said, "No, I don't hunt in my own yard. I've learned that lesson," with a hint of regret.

I didn't ask if he meant Padget, Luther's half-sister. It was apparent he'd been hurt by her treason just as much as I had. And yet neither of us felt that betrayal as Luther, who took her in and treated her as close to a sister as he could without the public acknowledgment, had.

I often wondered if the revelation of Padget's actions triggered the change in Luther towards me. If I recall correctly, it wasn't until her trial that he first talked down to me. Maybe Padget was the trigger, Hartwin's revelation as my lover was the catalyst, and Utz's betrayal was the straw that broke the bar on the scale.

As I followed Jervaise into my inner quarters, I decided it didn't matter. What was done was done. There was no taking back words said and actions enacted. It was called the past for a reason. Moving on was not optional if sanity and living mattered. That didn't mean you forgot. History was an ever-present lesson. Forgiveness? That was optional, and right now, it was not considered.

Chapter Twenty-Six

P icking up the teacup, I inhaled deeply, the reminder of home, of playing hide and seek with my brother while our carers tore their hair out in frustration, putting a smile on my lips. Taking a sip of the Kudai tea, I enjoyed the fruity flavor that filled my senses and put the cup back on the table.

"The summer palace gardens were filled with the Kudai plant," I told Ammita as she finished pouring her tea and sat across from me. "Every time I smell it, I'm transported to the happy memories of my childhood there with all its orchards and herb gardens."

"I have similar memories of my childhood home. We also had our own supply of Kudai in our garden. The cook taught me how to harvest it, dry the flowers for tea, and jam the fruit. Lucky for you, or you wouldn't be enjoying that cup right now," Ammita chuckled.

"You grow Kudai here?"

A smile playing on Ammita's lips, she lowered her eyes coyly. "Some years ago, when I decided to leave my home, I potted a few of the bushes and took them with me. When I found a new home here, I planted those trees as part of our joining ceremony to symbolize setting down new roots with the love of my life."

"How beautiful."

Shrugging a shoulder, Ammita stared at her tea. "It was sentimental foolishness to him, but I tended those bushes like I tended our marriage. After his death, I gave them the love and care in his absence."

Her heartache was tragically beautiful. "Do you believe we can learn to love another? If the one we first devoted ourselves to is taken from us?" I asked.

Inhaling the Kudai steam, Ammita released a sigh on her exhale. "You are young. It's a possibility. My children were fully grown when my heart was ripped from me. I had too long with it beating only for him. Another heart would be too foreign for me to endure after all that time." She took another sip, as I did, then met my eyes over the rim. "Has he been long from your life, your first love?"

"He was taken from me two years gone. It's made my joining with the prince harder to accept. Still, before the attacks, I had started to develop an inkling toward my guardian," I admitted.

"Let the grief of your recent loss scab over, then nurture the bud that grew before it. You might yet feel your hearts beat in sync with one another."

Swallowing another sip, I hoped Ammita's wisdom could be true. Setting my cup on the table, I glanced around the winter garden where we sat by the fireplace. My Elite were dispersed amongst the foliage, giving me an illusion of normalcy. Inhaling, I checked the time, smiled, and put my hands on my lap. "So, how was your meeting with Aldous today?"

"Entertaining. That snivelling twat thought I would fill your calendar with any soirée he deemed you should attend and not question it. As you instructed, I limited your public outings with the Prince to those related to charity or family commitments. I also suggested dates for you to meet with a designer to decorate your new suites. He gave me the tentative dates for the renovation meetings. The prince will be present at those, but as it will just be the building team, I shouldn't think you would object?"

"No, those are fine. It's his palats. He's right to ensure the design complements the existing beauty and intricacies. The prince will have the final say in anything external to my suites. Still, all final decisions for interior design will be mine to make," I confirmed. "Did you manage to get hold of the Native Council?"

"No, by the time I finished with Councilman Aldous, it was late in Praldia, so I thought I'd contact them later this evening. I've also looked over your old daybook. I will contact some of the other charities to organize attendance to any fundraising that you can be involved in with them."

"Hold off on that for now. We don't know what my return to Praldia will herald. I'd prefer not to over-commit and then pull out because of danger or the Prince's control issues," I decided. "Did you put that list together for me?"

"Yes. Just the names you gave me," Ammita handed me the list to check.

"And the other thing?"

Ammita handed over another note with directions and a map of the homeworld. "Can I ask your intent?"

"Kaynon sacked the temple to arm his man against me," I answered, placing both notes on the table beneath the tray Ammita carried the tea out on. "He's proven he can't be trusted with such precious relics."

"I still have some contacts if you need someone to unburden him," Ammita offered.

"I would trust another mercenary even less," I stated plainly. "They are relics of our people. They should be kept safe and not used for selfish exploits. I have someone who can secure them for me." My comms buzzed. I checked the message and then deleted it. "Why don't you go see if the Native Council is up yet, then take the rest of the night off."

Eyeing my comms, Ammita smirked, bowed her head, and set her cup back on the tray. "Should I take the tray?"

"Leave it for now. I don't like to be wasteful." Picking up the teapot, I refilled my cup, then picked up a finger of the snacks on the tray and nibbled as Ammita left for the night.

Chas wandered out of the garden and helped himself to a cheese and pastry scroll. "There's a third cup on the tray?"

"I'm expecting my friend from Praldia to call this evening. He's on his way now."

Chas swallowed the mouthful of food and eyed the plants. "I'll tell the others to give you some privacy." Without another word, he sauntered off.

There'd been a change in Chas since he'd been suspended. He was back on the night shift but never offered me the affection he had before. In fact, he was very hands-off, which unnerved me a little since he was the one to suggest to my Elite back in Praldia to make physical contact to build trust. Still, he stayed in my bed and held me for the babies I carried. There was no need for him there now, yet I missed him. More so now that he was located just across the room from me.

A Cyran emerged from the foliage and, after ensuring I had noticed him, took the seat Ammita had just abandoned. "Princess." Taking my hand, Ethelred kissed it, then clasped it. "I heard what happened. I grieved for you."

"The prince?"

"His spirits have been low since it happened. I assumed the reason and, on seeing you tonight, knew it to be true. The grief in your heart shows in your eyes," he told me gently.

"Thank the stars that the broadcasters are not as familiar with me as you are to know such things," I whispered, taking my hand back and pouring him some tea. "This is Kudai flowering tea. It's from my homeworld and is good for one's complexion and constitution. It is a tradition in Avalonia to share the tea with family and friends whenever one comes to call."

"I'm honored." Ethelred smiled as he took his cup and sipped. "Very nice."

Sitting back, I watched as Ethelred consumed the tea. When he was done, he set the cup down and sat back, his eyes focused below mine. "I can tell you nothing."

No, that wasn't happening. We'd bargained and come to a deal. "But we agreed," I insisted.

Taking out a tablet, Ethelred repeated, "I can tell you nothing; I will not betray my prince." Giving me a hard stare, he handed me his tablet. On it were photos of the mission board in Luther's office, screen grabs, and videos of Luther discussing their plans with his war council.

Without hesitating, I sent myself the file and handed his tablet back. "Fine then. I have two more requests for you." Taking the notes Ammita gave me, I handed them to him.

Unfolding the list of names, Ethelred read it and lifted one of his brows at me. "For later," I told him. "I'll have further instructions when and if needed."

Placing that note in his coat pocket, Ethelred considered me. "You have been plotting in your grief."

"It was better than being trapped in the heartache. I am not set on this plan. Not yet. I have some homework to do first, but I'll need you to act quickly if I'm correct about my assumptions."

"How quickly?"

"I might only be able to give you a day's notice," I confessed.

Considering me, Ethelred sighed and turned his gaze to the fire. "Depending on what you are asking, that may not be enough. My reach is not limitless." Looking at the map and directions, a smile crept onto his face. "And this?"

"Is where the item Utz used against me originated from," I answered, making Ethel's eyebrows jump. "Don't damage the temple in any way, but relieve it of its treasures. I will ask that you give me the first pick from your loot before selling to anyone else. What I don't take, you keep as payment for both jobs," I negotiated.

Tilting his head, Ethel smiled as he slipped that note away too. "What if there is little value there?"

Picking up my tea, I didn't rise to the bait. "Then the landholder obviously robbed it first, in which case, feel free to unburden his estate of such valuables."

"And his name would be?"

"Lord Kaynon. A close friend of the former king. A murderer and thief. But one with a significant influence and control over an arm of the Avalonian army. You may have to avoid them to get to the temple."

That made Ethelred laugh. "Oh, Princess. I get to pillage and plunder? All you need add is a beautiful woman to sate myself with, and it would be the best offer I'd had in a while." How Ethelred's eyes roamed my body told me which woman he'd take for that pleasure.

Setting down the cup, I rose and moved to stand beside him. "I'm not the same woman I was when we were lovers. I foolishly gave my heart away. It aches for him with every beat. And then there is the prince to consider."

"True," Ethelred replied as his hands snaked my hips and guided me gently into his lap. "But you were there for me and took my pain when I needed an outlet. I can do the same for you."

Tempting. So tempting. After all, Luther caused my grief when he bedded his mistress. He'd have no recourse if I took another to my body to ease the pain.

Gripping my chin, Ethelred brushed his mouth over mine. "You are my Princess; you only have to ask."

Turning my face, I broke his grip and placed a seductive kiss on the corner of his mouth. "I'll keep that in mind." Rising to my feet, I stepped away and then stopped. "Stay the night. I'll have my plan set by daybreak."

"If you give me a bed, I'll happily lay in it," Ethelred responded softly.

Smirking, I turned my focus to the garden. "Elite Chas," I called, raising my voice just above what I'd used to converse with Ethelred. There was no way my Elite moved out of hearing distance.

"Princess," Chas addressed me as he emerged from the foliage.

"My friend will be staying with me the night, but first, I would like some time to myself for some quiet contemplation. Ensure your Elite knows to let him in when he comes by in a few hours."

Despite his jaw tensing, Chas bowed his head obediently. "Yes, Princess."

Huffing, Ethelred stood up. "Well, I best go visit my mother. She'll be agitated if she found out I was home for the night and failed to call. I'll be back when the moon is high."

Giving him a nod, I headed for the path inside. Chas whistled, and my Elite melted out of the garden to surround me. I had home-work to do and my own plans to shore up before morning.

Chapter Twenty-Seven

The flames danced around the fireplace as Chas stood by it, watching me. He'd been silent since we returned to my rooms three hours ago. Chas stared out the window while I bathed and changed into my nightwear, not turning back to look at me until my robe was wrapped tight around me, and I'd dropped onto the sofa and started reading. Then, as the hours ticked by, he moved around the room, slowly making his way closer until he stood beside me.

I finished watching and reading the information Ethelred provided me after the first hour. I studied everything a second and third time in the following hour. Luther had spoken the truth. They'd eliminated every other possibility, and still, the casualties would be high.

For the last hour, I'd doodled ideas on my tablet, changing my mind and adjusting the plan that had slowly been building over the previous month. There was a way for the civilian casualties to be zero, but the cost...

My eyes drifted to Chas. "Say what troubles you."

"I don't want that man in your bed," he told me honestly.

His admission didn't surprise me. "Jealousy or protectiveness?"

"I don't think I could choose."

"Do you feel that way when the prince beds me?" I poked this possessiveness for its tether.

Chas stood a little taller. "No. He is the prince and your companion."

"Hartwin?"

Frowning, Chas considered that one. "Nor him."

Sighing, I sank into the comfort of the lounge. "So, as long as he is Elite?"

"I respect Ethelred. He gave up his career for love and, amid grief, built himself a very profitable business. But he is not someone a Princess should associate with, nor should you enter an affair with him."

"Ethel and I were lovers before Hartwin found the courage to pursue me," I confessed. "He is a known quantity. A safe choice for me."

"Physically, that may be so. Reputationally, not." Chas sat across from me, leaned his elbows on his knees, and considered me. "I know he is your friend, but he would betray you for the right price, Princess. He puts his business above all else, even his own life."

"Because he is tempting the stars to take him so he can be with his beloved," I told Chas, dismissing his concerns. "Ethel will not harm me, Chas."

"You can't be sure," he argued.

"Yes, I can," I told him gently. "Just as I know you would never harm me."

Chas swallowed hard, looking at the fire instead of me. "I still don't want him in your bed."

"Because you want to be there instead?"

Chas's gaze swung back to me, his mouth pulled tight, the veins in his neck pulsing visibly with his heart rate. Slowly, he eased back and rose to his feet. "You are my Princess; if you need me that way, I will please you as long and hard as you desire. It would be an honor."

For a moment, the tension between us was too much. I could barely breathe with the intensity in Chas's gaze.

Forcing myself to my feet, I moved to stand before Chas. My hand swept up his chest and stopped above his heart. I could feel it like a drum beneath my palm. "Fidelity may not be in my joining contract, but as changed by my time in Praldia, I'm not sure I could look at myself the same way if I were to casually take a lover. Hartwin was one thing. He has my heart, and it was hard to ignore that. A spark ignited with Luther, and I had hoped..."

Dropping my head, I closed my eyes on the disappointment and grief. Taking a breath, I raised my eyes to Chas and implored him to understand. "You are my Knight, brother. I love and respect you as if you were my kin. If I were to succumb to this attraction that developed between us, it would set me on a path I may not be able to come back from. It could ruin my chances of being queen to my people and destroy any chance of Luther and I reconciling."

Dropping my hand, I moved to the fire. Chas took a moment, then headed for the door. When he was halfway there, I had to tell him the truth. I couldn't let him believe it. "It's revenge," I stated.

Chas stopped, but he didn't turn to face me.

"I know Ethelred staying in my room will get back to Luther. I want it to. I want him to hurt like he hurt me when he chose that woman over me and his children. It's the closest I can come to sticking a dagger in his heart, and I want to do that so badly. So, I will let you all think my former lover is in here bedding me all night if it puts that proverbial knife in my hand to twist it. But I won't physically betray my heart or my belief in marriage."

Turning to face me, Chas returned to my side and tenderly wiped the tears streaming down my face. "Then I'll stay in here with you. Let the others think I watched or joined in, but I'm not leaving you alone with him. You are as angry as you are grieved, and Ethelred is smooth enough to work your emotions to his benefit. Before he met his wife, he was just like Jervaise, and he already knows your lust to wield it against you."

241

Nodding, I didn't fight when Chas pulled me into his arms and let me cry on his chest. Vengeance was a need, but it tore me apart as well. Because as much as it grieved me to admit it, I realized to hate Luther as much as I did, I had to have loved him first.

It wasn't the consuming love I felt for Hartwin. Or the way I had come to care for Chas. But it had crept into my being, a tiny ember of the emotion that could erupt into a bonfire if fed the right fuel. Instead, I was smothering it with a blanket wishing it would die out, not admitting that I was suffocating myself. But I couldn't forgive Luther. Not yet. Not while my grief demanded I hurt him like he did me.

Chas's comms dinged while he held me. Glancing at it, he kissed my temple and eased me away from him. "Go wash your face. Your revenge is here. I'll delay him until you are ready to face him." Heading for the door, Chas stepped out and closed the door after him.

As Chas told me, I washed my face, grabbed my comms, and went out to the balcony. Nyla answered on the third ring. "Princess? Is something wrong?"

"Not with me. Is your husband there? I think it's time we talked."

It was early morning in Praldia, so I hoped to catch my Uncle Ravid still in bed. Yet, by calling Nyla, my call could be explained away as seeking medical advice or needing to talk to a woman I'd spent my life with.

"Yes, I'll put him on," Nyla replied without hesitation. "I'll go make some tea," she told her husband as she handed over the call.

"Princess." Ravid came on the line. "I was wondering when you would contact me. Are you ready to plan your war?"

"You didn't think I would abide by Luther's plan?" I asked, surprised.

"His plan works for the war, but he is not Avalonian. As much research as he has done on our kind, and I'll admit it's been limited by what is known outside of our own people, he doesn't understand

242

what our natal scales mean or how they could benefit in a more direct approach."

"Abaddon has an ice maker?"

"Yes. Three of them are on rotation, but they are not barbarians and not as loyal to him as he thinks," Ravid revealed.

"But are they loyal to us?"

"No. Like most ice makers, they have cold hearts and lack compassion but are highly logical. So, they may not act as commanded if they feel it benefits them to stay their hands."

"I can work with that. I have more questions, and then I need to make my decision. Luther will be here tomorrow evening, so I need to have my mind made up to know how I need to approach him."

There was a rustle of sheets and a sigh as my uncle relaxed. I would have preferred to do this using the 4d digitization, but I couldn't risk him being seen if someone walked into my room.

"Ask your questions, Princess. I am your loyal servant; my men are yours as you need."

My planning over the last month had already garnered a handful of questions. Still, Luther's plan affected mine, and I needed facts to help make my decision. I wouldn't move against Luther. He was my prince despite the situation of our joining. Yet, I couldn't agree to his plan and watch my people die if I didn't explore my other options first, and I did have another option. I just had to ensure it could work first.

After Ravid had answered all my questions and given me as much information as he could, I disconnected the call. I stood staring at the stars for a long time. Eventually, Jervaise came to find me, worried I'd been left alone too long.

"Princess, your guest is waiting." The tightness in Jervaise's tone indicated he was just as unhappy with the idea of me sharing my bed with Ethelred as Chas, but possibly not out of jealousy, and instead loyalty to his Prince.

"If I left the Prince. If I decided I couldn't be his after everything, would you follow me or choose to return to him?" I asked.

Jervaise blinked, and his mouth dropped open, but then he closed it. "I don't know. I'd want to know you are safe. I couldn't bear to discover that your decision caused you to fall in harm's way, but if you ended your marriage, your Elite would be recalled. My duty is to the royal family or, as assigned, Princess."

Accepting that answer, I started to move inside, but Jervaise blocked the way. "Don't leave him. I know you are distraught after your loss, and your blame falls rightly on the prince, but it would kill him if we left you unprotected and..." The words failed him. "We'd all hate ourselves for it. Especially Chas. You'll find a way to make it work. Even if you are his in title only, don't give up your safety and crown because he broke your heart. Stay and make him suffer for it. Make the prince crawl and beg at your feet to be forgiven every day for the rest of his life. Leaving lets him off the hook. So don't do it."

A smile pulled at the side of my mouth even as a tear raced down the side of my nose. "You present a playboy joker to the world, but your wisdom and heart occasionally show through. I find myself admiring you for it."

"I want him to win you back, Princess. I do. But I want you to make him grovel first. If that's why your guest is here, then I can't be angry at you for it. I will say, you fight dirty, Princess. I doubt the prince knew what a wild thing you are beneath your grace and nice dresses. Still, I think he's quickly learning that his delicate Princess is actually a hellion in disguise." With a wink, Jervaise pushed the door open and held it for me to return to my room.

The fact Jervaise caught onto my plan this evening didn't bother me. I knew it wasn't him reporting back to Luther. So, I put a smile on my face and focused on getting my revenge while simultaneously moving my pieces for the coming war into place.

Chapter Twenty-Eight

"The prince is in transit," Kylar informed me from where he stood by the door.

Looking up from my reading material, I checked the time. "He's three hours early."

Kylar didn't respond. All my Elite, even those usually chattier, had been tense today, probably in anticipation of how the prince would take Ethelred having spent last night in my rooms.

Since I wasn't due to see Luther until the morning when he would collect me for the Queen's parade, I returned to my reading. Tonight, Luther would liaise with the King about the war and probably socialize with his friends here. I got to enjoy the comfort of my company and the fireplace.

I'd already bathed and had my nightwear under my robe so I could fall into bed when exhaustion overcame me. After Ethelred arrived last night, I told him my plan while we stood together at the fireplace. Instead of sleeping together like my Elite assumed, we'd stayed up all night talking through my idea and making plans.

About five minutes in, Chas joined us, offering his expertise. Neither was happy with my plan, purely because it put me at risk.

That Chas's life would also be at risk didn't alarm them as much. Still, neither could argue that my plan had the potential for far fewer casualties and a lot less bloodshed, so they didn't threaten to block me.

With Chas on board, Ethelred showed him the list of names, and we finalized it before Ethel left in the morning. Tomorrow, while the Prince was busy here, Ethelred would pay my uncle a visit in Praldia and bring him into my strategy.

The doors opened, and Luther strode in; my Elite in the outer quarters were arguing with Anberon and Hartwin while Kylar looked from his prince to me with wide eyes. Luther didn't even pay him attention as he went to my wardrobe and deposited a garment bag inside.

"I already have dresses for the parade and the birthday party," I called.

"That has my uniforms in it," Luther answered as he returned, his current uniform shirt hanging open, exposing his Elite body to me.

Hate aside, Luther was a gorgeous specimen, and those months of intimacy before my coming here destroyed us had created an automatic physiological response to seeing Luther's flesh.

Going to the bathroom, Luther started the water running. "Thank you, Kylar; you can finish your shift in the inner quarters with Erhaird," Luther dismissed him.

Kylar didn't move, his eyes coming to me instead. "Why would Kylar leave? Your father ordered one of my Elite to always have eyes on me. And what is wrong with the facilities in your suites?"

Disrobing, Luther kept his eyes on me as he exposed every delicious inch of his flesh. "I think we can be sure you are at no risk of self-harm at this stage of your grief. At least not the sort that puts your mortality on the line," Luther grumbled the last and stepped into the bath.

Heat pooled between my thighs, my mouth watered, and my nipples hardened as Luther picked up a sponge and washed.

No! I will not be tempted by him. Get your libido under control.

Huffing, I looked at Kylar and tilted my head toward the door.

With a slight nod, he stepped out and shut the doors. Sighing, I put my tablet down and went to the bathing area. "And what is wrong with the bath in your room?"

"Nothing," Luther answered as he lathered his hands. Standing up, his entire torso was visible, dripping water from where he had dunked himself. The top of the V from his hip to his groin was just above the waterline, but since the water was still clear, all his muscular strength beneath the water was also in full view.

Stars! Why couldn't he be ugly and rotund like half the Native council?

"I heard you were lonely and willing to share your room with ex-lovers while they are visiting Cyra, so I decided I'd be generous and keep you company." Having soaped his body, Luther started scrubbing his lathered hands through his hair. Then he stepped onto the ledge that formed a seat and cleaned his abundance of manhood.

"Don't worry; I can see you're exhausted from your 'friend' keeping you up all last night. I'm happy to sleep beside you so you don't feel alone."

How he knew just how much I hated the emptiness of my bed these days, I didn't know. I opened my mouth, ready to tell him to get out that I wasn't interested in sharing a bed with him, but the challenge in his eyes stopped me. It's what he wanted. What he expected. For me to kick him out and to take this chance to hurt him and get my revenge. It's what I'd planned when I let Ethelred stay last night, but that look in Luther's eyes made me shut my mouth because he didn't believe I'd done it.

But why? He used to get jealous about Chas and Hartwin in my bed when they held me. Why did he doubt I'd been intimate with Ethelred?

Inhaling, I forced my body to relax and acted non-plussed. "That sounds lovely. I enjoyed having a bedmate again last night; two was even better. They left me thoroughly sated," I told him, insinuating Chas joined in. "In fact, I should ask Hartwin to join us. It'd be unfair to invite one ex-lover to my bed and leave another on the other side of the doors."

The challenge in Luther's eyes vanished, instantly replaced with the hurt I'd longed to see. I caught a glimpse as I turned my back because I wouldn't stand over him to bathe in his pain. That would be the equivalent of stabbing him in the heart and then rolling around in his blood while he bled out. Knowing I'd hurt him like he had me was enough.

"Zira," Luther called when I'd moved only five steps away.

"Yes?" I turned back to see his eyes fierce with pain and anger.

"Leave Hartwin out of this." He didn't mean tonight. Luther meant out of this fight. Was that the right word? We weren't actually fighting, but the game seemed wrong. Maybe vengeance? That's what this was, after all, and Luther was right; Hartwin had no place in it right now. Yes, Hartwin shattered my heart a few years ago, but he would just be one of the cards I discarded in a game of Kort until I could get the Pip I needed to win the hand. Hartwin didn't deserve that. This entire situation, me joined with his best friend, and him having to watch our misery was revenge enough for the pain he caused me.

The side of my mouth twitched in a smirk. "As you say, my prince." I turned and went to bed. Glancing over my shoulder, I watched Luther submerge to rinse himself clean.

Closing my eyes, I wondered for a second if I could do this, but as I exhaled, I relaxed. I'd been raised a Princess who would submit to men. To my uncle, the King, my brother, the future king, and the warrior chosen for me to be my husband and father of the prospective heirs. I'd hidden who I was for half my life; even after we escaped to Praldia, I still played the part of the submissive lady, only allowing my true self to show to those I let close.

Pulling the covers back, I waited until Luther was above water again to release my robe and throw it on the end of the bed. I don't know why I'd chosen one of the gauzy Avalonian-style rompers Luther purchased for me to wear to bed tonight. Still, now that he was trying to call my bluff, I was glad for it. This one, in particular, had a low-slung back exposing my full natal scale, not that the material hid anything.

Satisfied with the growl I heard from the bath, I switched off the lights so only the glow of the fire illuminated the room and climbed into bed. A few minutes later, Luther joined me; the heat from his naked body radiated across the bare skin of my back.

The room was silent, just the crackling of the fire. I jumped when Luther's lips kissed the top of my spine. "What are you doing?" I asked, suddenly tense.

Tracing the symbols of my natal scale with his finger, Luther followed each completion with a kiss to the glyph. "Do you mean to tell me that all you did with Ethelred was sleep?" Again, he challenged me, daring me to rub his face in it.

"There was no sleeping. But you said you could see I was exhausted and would let me sleep," I reminded, rising to his challenge.

"Hmm." Luther placed a kiss on the symbol at the dip of my spine. "That hardly seems fair, though, does it? To give one ex-lover a night of your passion and deny another the same. There must be equity in how you treat us, Zira," Luther lectured, starting on the lowest of my scale.

"But there isn't equity in how things ended. Ethelred and I were only ever a casual affair. There was no bitterness or regret when that affair came to a natural conclusion. Hartwin ripped my heart out and abandoned me to the torture of my soul, fading agonizingly slow. You neglected me and caused me insurmountable grief. The way our relationships ended varied significantly. Therefore, there can be no equity."

Luther didn't argue; he reached the last glyph, the one for procreation, and traced it twice. When his mouth touched my skin this time, his lips lingered, and then his tongue traced the pattern. Shivers raced up my spine, and my core melted despite the outrage that burned at his gesture.

How dare he! Of all the symbols.

Before that outrage could fester, Luther's hands gripped my hips, and his forehead pressed to my lower back. That's when I felt the drops of moisture pass from his cheeks to my skin. Tears. Luther was grieving in that action, not trying to seduce me.

I wouldn't have it. I couldn't. Luther didn't get to grieve what he caused in my presence. Rolling to face him, I hardened myself. "Is that what you want? To do with me what Ethelred did?"

Luther's eyes cleared of grief immediately as the denial of the claim returned. "Zira, I know you well enough to know you would never-"

I grabbed Luther's hand and placed it on my breast, forcing his palm to mold it. "Is this what you want, my prince?"

Luther growled. Pain and jealousy aside, he was a Cyran male, one of the Elite who restrained their lust so severely that it was as hot and violent as a solar flare when they released their need.

Rising above me, Luther stared down at me, his jaw tense as his eyes focused on how his hand kneaded my flesh. His eyes flashed to mine, hesitancy taming his lust for a few seconds of reasonable thought.

"If it's what you want," I murmured, sliding the strap from the opposite shoulder and folding the material covering the untouched portion of my chest to expose the hardened peak.

"The same rules apply," I told Luther. "There will be no cuddling or sleeping in each other's arms after. Once we are done, you leave. That's how it always was with Ethyl. That has always been the limit of our physical encounters."

A slight lie, he always held me while we recovered, and then we usually shared a meal and talked. "You will get more than he or Hartwin ever did since they never had me naked. But if equity is what you want..." I folded the material back up to cover the pale nipple. A growl echoed from Luther's chest. "It's your choice, Luther. Be happy to share the bed and sleep, or slake yourself. You don't get both. Not anymore."

Jaw grinding, Luther stared into my eyes. I didn't need a psionic link to see the war inside him. But as I watched, the side of Luther's mouth straightened into a Cyran smirk. "There is a third option, so I will negotiate," Luther decided as he shifted his position to roll me on my back and kneel between my thighs.

"A third-?"

"I will not have any sexual release, and I will sleep beside you, but you will be sated so you can rest well," Luther decided. Before I could puzzle that out and argue, Luther dropped his mouth between my legs and sucked me through the gauzy fabric. My back arched, and a gasp of pure need left me as his tongue finished the action by pressing against the nub of my desire ending with a hard flick. It felt like it had been forever since I'd had any physical pleasure, and my body was more than eager.

"Yes," Luther chuckled as he pushed the loose legs of the romper out of his way to breathe over my bare core. "That will be how this works. For now." And without further ado, Luther put his plan into action. His tongue drew through my folds, circling my nub, before closing his mouth around the sensitive bundle and sucking hard.

I shouldn't have allowed it. I should have shoved Luther away and told him to leave my room. I knew I was weak to allow it. I knew it. Especially after I'd told him it would never happen again. But Stars, I missed intimacy, and Luther, like Ethyl, was a known quantity.

"I hate you!" I cried as my body tightened beneath his administration, my back arching as the precipice of pleasure loomed just out of reach. "I hate you so much!"

"I know," Luther murmured as he rose over me to stare down at me. His cock slipped through my folds, and with a snarl, he buried himself deep inside me and started thrusting hard and fast. "I know, Zira. Hate me. I'll take it. For as long as you need, I'll take it until you love me like I love you."

My nails dug into his biceps as the violence of his fucking drew my hatred out of the depths of my soul to join with the lust of our bodies, the two merging to tip me over the edge of oblivion.

Luther's grip on my hips became painful as he gritted his teeth and held himself together as my body tried to tempt him into going back on his word. But being the Elite soldier he was, Luther endured my pleasure, withdrew with a pained groan that told of his agony and fell to the bed beside me. His cock still stood hard and thick, pointing towards his head as he yanked the covers back over us, then turned me away from him and wrapped me in his arms.

I tried to hold my emotions in check, but as the tears streamed down my cheeks, Luther kissed my shoulder. "I deserve your hate, Zira. So you go ahead and despise me, because I love you enough for the both of us."

The sob escaped, Luther held me tighter, and I fell apart in his arms, crying myself to sleep while his erection dug into my back.

Chapter Twenty-Nine

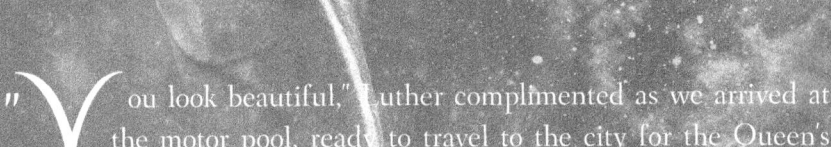

"Y ou look beautiful," Luther complimented as we arrived at the motor pool, ready to travel to the city for the Queen's Parade.

My dress was similar to the court dresses I'd worn when attending formal events as a Princess of Avalonia. Before the Barbarian tore my life apart.

"Thank you," I murmured.

This morning, Luther had been gone before I woke, and when he arrived at my room's fifteen minutes ago to escort me, he didn't say a word or even give me a look that spoke of last night. I wondered how he'd slept because his cock had stayed hard through my submission and until I fell asleep, at least.

Arriving at our transport, Luther followed me into the middle cab, and the door closed us into privacy. "The parade takes two hours," Luther explained as we started moving. "When we arrive at the starting point, we will sit on the Queen's float, a step below my parents. Our Elite will keep us safe."

"I've played the well-behaved Princess half my life; I know how to do it."

Luther peered in my direction. "I never said you didn't. I'm just giving you the run down today.

"After the parade, we attend the picnic and interact with the citizens. Due to recent assassination attempts, our Elite will scan anyone who wishes to greet us before allowing them near.

"My extended family will also be at the picnic, so you will meet my cousins from my mother's side and distant cousins from my father's. Should I die or fail to produce heirs, the latter is next in line for the throne. They will be excited if you tell them our marriage is a sham and I will be the last of my father's line."

Meeting Luther's eyes, I frowned. "I agreed to put on a good public face. Besides, if you live long enough, they will not take the throne, but their grandchildren. Besides, you'll have your mistresses. I'm sure-"

"No."

"No?"

"I won't be taking on another mistress. I have a companion. Even if it's in ink only, I understand now how high your people hold fidelity to your moral expectations. You will be the only woman in my bed for the rest of my life, Zira."

"I won't be in your bed."

"Then no other woman will be either. I will keep it empty in case you change your mind."

Swallowing, I averted my gaze. "Last night was not forgiveness."

"I should hope not." Luther didn't press the subject. "After the picnic, we'll return to the palats and prepare for the gala. Tomorrow, there is lunch in the winter garden with all the dignitaries and high society. Tomorrow night is the actual birthday party."

"It sounds exhausting," I muttered. I couldn't fathom my birthday party lasting two days.

"Thankfully, you slept well last night to restore your energy for it all," Luther replied.

Before I could use the segway to raise last night's issue, the door was opening. A minute later, we were being shuffled through our

Elite and onto an open-top transport with a raised dais at the back that was canopied to prevent the snow from falling on our heads.

Ammita approached with a fur to wrap around my shoulders. "I know we don't feel the cold quite like them, but they will think you insane if you don't have a shawl and a blanket to warm you in this weather."

"Thank you."

Luther was studying Ammita as if she was a secret weapon. "Prince Saboa, my new assistant, Ammita Sreechie."

"Elite Chas speaks highly of you. You raised quite an exceptional Elite," Luther praised. "I believe your son is also in the Royal Guard?"

"Yes," Ammita sighed, her eyes taking Luther in and appreciating his good looks. Still, I noticed her eye wandering to where Commander Stark directed our Elite. "My son is in the advanced company. He was with you when your father sent you to Praldia and still serves under you."

Luther's eyebrows lifted. "Chas never told me. The advance company is in Turbina right now. I'm surprised your son didn't try for Elite with Chas."

Ammita laughed. "My son thinks the Elite has the most boring job. Standing around all day making sure no one kills you. He prefers the action of the advance company."

"You have men in Turbina?" I butted in, disturbed by this news. "Why? When?"

Luther glanced my way. "I told you, your compassion will be needed on behalf of our people sooner than later. Excuse us, Ammita, my parents just arrived."

Taking my hand, Luther moved me towards the dais, creating space between us and our Elite. "Consider Turbina your first project as my heart when you come home, you can have Ammita gather up the information from Aldous for you, and when you are ready, you can come to me with your petition during a closed or open court, but I will not be discussing it now, or even later with you in private."

Blinking at Luther, I remembered when we first negotiated our joining. "This is like Dåligalandar, where my work to give the natives a better life goes against your plans?"

"Not quite," Luther muttered. "I didn't go into Turbina willingly nor for resources. Now, that's all I'll say on this between us. When you think you have the facts, you can petition me in court for any compassion you feel is needed, but I won't bring Turbina into our marriage."

Before I could respond, Luther turned from me, smiling as he greeted his parents and wished his mother a happy birthday. Swallowing my concern for whatever happened back in Praldia, I smiled at Galiena and wished her a blessing for her birthday. In response, the Queen pulled me into a hug.

"Things looked tense between you two when we arrived," Galiena stated.

"It wasn't personal, just some happenings back in Praldia with the civilians that made me uncomfortable to hear," I explained.

While Searle and Galiena knew I'd tried to leave this joining, they also seemed unified in not allowing it, but for different reasons. Not that I'd asked. I didn't care. It was my life and relationship. Thankfully, other than Searle refusing to grant me a divorce, they seemed happy to let Luther and I manage our situation however we chose, as long as it wasn't made public.

"Oh, you see, this is why I stay out of the political side and let Searle deal with that. We'd hate each other every other day if I made my preferences known about how he runs his worlds." Stepping back, Galiena looked me over. "You look beautiful. So regal. I might have my designer weave some of your styles into my next season."

"Your majesty," Galiena's assistant interrupted, pulling her away as the event coordinator called out the countdown now that everyone was on board.

Searle stepped away from his private conversation with Luther, a grin in his eyes as he observed me. "Zira. Beautiful as always. You look well rested today." He moved up to the dais before I could even say thank you, leaving Luther and me to be herded into our seats on the next step down.

"You told him," I accused.

"My father knew I spent the night in your room, just as he knew who was there the night before me."

"Don't say it like that. You make it sound like my bedroom has a revolving door."

"Well, you pointed out Hartwin had been left out. If you invited him to stay tonight, it would be as it appears," Luther muttered.

Clenching my jaw, I scrunched my dress in my fists. "Watch yourself, my prince. Fólk í glerhúsum ætti ekki að kasta steinum," I murmured. I knew he spoke Avalonian fluently and understood my words.

"And I'm the person in the glasshouse in this scenario?" Luther asked, seeming intrigued.

"Throwing boulders instead of stones," I seethed.

Luther watched me for a moment. The event manager was calling out, and then the float hovered toward the crowded streets blocked off for the parade. Luther worked his jaw, then faced forward, folded the thick fur blanket over both our laps, and took my hand as he smiled, waving at the small number of people gathered on the sidewalk away from the main parade.

"It's interesting. Hartwin tells me his father busted you together because you were quite vocal in your pleasure. Every time we've been intimate, our Elite has known it. Even last night alerted the neighboring rooms to what was happening in your bed."

Somewhat embarrassed by the truth of his words, I gritted my teeth and asked, "What's your point?"

"You would have me believe that Ethelred spent an entire night in your bed, fucking you senseless, yet your Elite didn't hear a peep. So, forgive me, Zira, if I speculate that Ethelred's night in your room in no way involved his cock between your thighs, or he was incapable of pleasuring you satisfactorily and therefore isn't a threat to our joining."

If we weren't rounding the corner where everyone could see us, I'd double down on leaving my palm print blazing on his face again. Instead, I settled for smiling as I waved at the Cyran crowd and said through my teeth, "I hate you."

Luther let a beat pass, then replied, "I know."

A minute passed as adoring citizens cheered and threw confetti toward the float. At the same time, the King and Queen tossed Cyros—Cyran money—into the crowd.

"You can show me how much you hate me anytime. I'll abide by last night's rules. Your pleasure while mine is denied."

Frowning, I glanced at Luther. "Why would you want that?"

"Call it penance. Your pleasure, my agony. After what I put you through, it seems fair. Smile," Luther warned after a moment.

Blinking, I turned my focus back to the crowd, forced a natural smile, and waved. "And you won't take your needs to another? You'll suffer the agony of unfulfillment to prove what?"

"That I'm sorry, Zira. What better way to make a man learn from his mistakes than to demand you be pleasured and deny him the same?"

Considering that explanation, I thought about my plans with Ethelred. I wondered if last night would even matter in two days. I knew it wouldn't, so I didn't see why I should feel guilty for it.

"I'll think about it," I told him. And I did. For the rest of the parade and the picnic, I could only think about how amazing last night had felt, even crying in his arms afterward.

I evaluated everything Luther had told me in the car on the way back to the palats. "You won't take your need to another?" I asked out of nowhere.

Luther's brows drew together but then smoothed again. "No. And before you ask, last night was the first time I've had any sexual activity since the last night I was with you."

That was nearly three months ago now.

"Don't look so surprised. I survived the five years of celibacy to become Elite," Luther reminded me, obviously affronted by my response.

"Would you be celibate for five years to earn my forgiveness?"

Turning to face me a little, Luther considered me. "If you asked it of me, I would, but that would impact you. Consider that before you make me vow to it."

"I lived a celibate life after Hartwin abandoned me," I reminded him.

"Two years. That would still see me earn your forgiveness before the time set about in the contract to start our family."

Scoffing, I slouched back in my seat. "I told you I won't make that mistake with you again."

"You will need heirs for Avalonia, or you will not keep that crown on your head a decade," Luther warned. "You are angry and grieving, and it's well-deserved, but don't be blind and make premature declarations before considering the long-term ramifications. Tell me you hate me. Deny me pleasure while you take your own, don't talk to me except through our advisors if you so wish, but don't be fool enough to think denying me heirs affects only my throne. You are claiming your crown based on the purity of your blood and that the men of your bloodline have abused that for years. How will your people react to their queen refusing to breed the next generation? How long until another male uses your choices to call your rule into question?"

I thought about everything I knew was coming, what I would need to do. "You're right," I agreed. "A year."

"A year of celibacy or restraint?" Luther clarified.

"From the moment we leave Cyra, you'll go a year without any sort of release, and when that year is up, we will discuss heirs again. That should give me time to forgive you for your actions and inactions and brave trying again."

"A year?" Luther considered as he studied me. "But not until you leave Cyra in two days?"

"Correct."

"And until then?" Luther tested, his voice a low growl.

"I get to hate you and deny you as much as I like."

The side of Luther's mouth lifted. "I agree to those terms."

Inhaling deeply, I wondered if I was insane making this agreement. Yet, it was clear I wouldn't be let out of this contract with Luther. If I failed to provide him the agreed-upon heirs, Luther could divorce me, yet I knew he wouldn't hold me to that if it meant losing me. I would have no choice inevitably but to forgive Luther and let him seed my womb again. Just not anytime soon.

So, I hated Luther for now. Once at the gala, in a storage room Luther dragged me into. Twice again in my bed that night. Again in the winter garden during his mother's lunch—for which Luther had to cover my mouth to prevent me from alerting the other guests to how much I loathed his existence. In the bath while we readied for his mother's birthday party, and twice more before we fell exhausted and sated, on my part, into slumber.

True to his word, Luther never finished, and it was evident with each consecutive expression of my loathing that he was in more and more agony, holding himself back. Honestly, Luther deserved worse, but a part of me niggled that I could enjoy his pain. I'd never been that kind of person, and it made me think of Ammita's reminder about Salarneytandi. The demon who fed on grief. The Avalonian lesson about how letting my grief control me would lead me down a dark path. I needed to heed that warning, or I wouldn't be worthy of the crown of Avalonia. Instead, I'd end up Andlaus, just like the Barbarian.

Chapter Thirty

T he doors to my rooms opened, disturbing my reading once
again. Luther came in, ignoring Kylar's presence by the fireplace, and sat across from me. Luther spent our last day in
Cyra with his father and the King's war council, detailing the plans
for his Avalonian invasion. I'd attended the morning session, hearing
the plan from Luther's lips for the first time. In the afternoon, when
Searle's council started speculating how they could profit from their
control over Avalonia, I'd excused myself.

"Are we leaving now?" I asked Luther. My bag was packed. Chas
would carry it through the teleportation for me; the rest of my clothes
would be shipped back to Praldia after our departure.

I was going to miss these suites when we left. Not that the
prince's palats in Praldia were any less luxurious, but there were no
fireplaces since the Praldian winter was nowhere near as cold. The
architecture in Praldia was also all steel and glass. A lot more sterile
than the warmth of sandstone.

"In about an hour. I want to arrive while Praldia sleeps and in line
with the return of one of our cargo ships." Luther leaned forward and

scavenged the leftovers of one of my afternoon snacks. "Our Elite are just making the final arrangements now."

Turning my focus to Kylar, I set my tablet aside. "Elite Kylar, you should get ready to go and be involved in any final arrangements."

Bowing, Kylar left us alone. Rising to my feet, I touched the tab on my dress and opened the seam.

"Zira?" Luther's gaze grew heavy, his interest as I let my dress fall to the floor undeniable, especially with the growing tenting of his pants.

"It's the last chance to be inside me and pleasure me for a year," I reminded Luther as I stepped between his thighs. "Will you deny me?"

The side of Luther's mouth twitched. "Never again. I learn from my mistakes, Zira. The next time you demand my affection, I will forgo all my princely duties until you are sated and free me to do my menial tasks."

Kneeling between Luther's legs, I freed his desire from his uniform. "You'll make me your priority?"

"You'll always come first," Luther assured. "In every way."

His grin was infectious as I stroked his manhood's hard, silken thickness. Luther groaned. "Zira, my love, if you wrap that pretty little mouth around my cock, I may break our agreement. After denying myself so often these last two days, I'm unsure if I could resist the temptation. My control is a fine wire ready to snap."

"It's your penance, Luther. Take it like a big boy." My mouth covered him, sucking and tasting. His spicy earthen scent filled my nose, flooding my body with want as I swallowed him into my throat with every second inhale. Luther's fingers wove through my hair—not fisting it, he knew better—to cup my head while he urged me on and tried to restrain me simultaneously.

A curse left Luther's lips as his need pulsed in the heat of my mouth. Luther slipped his hands to my cheeks and gently removed me from him, then he grabbed the base of his cock. He squeezed tight, lifting his head to the ceiling, focusing on whatever allowed him to pull back from the edge. Luther's chest rose and fell quickly, his engorgement so strained the veins stood out, and it seeped his seed. I wanted to lick it clean but knew that would unravel him.

Standing up again, I eased the straps of my underslip from my shoulders. This one was a pale blue silk in the Avalonian style. As Luther lifted his head, his eyes blinked back to focus on me and then grew heavy with his desire again. Extending his hand to me, Luther helped straddle him, and then before he could warn me off, I sheathed him inside me entirely.

Cursing, Luther gripped my waist tight. "By the stars, woman. If I'd known making that deal you would take to torturing me so thoroughly, I would have thought twice about it."

Placing a finger over Luther's lips, I met his eyes and let the psionic link click into place. "It's about to get a lot worse, Luther." Slipping my hand down, I pressed the tab on his shirt and spread it wide open as it unraveled. My hands roamed his skin, the hardness of his muscles beneath the soft flesh. "Touch me, Luther. Worship me."

Luther's fingers clenched tighter at my waist. "Zira-"

"I have control. You won't finish," I assured.

A laugh escaped Luther's lips, and he shifted his hands to caress my body. "Is that so?"

"It is. Do you wish me to prove it?"

When Luther raised a brow, I couldn't help the dark smile I gave him. Non-magics consistently underestimated the Avalonian psionic power. Pressing into Luther's chest, I started riding him hard and fast. He grabbed my hips and tried to stop me, cursing and begging me as his body reached for that final bliss. That never came.

Slowing my ride, I eased us to a stop. Luther was grimacing, panting, and as I watched, a heavy frown settled over his brow. "What in the blackness?" Luther murmured.

Smirking, I leaned into him, a shiver racing through his body as my lips traced his ear. "I've tethered your body's ability to climax," I murmured. "Your pleasure belongs to me now, just like you promised."

Luther's hand cupped the back of my neck as my lips whispered down his neck. "Zira. How?" He swallowed hard and groaned as I circled my hips on him.

"You should know better than to underestimate me by now, Luther."

As I met his eyes, Luther smiled. "No, my love, it is not that I underestimate you; it is that you are a goddess, able to bring the stars to her feet, and I am merely a man, clumsy and foolish in my pursuit of your heart."

Before I could laugh or cry, Luther was lying us down before the fire and driving into me hard and slow. His hands and mouth worshipped me while he took me the Avalonian way, sweet, tortured agony marring his features the entire time, especially as he brought me to orgasm and my body naturally called him to follow.

Luther held himself above me as I recovered, cursing and praying to the stars. His entire body shook with effort. His head bowed, and sweat dripped from him. "Luther," I cajoled, urging him to look at me.

"I never knew such pleasure could be torture. Your ability to let me ride the edge but not fall over is twisted. Like finding bliss from being stabbed and bleeding to death," Luther murmured.

My mind spun to my desire of wanting to slip a dagger into his heart. I thought Ethelred had been my weapon, but even if Luther was hurt for a moment, his cunning stopped my blade from ever hitting its mark. But this surrender to my hate and desire had achieved the goal.

When Luther went to roll away, I gripped him, making him whimper when it drove him deep into me again. "Zira, I know you hate me, but don't be cruel," he begged.

"Look at me," I demanded gently.

Lifting his head, Luther met my gaze. Those midnight blue eyes pleaded for mercy as I cupped his face, and I crunched up to press our mouths together, distracting him as I reached down that link and untethered my hold on him.

"Zira?" Luther moaned as I rocked against him. "I promised."

Cyra

"And you kept your promise. But after we walk through those doors, you will not touch me for a year, and I am not so cruel as to show every other creature compassion except you." Laying back, I caressed my hands down Luther's sweat-slicked back and grabbed his ass. "Take your pleasure, Luther. It will be the last for quite some time."

Growling, Luther thrust forward, driving into me with a need only the fear of eternal blackness could bring out in a man. My back arched as the friction of our bodies brought me quickly to the edge, and as Luther jerked and lost himself to his release, stars exploded behind my eyes, and I fell into sweet oblivion.

"Thank you," Luther murmured to my hair as he held me. "I didn't deserve it, but thank you."

Rolling away, I sat up and stared at the fire while I gathered together the shards of myself.

"Zira?" Luther sat up behind me, his hand massaging my arm while his lips kissed my shoulder.

"I haven't forgiven you. These last two days have been hate and grief, that's all."

Squeezing my arm, Luther kissed me again. "I know, Zira. I never expected anything more. As I said, I'll love enough for the both of us, and maybe one day, you'll look at me like you used to before your parents kneeled for my sword and Stark dragged you to me, and your eyes were filled with fear and acceptance."

Frowning, I turned to see Luther's face over my shoulder. "I respected you, but I never desired you like that."

The side of Luther's mouth smiled back at me as he set a kiss right to the point of my shoulder. "There was a day when you came to warn me about a danger to my soldiers. Do you remember it?"

Blinking back to that time, I recalled the day he was talking about. It was during the Winter Rose Ball, one of the big fetes Luther held every year as a fundraiser for the children's clinics he'd set up all over Praldia. During one of my less-than-legal dealings with my favorite black market smuggler—not the one whose name I gave to

Ethelred—he'd warned me against going on one of my scheduled charity visits to one of the more hostile countries. That a rebellion against the prince was about to take place.

It was before Hartwin or even my affair with Ethelred. I'd feared for the lives of innocent women and children if the rebellion attempted the coup. So I'd taken one of my mother's nicest ballgowns and snuck off to the palats.

Luther's thumb drew circles just beneath my shoulder. "I had you dance with me while you shared your warning and then asked you to stay while I conferred with my men."

"Then you asked to dance with me again to ask some more questions, but other than asking me to dance, you asked nothing," I remembered aloud. "You held me so tight to you; I felt every shift of your body, and the way you led me around the floor made my heart beat so fast. For one terrified minute, as the dance wrapped up, you lowered your face to mine, and I thought you might kiss me, but then you looked past me and simply thanked me instead and had two of your men escort me home."

"I wanted to kiss you," Luther confessed. "I was going to. The way you stared at me with such awe that night. How you blushed as I held you tight to me. I didn't even know an Avalonian could blush until that evening. I was sure then that you were still innocent."

"I was." I'd only been eighteen then, still looking for the right man to be my first. I'd wanted Hartwin but was terrified of the Cyran countenance.

Luther chuckled, placing another kiss on the top of my spine. "I fantasized about taking you back to my suites, remedying that problem for you, and never letting you out of my bed until you agreed to join me."

"Why didn't you?" I asked, then quickly clarified, "Kiss me?"

"Your parents spotted us, and your mother started storming over to get you away from me. I had my men take you home so you would not be caught up in whatever words were exchanged. I should have had them take you to my rooms and followed you after I dealt with your parents."

"What made you think I would have done that? Been with you that night?"

Leaning his head next to mine, Luther sighed. "There was a yearning in your eyes that night, and when we danced, I saw a spark of your desire. I think you were thinking about another and dancing with them that way, but I hoped, had I kissed you, you might have surrendered that yearning to me."

Thinking back, I might have. "The stars lead us where they need us." Getting up, I crossed the room and went to wash the past hour from me. Luther followed, and then we dressed and went to join our Elite, who were waiting for us to get on the way.

"Zira," Luther took my elbow and pulled me into him one last time. "I love you. I'll see you at home." He kissed the star beneath my eye, causing tears to cloud my vision.

I wanted to tell him I loved him too, but I wasn't ready for that declaration, not while my loathing still wreathed in me like a living thing. Instead, as Luther released me and stepped amongst his own Elite, I moved well away, ensuring I was out of range. A buzz filled the room, and I watched Luther and his Elite disappear, entering the long-range teleport to Praldia.

"Princess," Wolfe came forward. "It's been an honor."

Behind Wolfe stood Hildebrand and Didrika. Pretending my tears were for leaving them behind, I lunged into Wolfe's arms, causing him to laugh as I hugged him tight. "Thank you. I wish you could come with me."

Patting my back, Wolfe gave me a squeeze and then stepped back. "Shh, none of that. We'll see you again in only a few weeks for the Solstice ball."

Swallowing down my emotion, I forced a smile to my face. "Yes, of course."

Giving me a chuffed look I think he typically reserved for his daughter, Wolfe stepped aside, and I farewelled Hildebrand with a bit more decorum. Still, when it was time to say goodbye to Didrika, I struggled to let go.

"Your friendship meant so much to me these past months," I told her.

"You're like the sister I never knew I had," Didrika whispered. Pulling back from the hug, Didrika kept hold of my hand as I went to step away. "He loves you. I can see that as bright as day, and I know you'll find a way to forgive him, but don't ever let him treat you like he did when you came here again. If he starts that nonsense, you use your Avalonian magic and kick his ass like you did these newbies in the trials." She indicated my new Elite.

Patting the top of her hand, I let go. I stepped into my Elite, them making room for me to be in the center, surrounded by Chas, Kylar, Erhaird, Hamlin, Rylan, and Ammita.

"Are you ready for this?" Ammita murmured as the buzz of the channels filled the room.

"You make it sound like I have a choice."

The teleportation closed around us with a large crack, like lightning splitting the air above our heads; it echoed through my skull like the last long-range teleport. My stomach lurched as the world blurred, a galaxy of stars zipping by at speed, twisting and turning as the channel drew me away.

After only moments, another crack of lightning shattered my skull, and I was yanked in a different direction. Around me, it was like the galaxy split. Some colorful stars racing with me followed me, and the rest stayed on their trajectory.

Clenching my teeth, I dug my nails into the palms of my hands to not pass out, puke, or both. Then the channel spat me out, throwing me to the ground so hard that dirt and leaves exploded around me. I grunted and took a moment to curse beneath my breath and assess if I'd hurt myself badly in the fall.

Looking up, I took in my surroundings, and my heart started beating hard. This was not where I was meant to be.

Chapter Thirty-One

Luther

Whenever I thought I had Zira figured out, she surprised me again. First, when she let me climb into her bed without a fight. I'd gone to her room, trying to draw her out. To have her lie to my face about Ethelred and try and rub my face in it. While it would have hurt, I knew nothing happened between them, so it would have just been her words that stung. I was willing to let her have it. To punish me that way. Zira didn't just play my game; she turned it back on me.

Zira shocked me when I cried over the glyph for life on her sacrum, and instead of pushing me away and getting angry, she challenged me. Not that I expected sympathy. Not from Zira, at least. She shouldn't and wouldn't give it to me. Instead, Zira subtly weaved her words into a flesh-tearing whip and, by offering sex to me, in turn, suggested what happened between her and Ethelred. I knew better, but it hit its mark.

Yet, I couldn't pull out of the game I'd started by going to her room. I rose to Zira's challenge and found a new way for her to have her revenge. Take her pleasure and deny me. And after four months without her in my bed, the ache in my groin was severe enough to bring a lesser man to tears. Blackness, I nearly did cry from the pain when she hit her euphoria, and I had to resist.

The Elite thought five years of celibacy was hard to endure. They should try refraining from your natural urges while your wife's tight body milks yours. It was sheer torture. Enough to drive me to insanity. And that was just the first time. When Zira opened the door for the entire birthday weekend to be a hate-sex fuck-fest, I was over the moon and angry at myself for the offering.

Still, a woman scorned with no method of revenge was a danger. Considering the video Gallows shared, the sooner I gave Zira a way to punish me that didn't cause bodily harm, the better. Not that I thought Zira would ever purposefully harm me, but with her power and skills, the King and I agreed it wouldn't take much for her to lose her temper. Her control and reason could follow easily. Hate sex hadn't been my intention, and I still wasn't sure if it was better or worse than Zira convincing me she had taken a lover. Until we woke this morning and Zira used her abilities and body to cause me such sweet agony and then showed me her mercy.

As my Elite and I teleported back to Praldia, I had a few minutes to ruminate on the last few days and steel myself because when the channels closed behind me, I wouldn't be allowed to touch my wife for a year.

The royal guest suite at the other end of the upper level of my residence was ready for Zira. It was where my parents usually stayed when visiting. Now relegated to the smaller guest room between Zira and me. It was important to me that Zira was comfortable and happy. I'd prefer her to be in my bed every night, but I earned her hate. Now I had to endure it.

At least a year. And even then, there was no guarantee Zira would share my suite regularly. All Zira promised was that we could discuss heirs in a year. She may never return to my bed except for pleasure and to conceive our children. After what I'd done, I'd be lucky to get that from her.

Our marriage had started to look like my parents' when they were on the outs with each other. That's not to say it had always been like that. But, as cold as Cyrans could be emotionally, we loved and hated like every other species.

Behind our stone facade lay passions that burned hotter than the surface of Risastór sól. When my parents hated each other, they were each other's worst nemesis, but when they loved, they did so fiercely, and god help any who tried to come between them.

The teleportation channel slowed. Lightning cracked, and I relaxed my knees in readiness as my feet touched earth again. Then I was standing in the entry courtyard of my palats in Praldia.

My home away from home.

"Clear the way," Anberon called.

With a sigh, I immediately moved off to the side so we wouldn't cause any collisions with Zira's Elite. "How are we for timing?" I asked Hartwin.

"The ship from Cyra landed five minutes ago, so we've timed it perfectly," he answered. He eyed me but didn't say anything else. Things between us had been tense since Zira escaped to Cyra.

The entire situation with Adima and how I treated my companion tested Hartwin's loyalty. We both loved the same woman. He'd stepped aside for me before I knew there was competition, but that didn't mean he stopped caring for her. After Zira put her foot down and called me out for my treatment of her, then dismissed Hartwin, he'd asked for a few weeks' leave to get his feelings under wraps. And while he'd been away, Zira miscarried and nearly lost her life. I remember his words the night I visited him, looking for my best friend to hear my grief.

'She warned you. Zira begged you, and I had to stand there watching her struggle to cope and be your friend and soldier while she unraveled. You have my loyalty, but you'll get no sympathy from me for a situation you could have prevented if you just listened to her,' Hartwin told me through gritted teeth.

'I know. I just never imagined things would be like this. That she wouldn't trust me to protect her."

'Can you blame her? You nearly killed her!'

'Hart, I didn't want to go to that funeral. The King ordered me.'

Grabbing me by the shirt, Hartwin yanked me close, spittle on his lips as he yelled, 'Get your head out of your ass! The funeral was the tipping point, but if it had been that and that alone, she would be whole, and your children would still be alive.' Shoving me away, Hartwin backed up and swiped his hand through his hair. I could only stare. Hartwin had never assaulted me away from training.

'It wasn't the funeral,' Hart repeated with more control and less volume this time. 'It was the infidelity, the dismissal of her needs, the resentment you drowned her in instead of the love and adoration she deserved. Everything she has suffered, Luther. The Barbarian, her parents' betrayal, the abduction attempts, and me. All you needed to do was be patient and love her. That's what she needed, and you failed her.'

'Patience is not my virtue,' I muttered.

Hartwin met my eyes. 'You must make it so, because she'll never truly be yours without it. Not now. Not after this.'

Lightning cracked throughout the courtyard as Zira and her Elite approached. Light scattered across the circular enclosure; I sucked in a breath and stood straight. Patience would need to be my virtue.

Bodies materialized, and I stepped forward, ready to escort Zira inside with me, but she wasn't there. In fact, several of her Elite were missing too.

"Where's the Princess?" Anberon was quick to ask Jervaise.

By the way, Zira's Elite was looking around at each other; they were just as surprised by her absence as I was. Jervaise's eyes widened, and he strode straight for me, Anberon coming alongside.

"Zira was with us. Those standing closest to her are also missing," Jervaise reported. How his throat worked and how he kept looking around us while keeping his voice down betrayed Jervaise's nervousness. I'd never seen him so off-kilter.

Turning on my heel, I headed through the doors to the control room. Anberon, Jervaise, and Hartwin followed while Tancred gave orders to Zira's Elite. Commander Stark was standing in the room, monitoring a feed. He frowned when he saw me, then looked behind me. "The Princess refused to return?"

"No," I said, approaching the teleportation section. "Jervaise assures me she was with her Elite when they left, but her and," I looked back at Jervaise, pausing. "How many are missing?"

"Ten Elite in total plus Ammita," Jervaise answered, already typing into his comms. "I'm not getting any response from Chas. I'll try Kylar."

"They didn't come out of the Teleportation," I finished for Stark. Turning to the soldier at the controls, I focused on the screen while the others started trying to contact the missing. "Track all the channels that left Cyra. How many left after my team?"

The tech started typing away and, a moment later, had columns of numbers on his screen. "Twenty-one in the initial teleport. All arrived. Twenty-two entered the second." The tech's face pinched. "Only ten arrived."

"Check the missing ten destination codes," I ordered.

"They're all the same. All forty-two approved teleports had the same locked destination. Here. Specifically, the courtyard outside." The tech kept typing.

Turning to Stark, I threw him my comms. "Get Aldous out of bed. He had Ammita's contact details. Get them and track her. She'll be with my wife."

Bowing, Stark stepped out of the room.

"Anything?" I asked the others.

"No one is answering or responding," Anberon grumbled. "This doesn't make sense. There is no way that if the channel was set to bring them here that they shouldn't be here."

"Could it have failed mid-flight?" Hartwin asked, looking pale. "Could something have disrupted it and spat them out in the middle of space?"

"If it did, they're all dead by now," the tech muttered as he kept typing.

"No," I refused to believe that. Plus, in all my years, the channels had never just dropped out and spat someone out before their destination. "Something else happened. Jervaise, did you see anything?"

Still looking nervous as anything, Jervaise shook his head. "I always keep my eyes closed until the channel connects."

Studying the Elite, I moved over to him. "But you suspect something."

Swallowing exasperatingly, Jervaise dropped his gaze. "The night before you came-"

"The night Ethelred stayed?" I asked to clarify.

Jervaise nodded. "Just before he arrived, the Princess, out of the blue, asked me if she left you, would I go with her. I told her my loyalty was to the crown, and if she left you, the King would withdraw her Elite protection. I also told her leaving you would let you off the hook. I didn't think she actually meant she'd leave you."

My jaw worked over this news. Zira asked for a divorce, told me I wouldn't be forgiven, and that she wanted nothing to do with me. I knew the last two days weren't forgiveness, but she'd promised to play the part of my wife, if only in public. Could it be she was just biding her time?

"She asked you this before Ethelred arrived?" I checked, my mind putting pieces together.

"Yes."

"And then they were together all night, but the usual sounds of her pleasure never reached you?"

Jervaise frowned, then his face became pale. "She wasn't cheating; she was-"

"Planning her escape," Anberon finished, then cursed.

"No," I refused to believe that. "Not her escape. Zira is a woman of her word. She made me promises. She wouldn't just run away from her responsibilities."

"Nor her people," Hartwin added. "Caring for those who couldn't care for themselves was everything to Zira. She wouldn't abandon the people of Praldia. She would endure the prince and use her position to help others."

"My prince," the tech called my attention. "I've found it. The route wasn't altered from our side. Mid-teleportation, a signal hacked the channels and rerouted the Princess and those surrounding her."

"Hacked?" I checked. "Who the hell has that technology?"

"I don't know," the tech answered. "I've never heard of a channel being hacked. But that's what happened. A signal hit the center of her team and caused them to change path." He typed continuously, copying a number and pasting it into a different window, bringing up a shot of a blue planet with auroras of blue and green swirling around it. Then it zoomed to show a world mainly of water. Then zoomed in again to display a landmass. And that's where it stopped.

"That's as far as I can trace it. Weirdly, a second signal was sent when they reached this location, which sent them off-course. I can't track where they landed because no destination was provided with that signal."

"Where is that?" Anberon asked behind me.

My heart was beating hard despite how still my body was. "Hart, get your father. Find me, Ethelred. Now."

Hartwin, looking just as angry as me, moved. Anberon looked at the tech. "Where is she?"

He didn't really need to ask. We all knew. There was only one planet with that much water in our solar system.

"Avalonia," the tech answered, confirming my worst fears. "Whoever hacked the teleportation sent the Princess to Avalonia."

To be continued in Avalonia...

Glossary

Älskarinna (älskare) - mistress (mistress's), paramour, kept woman, fancy woman

Ánægjuhóra - Pleasure whore

Broadcaster - A media recorder

Brutnalöfte - Broken Promise - A law in Cyra where a promise broken can have payment extracted to equal physical consequence.

Cyran Skvaller - Cyran Tabloid Broadcasters

Glossary

Dödfödda - Still Birth

Hälsodryck - A drink made to provide all the required nutrients for an expectant mother. Avalonian in its origin, it is also used by Avalonian's when they need an extra burst of energy.

Is (Pronounced Eas - Like East without the t) - Black stone used in flooring that sounds like cracking ice when you walk over it.

Missfall - Miscarriage

Palats - Palace

Öfugt - (o-vooff) Unfavorable

Sadisten - Sadist

Dark Romantasy / Paranormal Romance by Ebony Olson

STANDALONE BOOKS

Of Shadow and Light

Boundary

Silver Rogue

Halos

The Grave Keeper: All Hallows

ANGELIS SERIES

Spectra

Angelis

HIERARCH SERIES (DARK ROMANTASY)

Succumb

Numinous

Masked

Exodus

Burning Immortality

OREY GELUS SERIES

Gelus Hearts (Compilation of Orey Witches & Edge Gelus)

Vidal

CHAOS STAR TRILOGY (SCI-FI ROMANCE)

Praldia

Cyra

Avalonia

ANTHOLOGIES

Booktober: A Halloween PNR Anthology

Romance Suspense by Ebony Olson

Hotel Series

HOLLY CLAIRE TRILOGY

Holly's Trilogy: Books 1-3 Hotel Series

(Compilation of Henderson, Cassidy, & Holmes)

JESS BUTLER TRILOGY

Best Sunset: Books 4-6 Hotel Series

(Compilation of Best Man, Best Layover, & Best Knight)

Black Mark Series

Black Mark: The Complete Saga

(Omnibus of Resistance, Secret, & Heart)

Black Mark X

Standalone Books

Calypso

Rain: A Dark Past Romance

Protective Instinct (On KU as Hunter Enemy & Lover Enemy)

About the Author

Ebony lives in Sydney, Australia, with her husband, daughter, and six rescue cats. She loves to read fantasy, thrillers, and paranormal romance, spending most of her free time with her nose in a book or writing.

Having always possessed an over-active imagination Ebony spent her younger years regaling friends with fantastic stories, holding her audience captive with the passion and suspense of her characters plights. In adulthood, she shows no signs of stopping her imagination from spreading across as many pages as it can find.

Website: http://ebonyolson.com/
Ebony's Mischief & Mayhem Peeps

facebook.com/EbonyOlson.Author

instagram.com/ebony_olson

amazon.com/author/ebonyolson

bookbub.com/authors/Ebony_Olson

goodreads.com/Ebony_Olson

tiktok.com/@ebony_olson